The Runaways

Table of contents:

Prelude: 3

Tragedy: 6

Dreams: 27

The Monster: 44

Runaway: 60

Danse Macabre: 75

Recital: 90

A-maze-ing Grace: 106

Entry of the Gladiators: 122

Eye of the Tiger: 144

Intermission: 161

Sound of Silence: 168

The Ultimate Show: 185

Waiting: 206

In the Hall of the Mountain King: 212

Grief: 232

Wendigo: 237

Ghost: 258

Curtain Call: 281

Prelude:

Thunder cracks across the sky as the winds bellow, and the storm rages. A group of cloaked figures celebrates as the screams of the dying can be heard echoing through their old and disheveled halls. Their leader, a terrible creature with a wicked smile, laughs as she passes away on the delivery table, for what use was she to him now? She had already provided him with five perfect sons who knew not to question his authority and obeyed his every word, and now with this delivery, he had the sixth.

The old crow's eyes shined as he approached his former wife's corpse on the table, and he reached down, not to clean her blood, nor remove her body, but instead to recover the darkly colored egg that she had just given birth to.

"The time has come my children." he cooed softly over the cries of his youngest two who sobbed and clung to their mother's sides. The eldest three stood back, for they knew what getting close to her meant. He would have to punish the smaller ones later, but for now, he was in too good a mood to do so. "The end of all things quickly approaches us. In just a few short years, we shall claim the right our family was promised! So mote it be!" he bellowed.

"So mote it be." The elder three responded in unison.

"One, take your mother outside, bury her. I don't care how. Two, go prepare the newborn's room, I don't want him escaping..." he pauses, thinking, this child is too valuable to let be harmed or to escape, he would need a way to ensure that his plans would succeed, and to keep a constant eye on him. He thinks back to the books he read as his father before him had. The dark manuscripts and ancient tomes of forbidden knowledge and cursed black magics that their family had employed for generations. Surely there was a spell or skill he could use in this- and then it hit him, and he flashed his evil smile across his beak.

His eyes, glassy and yet so full of anger and hatred fell upon Three. Three's heart sank; he hated it when Zero looked at him. "And as for you Three, I have a very *special* job for you."

One and Two set to work, doing their jobs as their father had demanded, and they gave gratitude to whatever dark god that was listening that it wasn't either of them that Zero wanted for this special job. Even after they had finished, they could still hear the screams of Three coming from the mine below.

Tragedy:

Why must all stories start with a tragedy? Perhaps it's because there would be no story if the players all started with their happily ever after, or perhaps it's because there needs to be an obstacle to overcome. Regardless, whether it be large or small, every story begins with a tragedy. It's a quiet neighborhood in Orange Bay. Not a lot around, just streets upon streets of houses and convenience stores, the elementary school, and the old hospital next to the police department. There's the nearby beach of course, but it's still a good hour's long drive from there to any of the "big" places, like Destinyworld.

None of this mattered to the young rabbit Lute, however. He would have been perfectly content living in his quiet home at the end of the cul de sac with his mom and dad, attending school, he might even have paid attention in class or tried studying if it meant avoiding his tragedy.

But no, this one has no cause, at least that's what the doctors could determine. A one in a million rare disease that came on quickly and left with his mom just as quickly. The funeral was small, and poor Lute didn't stop crying for a whole week. He never had the best relationship with his dad, he has always been more of a mommy's boy, though they got along as well as any family would. After his mom's death though, something seemed to change in his father. He seemed quieter and would come home later with a funky smell to him.

A few months later, summer ended, and Lute begrudgingly had to go back to school. Fifth grade, the final year in elementary school before heading off to middle school. Only two weeks into the new year, and already he had adapted to his new schedule.

7:00 am. Wake up, brush his teeth, get dressed, and make himself breakfast. Usually, whatever cereal was around with maybe the occasional bit of milk that's a day past the expiration date. Maybe some Plop Tarts or Warm Pocket sandwiches if he was really lucky.

7:30 am. Get on the bus, and try not to make eye contact with the other-

Flump. He falls over as the bus laughs. Someone had tripped him. "Ha! Nice fall, loser!" He knew that voice anywhere. *Of course, it had to be Randy.* Randy Fang, a Black Bear that was held back more times than Randy could probably count. If Lute were a straight C student, Randy was a straight F student. That's not to say he's dumb, but rather he simply doesn't care about doing the work. Randy proved to be quite smart, able to easily manipulate people into trusting him, or doing what he said.

Thankfully Lute had already gotten a reputation for being "the class clown", so he simply hopped up, dusted himself off, and tried to play it off as if nothing had happened. "Yeah man, guess it's true what they say about us bunnies and big feet. But hey, y'all know what they say about big feet, am I right?" he laughed, and in return got laughs and cheers from the other students, despite maybe only half of them knowing what the phrase means. He takes his seat in the back of the bus, next to the only "friend" he had at the school.

Boe P, a sheep who had the "fortune" of being in every class with him the past four years, as well as this year. It's clear they had some kind of friendship, but it's nothing too deep, often it amounts to nothing more than being group project partners when no one else wants to work with Lute. "You alright?"

"Yeah, yeah, I'm fine. Randy's a jerk, but whatever." Lute passes it off.

"Why don't you just stand up for yourself? You shouldn't have to take that from anyone." she shoots him a knowing glance.

"Dunno what you're talking about Boe, just cause I fell here doesn't mean he tripped me, and just cause I've got this bandaid on doesn't mean I got a scrape underneath." He lied.

Boe was top of the class and in a special "Honors program", so lying to her was hard, even at the best of times. If it weren't for her insistence that she wanted to go through every grade, she was probably clever enough to be in seventh grade already despite her age. But she also knew that Lute was stubborn, and would refuse to talk about this if he didn't want to. Worse still, he would start cracking jokes if she didn't stop, and the last thing she wanted to hear was about how he should call himself Humpty Dumpty for having a great fall earlier. So she just sighed and tried to change the subject.

"Probably doesn't help that you look like you're straight off of the farm." She says, "Seriously, this isn't the largest city in Eagleland, but still you dress like a scarecrow." She wasn't wrong. Lute's sense of "fashion" had always been questionable at best. A brown baseball cap, orange shirt, and blue overalls, simple, and easy to clean since he found that half the time he would need to wash his own clothes since his father wouldn't do it.

"Well golly Boe!" he said in a thick accent, "I always thought these clothes made me out-standing in the field of fashion!" he laughed as Boe let out an angry bleat.

8:00 pm. Class starts. The standard fare that any child his age would (and in his case does) sleep through. Basic Fogish that he already knew, and history and math he didn't care about. He would regularly and rudely be awoken from his naps by the teacher, Mrs. Fairgrove, a young goat, who would slap a ruler down on his desk. "We've been over this already Lute," she would say, "you can't sleep through this, it's important stuff that will help you one day! If you're going to keep acting like this, you're looking at going to detention!" She would then make him try to answer whatever question was being asked, and occasionally, he would get it right!

11:00 am. Lunchtime. Which for Lute would sometimes mean eating whatever he managed to bring with him. Other times it meant bumming some food off of the other students, mainly Boe, who always seemed to have a second peanut butter and jelly sandwich in her backpack. Of course, taking it from her meant getting a second lecture while he was trying to enjoy a nice sandwich.

"You've gotta stop sleeping in class, don't you sleep enough at night?"

"Of course," he lies again, "I just really like sleep. You could say I dream of getting more. Maybe you could help me with that. They say counting sheep is a good way to fall asleep. Watch! One." he drops his head to the table and begins to fake snoring loudly.

Boe just shakes her head. "Ha-ha. Cute, but seriously, why do you anger her like that? She's the teacher, and you seemingly do something to get detention every day! What, do you just like spending extra time in the classroom?"

"Maybe," Lute responds, taking another bite of Boe's second sandwich. "Not like there's a lot to do at home, I mean... aside from watching tv..." he shrugs, "at least here I can practice with the instruments from music class."

"Oh, wow, a recorder, that must take a lot of practice."

"Hmph, I'll have you know that the recorder is just as complex as the flute! Heck, I bet I could play your flute even better than you!"

"Hah, now I know you're crazy if you think I'm gonna let you anywhere near that. If you broke it, my parents would kill me."

"Hey, so would mine. I promise to be careful with it."

"No."

"Uhg, fiiiiine. How are the docs anyway?"

"They've been busy lately. Like, Dad seems to be working every night, and Mom seems to be super tired when she gets home." she shrugs, "the good news is we've been getting a lot of take-out recently." she laughs. "Now finish up, it's time for recess."

11:30 am. Recess. The school's excuse for "gym class." There's a teacher out here who has to spend their lunch break watching over two batches of students before the second teacher takes over. Always a different one and none of them really watch the students. They just cycle through and occasionally look around to make sure no one's hurt. Not like the students have it much better. The school surrounds two sides of the playground, and the other two are sealed in with a tall fence; the students would be reprimanded for climbing. It was just tall enough that students like Lute and other rabbits would come just short of jumping over it, and all the bird students would try to show off their flying "skills" only to faceplant before even making it halfway up. Aside from the teacher, there was the security guard, an old eagle who would hang out on the roof during recess hours to prevent any adult birds from trying to come in.

There are a few playsets out there, a swing set, a teeter-totter, a merry-go-round, and a slide/jungle gym. A small paved area the "teacher table" rested on is just wide enough for someone to draw a crude game of hopscotch on, and there is a full basketball court out there that gets used more by the fifth graders than any other grade.

While Lute seems to just lazily sleep through the entire morning, once the recess hits, he appears the most full of energy of anyone there. Recess is only a half-hour long, but in that time, Lute manages to run, well really hop, several laps around the entire playground, do some pushups and situps, and overall give himself a decent workout. Sure, he doesn't care about sports, but he knew it would be best to stay fit, mainly because of Randy. While Lute may have only started wearing overalls over the summer, he's always worn the hat, and Randy loves to play "keep away" with Lute's hat whenever he gets the chance. So Lute had to learn how to be quicker and outpace Randy.

Suffice to say that Lute managed to keep just out of Randy's reach most of the time, and it's why despite Randy's clear aggression towards him, the two would never get into a full fight. Because despite Randy's size and strength, Lute had more speed, stamina, and mobility, and chances are, would outlast Randy until a teacher or the security guard actually did their job and noticed what was going on and stopped him. That said, this is not one of Lute's luckier days, Randy managed to get the drop on him, and is currently running towards the fence with Lute's hat.

"Give it back, Randy!" Lute shouts while chasing him.

"In your dream, dork! This hat of yours is going straight over the fence!"

Now, please don't ask why Randy seemingly hates Lute so much as to steal from him, trip him up, and generally be a menace towards him. In truth, he doesn't single out Lute like this, and in fact, he tends to do stuff like this with all of his classmates, as he has in every fifth grade he's been in. There have been talks of sending him to juvie or otherwise just expelling him. Still, it had instead been decided that since he was in fifth grade, it would just be overall easier to let him slide through this year, allowing him to finally graduate elementary school, so he's no longer the school's problem. Someone might even have accidentally let it slip to his parents, and they might have told him that this would be his last year in fifth grade. This means, at least in Randy's mind, that he can get away with anything.

Keeping good to his word, a rare sight for Randy, he threw Lute's cap with all his might, and it landed on just the other side of the fence. "Haha! Looks like that's the end of that!" he cheered, feeling proud of himself for picking on a kid several years younger than himself.

"You're a jerk, Randy! Why did you have to go an' do that?!"

"For fun!" he smiled a wide grin, his teeth like polished razor blades. "And because I can. And there's nothing you can do to stop me, loser!" He just stood there, smiling and laughing at the misfortune he caused Lute. Lute had to act fast; otherwise, his hat would blow away in the wind, and he'd never see it again.

Thinking quickly, he notices the slide is close to this part of the fence. He climbs up it and turns to face the fence, still a good couple feet above him, no real room for a running start, he focuses intently on putting all his energy into one mighty leap! He jumps and grabs hold of the fence and lands just under the top of it. "Teacher! Lute's trying to escape!" he could hear as Randy went to snitch on him. Ignoring it, he quickly scrambles over and hops down, just in time to snag his hat as it gets picked up by a stray gust of wind.

Putting it back on, he starts climbing back up to return to the playground, only to hear a deep voice. "Just where do you think you're going?" turning around, the security guard is standing behind him, looking ticked off.

"Back inside." Lute tries to shrug it off, "Don't know if you've noticed, but I'm not supposed to be out here."

"I have noticed, and why are you out here then?" he asks as Lute returns to climbing.

"I fell off the top." he half lied.

"And you were at the top because?"

"I wanted to see if I could. It turns out I can."

"Yes. And you know what else you can do?"

"Is it report to detention after school today?"

"Hey, what do you know, you got it in one!" The guard flies up and back to his perch as Lute comes to a landing back in the playground, the teacher demanding to know what's gotten into Lute while Randy stands next to them, just smiling. He gives the same half-hearted responses he gave the guard before the bell rings, and recess ends, giving him a perfectly valid excuse to walk away and get back to class.

Noon. Which meant the first lesson of the day that Lute cared about was here. It was time for science, and like many of his classmates, he enjoyed watching the demonstration of the day's lesson on the projector screen. Most of the time, the entire lesson would be a half-hour long episode from an old TV show about a Billy Goat scientist explaining various subjects in creative and extraordinary ways. Their assignment would be done with a small sheet of questions they had to answer while watching. This one was about colors and light. It was interesting, especially the parts about how crayons were made, and how pigment works, and how what we see is just a reflection of light off of the objects we're looking at.

In a way, it almost seems deceptive. You look at an object, thinking you're seeing it for what it is. But in truth you never "see" the object, all you see is the light bouncing off of it, the object's depth merely the light taking mere fractions of a second longer to reach our eyes. Some things are even able to change their color on the fly, like chameleons, which will use this ability to hunt prey or hide from predators. You only ever see what they WANT you to see.

As the episode ended, Lute found himself quietly humming the theme song as he looked around, and he could have sworn that some of his classmates had a curious light shining off of their bodies. Boe had a curious shade of blue around her, and Randy had a red glow. Even his fur seemed to have been tinted an emerald hue of green. He stops and blinks his eyes a few times and the colors fade and vanish.

He needs more sleep if he's seeing things like that. Now's not the time for that though, he turns in his sheet with the rest of the class. Mrs. Fairgrove, having received an email about Lute's playground escapades, gives him a stern look, "We'll talk about this later." She says. "Just... try not to cause any more trouble today." she stands, "Alright class, everyone help me move the desks to the sides, it's time for music class!"

12:45 pm. Music class. This is by far Lute's favorite lesson of the day. For whatever reason, each of the grades had a unique lesson at this time. Kindergarteners and First graders had nap time. Second and Third graders had "health" class, really almost a second recess where they would learn about cleaning and diseases in class, and play games on how to have a balanced diet or do exercise in their classroom. The fourth and fifth graders got music class instead, however, where they would be taught the basics of how to read and write sheet music, as well as play an instrument... if they could afford one anyway. If they couldn't then they would be given a cheap plastic recorder that had been locked in the school's cabinets since the turn of the century and promptly forgotten about until someone needed one.

Despite the instrument's crude and simple nature, it was still capable of producing beautiful music in the right paws. And Lute had the right paws. He really took to the music lessons in fourth grade, and could easily read the sheet music in the practice books the class would use. As he read he could hear the notes play in his mind as if he were in the middle of a concert of violins and pianos and all manner of woodwind instruments playing these... admittedly simple songs. In truth, there was nothing special in these songs, composed of mostly half notes and whole notes, with a slow tempo, they were your basic beginner songs. *Baa Baa Black Sheep, Mary Was a Little Lamb,* classic nursery songs for beginners. That said, for some students, they were just as challenging as if you had asked them to perform open-heart surgery with a banana peel and a butter knife.

If Boe was the top of the class in science, math, Fogish, and history, Lute was the top in music. Mrs. Fairgrove had even considered bribing him at one point with his own music sheet, or the promise to let him take the recorder home if it meant he stopped getting into trouble. *He used to be such a sweet boy.* She would think to herself as the class set up the room. *And underneath his new personality, I can still see what he used to be. What on Earth happened?*

It was still early in the school year, and since most of the students were struggling with actually playing, she decided it would be a good time to review how to read sheet music. As she did, Lute's eyes began to wander around the room, the trick of the light from earlier still weighing on his mind. Why did he see the sparkles and why those colors? He tried to focus his eyes on his paw, and see if he could bring back his green shimmer. It was no good however, it was as if the light had never even been there. He shakes his head. At least he would have detention to practice his recorder.

1:30 pm. "Free time", as Mrs. Fairgrove called it. Really, it was her time to get the class to fix the room back to the way it was before music class, and then have a few minutes before the bell to work on the homework. You weren't allowed to get out of your desk once the room was set up again, you couldn't talk, and if you were like Lute, and didn't have one, you couldn't be on your cell phone.

2:00 pm. Detention. The bell rings and nearly everyone immediately runs out of the room and soon after the school, Randy leads the charge. The last three in the room would be Mrs. Fairgrove, Lute, and Boe P. Boe would wait to be the last out so she didn't have to deal with the crowds. At least, that's what she said anyway, in truth she stayed behind in the hopes that Lute wouldn't have detention, and have to be alone here.

Either way, she would leave, and that would leave Lute and Mrs. Fairgrove alone. "Lute..." she started, "this is the tenth time you've gotten detention this year," she says as she approaches him. "Last year, you got ONE from sticking gum under a desk, but this year... and this time you even broke out of the school! Honestly, just what are you thinking?"

Lute remained silent, he didn't know how to respond.

"You can't just stay silent on this matter. I need something, anything! Lute, I want to help you, but you've got to talk to me."

He looks down and away, not wanting to make eye contact. Mrs. Fairgrove had a reputation around the school as one of the kindest teachers, always willing to find a compromise or alternative solution to help the students. He doesn't feel right lying to her.

"If you keep acting up like this, I'm going to need to schedule a parent-teacher conference!"

"No!" he stands quickly, "anything but that." he curls his paws tightly into firsts as he tries to hold himself back. "Please. My dad's always working, he can't come in for that." he tries to brush off his sudden outburst.

"I see." Mrs. Fairgrove takes a step back at that outburst, "then what about your mother?"

Lute falls silent again.

"Is something wrong?"

It happened a few months ago, but he still doesn't like talking about it. Sometimes, even thinking about it for long enough can still make him upset. Tears form in his eye as he looks away again, Mrs. Fairgrove's ears drop, she understands without a word needing to be said. She approaches him and puts a paw on his shoulder. "I'm sorry, I didn't know. If you ever need someone to talk to about this..." she tries to comfort him.

Lute wipes his eyes and blows his nose, "Thanks, Mrs. Fairgrove. Can I go practice now?"

"Yes... just, try to relax, okay honey? I'm going to the teacher's lounge to print out tomorrow's lesson, I'll be right back," she says before leaving. Once more, Lute found himself alone.

The world always seems so quiet. There's noise in the distance if you listen closely, the sounds of passing cars and stray musical notes from people playing their radios too loud. But one must strain their ears to actually hear it, especially when inside, the noise falls nearly silent. Perhaps that's why Lute enjoys music so much, so he doesn't have to deal with the absolute silence.

There's a couple of songs he knows that aren't in the book. Songs that make him feel strange when he plays them. He decides to play one to try and get his mind off of how he's feeling. This song in particular usually makes him feel better, his mom used to sing it to him. It's a relaxing, somewhat upbeat song that immediately fills the minds of those who hear it with thoughts of springtime, and green fields full of flowers. Of bright sunlight and buzzing bees, the calm rains that come to feed the growing plants and the gentle breeze that blows through all of it. This song always helps Lute calm down. Any listener might even manage to catch a whiff of magnolias, and jasmine and other flowers as their minds play tricks on their senses as they connect the music with spring.

Mrs. Fairgrove still hasn't returned, and Lute does feel a bit better from playing that song, but there's one more that finds a way to calm him even more. He takes a deep breath and sets the notes out before him in his mind. This song is haunting to the listener. Low deep notes that sound like they shouldn't be able to come from the instrument he's using. The notes play slowly as they sound and reverberate around the room. He played it softly at first, allowing the music to fill every space of the room in its own time, like a thick goo that spreads outwards from that single point at the end of his recorder. Anyone who listens to it would find themselves haunted by the song, never truly forgetting it as the notes pierce their skulls and ingrain themselves in the minds of the listeners. If music truly is the voice of the soul, then this song is the words of pain, agony, and despair that a soul can scream into the void.

A sniffle and the sounds of tears cause Lute to end the song before he continues into the second verse. He looks behind him to find Mrs. Fairgrove entering the room, she wipes a tear from her eye. "That was beautiful." She composes herself, "I didn't know we had a song like that."

"We don't," Lute admitted, "I made it up."

She takes a step back, "You composed that yourself? But you're so young!"

"So was Wolfgang, and Bleet-hooven, they made great music, as you've shown us in class. This is just something that came to me one night."

"Still, that was beautiful. Have you written it down?"

"No, ma'am."

"Hang on, let me grab you a blank score so you can!" She says, rushing over to the supply cabinets, she searches around for a bit but comes out empty-pawed. "Strange, we seem to be out, I'll have to order some. Do you think you'll remember it until we do?"

"I don't think I'll ever forget it," Lute admitted reluctantly. He didn't want to write it down but figured it would be a good way to keep on Mrs. Fairgrove's nice list and to pay her back a bit for all the detentions.

"Well regardless," she decided to change the subject, "I know this must be a hard time for you..." She hesitates, a passing thought catches her attention, could the loss of his mother be the reason he was able to create such a beautiful dirge? Ignoring it, she knew the important thing was to comfort him. "But if you need anything, I'm always here to talk." She reaches out a paw for Lute.

"Thanks, Mrs. Fairgrove." He said, taking her paw as she pulled him into a hug. It was unexpected but honestly appreciated. He buried his face into her stomach, hugging her back tightly. When he pulled back, he could see the green sparkle on his fur again, and coming from Mrs. Fairgrove's fur, a shimmer of pure golden light radiated off of her, though it was very weak. He blinked, and the colors were gone again.

There was still time left in detention before he could be sent home, so he began to play the first song again, it's brighter, more friendly. The kind of song that works well after such a bitter and sad number to help cleanse the pallet. The upbeat nature of the song quickly helped both teacher and student get into a somewhat better mood. Mrs. Fairgrove begins setting up the classroom for the next day, getting all the supplies in place, and writing out the lesson plan on the board. That's one of the benefits of being in detention every day, he gets to see the next day's lesson, and hey, he seems to be able to focus on it more while playing, so bonus. It's honestly probably one of the only reasons he's not a complete F student and manages to hang on with Cs and Bs.

3:00 pm. Time to go home. Mrs. Fairgrove looks up at the clock now that everything is ready, and lets Lute know it's time to go home. He cleans and puts the recorder back into the locker with the rest of the music equipment. They leave the room, and as Mrs. Fairgrove locks up, she turns to Lute who's already walking away. "Hey, do you need a ride home?" she asks. "You normally ride the bus, don't you?"

"I do, but it's fine, it's only about a half hour's walk away, and it's a nice day out."

"Are you sure? I wouldn't mind like I said if you ever need anything..."

"It's fine, I promise." Lute smiled, as he left her behind and headed outside to bask in the wonderful sunlight and... bad-smelling air of the edge of Orange Bay's metropolitan district. It's not the safest place in the world, hence the need for a security guard. But as long as he doesn't go north into the city proper he's fine, which is also fine since he lives south of the school. The path home sends him down roads and roads of small shops and homes, the old post office, and the gas station that almost no one uses, and a couple of restaurants too.

The walk is long and somewhat boring in all truth, he hums to himself to keep his spirits up, and sometimes if he's really lucky, he'll have managed to get some money from the table in the kitchen, or the counter in the living room and will grab dinner from one of the restaurants on his way home. Today was not one of those days, so he had to begin thinking of what he was going to do for food when he got home. There's still some ramen in the pantry and a couple of cans of soup. There might even be some leftover takeout his dad brought home the night before, though he kinda doubts it.

Regardless, he makes his way back home, he knows the path like the back of his paw and has started to find a few additional ways, it's always good to have a backup plan after all. Arriving home he fishes the key out of his backpack and heads inside.

His house is dark and small. Yet no matter how many lights he turns on, or how many rooms he closes it never seems any less empty, any brighter, or any more homely. It's like there was some spark of magic that was here but is gone now, leaving the shell of a house behind. The house is dirty, with chips and cracks in the walls, and crumbs and stains of who knows what on the ground. Lute does his best to keep the place tidy, cleaning off the table every weekend, and dusting wherever he can reach. But no matter how hard he tries, or how high he jumps, there's still stains and dust just out of his reach. The vacuum broke a month ago, and the broom's bristles are beginning to fray and snap, and soon it too will be useless. He knows better than to ask for replacements.

His homework done already, he fishes out a can of soup and begins heating it in the microwave. Lute tries to make himself comfy on the big chair in front of the TV, there's a hard lump in it because of the tool his father keeps between the cushions. He flips on the TV and changes it from the news station to the local Public Broadcasting station. There's never anything good on, but it's still better than the news and its endless tirade about incompetent leaders and foreign terrors. The news is truly the worst thing on TV, unlike what he hears from Boe about the positivity and benefits that the world is developing, the news only focuses on the negative.

It's 2020... he thinks to himself, *people are buying advanced robotics, we have medicine that can cure many diseases, pollution is going down, and people are showing acts of kindness towards one another every day! Why does Dad's news station have to only focus on the scary and sad parts?*

The public broadcasting station isn't very interesting. Occasionally he gets something good, like cartoons about Dragons, or how to speak other languages. Other times he gets reruns of the science show from class, and other times still, he gets boring talk shows or local crazy people doing crazy things for fun. *They'd make more money online,* he muses, *but hey, they're still funny and this way I get to see them!*

He laughs at that and continues to laugh as the show that comes on features someone called "Captain Video". He's doing awesome, yet stupid things, like using a leafblower to make a motorized skateboard to roll around town with and perform various tricks. He eats his dinner just as it goes over, and some old black and white monster movie is about to come on. He loved these things. They were creepy, but also really corny. You can't really be afraid of obvious plastic props and fake blood made of chocolate sauce.

The movie ends, and it's late. He returns the TV to the news station and turns it off before placing the remote back on his Dad's chair. And quickly cleans up in the kitchen, making sure to leave his dishes out to dry and not to leave a spot or speck or crumb anywhere. He slinks off to his room, an average bedroom, it's got a bed, a desk, and an old bulky tv set. Mind you he doesn't get any channels on it, but he has a VHS player, though it broke a while ago. He considered saving up his dinner money to try and get a replacement or repair or maybe getting a job on a paper route or something if those are still a thing anyway.

Regardless, his is most likely the cleanest room in the house, Lute's dad stopped paying the exterminator a few weeks back, so he knew if this room got dirty he might have to deal with bugs at night, which he'd rather not do. Just as he closed the door, he could hear the front door opening. *Just in time.* He thinks as he quickly turns off his bedroom light. Dad's home, it's time for bed. He hops into bed and climbs under his cover, ready to begin the cycle all over again tomorrow.

Dreams:

Curious things happen in dreams. No matter how hard we try, we never remember them all, nor do we remember all the details of them. All the figments and fantasies, all the ideas that bubble through your skull as your mind digests the past and confronts the present. Some even say that dreams are your mind diving through your past to predict a possible future for yourself, but you can never focus, and so you only ever see bits and parts of it. Glimpses of the past and of what might come mixed with what you have never seen and never will see again.

One night, you can dream you're a knight riding on horseback and fighting a vicious dragon to save a princess in distress. Others you could be a pirate sailing the seven seas with your crew to find treasure and high adventure. Some nights you could be just a spectator, watching a screen as some movie plays on in your mind that doesn't exist. And then some nights... Some nights you get nightmares. We all get the same ones, for they are archetypes of bad dreams and fears that just about anyone can have, and while some can be wholly unique, others are quite common.

Birds will fear the dreams where while they fly, their wings are suddenly clipped, and they fall to the earth below them. Just about every child has the one about showing up to school in their underpants on the big test day they didn't study for. There's the dream where you have to leave home forever, being hunted by the law for something you have no idea of. And there's the classic one where you're standing in a sort of sun-god robes atop a pyramid surrounded by screaming women who are throwing tiny pickles at you. No? Why am I the only one to have that dream?

Regardless, many weird and wild things can and do happen every night. They're an escape from reality, from the outside world, and all of its hardships. Monsters can appear in dreams. Giant birds that command the storms and rain, dragons that seem snake-like, and dark figures veiled in shadow as dark as the night, and cryptids whose eyes sparkle like the stars in far off galaxies in space.

Perhaps, the strangest of all the creatures and monsters that a dream can produce, of all the giant abominations and ancient evils given new life and shape, the absolute strangest to find in a dream defies all of these ideas.

A friend in a dream, sometimes people can even bring them back into reality with them. The tulpa, or an imaginary friend, your Zannas and guardian angels. Figments of wild imagination that can have no true place in the waking world. They are kind voices that guide you, or friendly faces you can't quite place where you've seen them before, or even IF you've seen them before. Lute has one of these.

It was... cute, to say the least. Some small purple creature, it looked kinda like a malformed bunny with weird ears and crescent moons on its forehead and chest.

There were pink hearts on all four of its paw pads, and it had a long tail like that of a fox. Much like Lute, he would always be wearing a hat, some kind of bonnet really, but the rest of the time his clothes changed to fit the dream Lute was having.

Lute had met him at the best possible time to meet a friend like this too. It wasn't too long after his mother died. He just remembers the dream started that night dark and cold, and he just cried into the void before some giant figure started chasing him. It had gleaming red eyes and claws larger than Lute, it was chanting, "YOU DID THIS!" over and over again as Lute just ran away to try and hide. The shadows were catching up to him and overtook him too, but just before he could no longer see the world around him, a shining light descended from on high and dispelled the shadows. The light faded, and Lute's imaginary friend was there, and while he would love to say he was in some cool pose like from a superhero movie, in truth he looked even more afraid than Lute.

He stood there awkwardly, legs spread too far apart to have good stability, head tilted down, and visible tears in his eyes, he stuttered out to Lute, "T-t-t-take my paw!" The creature tried to grab them again, but Lute took his new friend's advice, and the world dissolved around him, and he found himself in his bedroom... still asleep, and holding the creature's paw. It let go and went to the other side of his desk, hiding from him. "S-s-sorry!" he shouts over to Lute. "I just saw you were in danger, and I had to help!"

Lute took a deep breath, trying to figure out what's going on. "Wait, how am I here? That's me, but... I'm here?" He placed a paw on his chest, and it phased right through it. "Woah! A-am I a ghost?!"

"N-no." the creature said as it sticks its head out from around the corner of the desk. "This is a... uhh... a dream... yeah. You were having a nightmare, but I decided to change it and bring you to your room..."

"Some dream." Lute rolls his eyes, "Couldn't have made it anything more exciting?"

"S-sorry. I'm not very good at this, I just started..."

"Good at what? Making dreams?"

"Yes! I mean no! I mean... uh... could we change the subject maybe?"

Dream Lute laughed, "Hah! So, what are you, I don't think I've seen anything like you before."

He comes out entirely, revealing his body entirely, he was dressed just like Lute dresses. "I'm... a friend. I can come to you in dreams." the creature hesitates. "You can call me Culania."

"Well, Culania, I'm Lute. Thanks for saving me from the monster." he smiles. "I've... been kinda dealing with that dream for a while now..." he frowns, "about a week."

"Y-yeah, I know, I wanted to help earlier but was scared," Culania admits.

"Hey better late than never. So... dream friend, can we do something fun?"

"Like what?" Culania tilts his head.

"Like... I dunno, how about a carnival? Or maybe an amusement park? We could play on the beach? This is a dream, I can control it right?" he tries to focus and make something happen, but nothing does.

"Err, well, actually, look at the clock." sure enough it was already 6:30, soon Lute would wake up.

"Oh, bummer. Well, thanks for at least ending the nightmare."

"Y-yeah... umm... I can't come back every night, but maybe... we could try this again soon?"

"I'd like that." Lute smiled as he returned to his body and woke up.

Weeks went by, and then months, true to his word, Culania did come back. Every week he would come back, almost always on a Friday, occasionally he would come on other days as well. The two of them would have fun, going through various dreamscapes, flying through the sky, riding on the backs of dragons, playing giant board games... one night Lute even performed a concert in front of a giant crowd. They were always fun, and Lute was glad to have another friend outside of Boe, even if he was only in his dreams.

He would still have nightmares, mostly on nights when his imaginary friend was absent. He would do his best to deal with them, but they would still cause him to have restless nights, and often even wake up in a cold sweat. That monster kept coming back in his nightmares, sometimes so close it could reach out a claw and smother him, other nights it would just stand off in the distance, towering behind the faraway trees and sometimes reaching off into the sky itself. Those nights were the better ones for the nightmares, he was the most afraid of that creature, but there were others, smaller monsters that would come and he would have to deal with them directly.

These were shadowy figures of predators and wild beasts. Giant reptiles would chomp and bite at him and try to consume him whole as he had to jump between them to reach a goal that always seemed further away. Faceless men with spindly limbs longer than their entire bodies, dressed in suits as black as the night would chase him through the woods as he brought keys to a wooden box in the heart of the forest, but no matter what he did, they would always catch him.

The worst nights of all, however, came when no monsters nor friends showed. These seemed... strange. Not even like normal nightmares. These always left him feeling drained like his life had been sucked out of him. He would wake up those mornings wanting to just go back to sleep as if he hadn't slept at all the night before. The one good part of those nights is that they were exceedingly rare. So far, since he's started regularly getting nightmares, he's only had these twice. As such, they were also the hardest to remember, as the rest recurred so often he could tell you just about all the details of them.

Whatever this type of nightmare was, he can only remember fire and smoke, the sounds of grinding chains, and the rusted metal rubbing together. A shadow descends from the city and swallows all light before it until nothing remains.

It sounds tame, but it feels real to him. Like the flames are actually burning him, and the smoke fills his lungs. Both times, there was a feeling of burning metal clamps around his arms and legs, and a sharp pain that stabs his chest just as he wakes up.

And of course, there are the nights where he has no dream. No nightmare, and no... whatever that last thing was, come to him. Everybody has nights like this, you fall asleep and wake up in the morning, rested, but you don't remember the night before. Sure these are common for most people, but for Lute they're uncommon. It's mostly nightmares and his dreams with his friend.

As for tonight, tonight he got a surprise visit from Culania. "Hiya buddy!" the creature said upon Lute "waking" in the dream world, some bright castle halls made of stone. In the few short weeks, he had gotten over his shyness and became quite close and affectionate towards Lute, even hugging him upon Lute's arrival. "Hope you don't mind me calling you tonight! I wanted to show you my home!"

Lute smiled and looked at his friend. He was wearing shorts and a cape, as well as a small crown. "Your home? Hah! I never knew you were a king. Well, your 'highness', I'm glad you decided to show me!" he jokes before pulling his friend into a nuggie.

"It's true! C'mon, I'll show you around!" he offers as he pulls out of the hold. The two of them go paw in paw down the halls and around the rooms, exploring the king's throne room, the library, and the court wizard's chamber. No one else was around, but that was fine. They ended in what Culania claimed was his room. It was filled with toys and games, a large bed, much too large for the small creature, and a sizable desk. There was fabric and fluff scattered about, as well as needles and thread, some scissors, and other sewing gear.

"This place is incredible!" Lute laughed, "shame I can't just move in with you."

"Heh, maybe someday!" Culania smiled.

"I wish," Lute said as he frowned and sat down, resting his head on his legs. "You saw my home, yours is so much nicer. This is just a dream, I'll have to wake up eventually."

"Yeah, but that's why I'm here." Culania sits down next to him. "I wanna help you make these dreams come true."

"That sounds nice," Lute admits, "but I doubt I'll ever see this one come true. That would be like magic if I did."

"Well? What's wrong with magic?"

"It's not real. If it was then..." he catches himself, "then things would be so much better."

"Magic is real though! Just try some when you wake up. Focus your eyes and look at someone, you'll see colors glowing around them!"

"Wait, what?!" The excitement made Lute shoot up in bed as he shouted those words. A loud stomp on the floor followed by a gruff shout of "QUIET!" and he quickly pretended to fall back to sleep.

Under the covers, Lute hides, covering his mouth and holding his breath, waiting until he's sure it's safe. If sounds come down the hall, then he needs to be extra convincing that he's asleep. He tries to keep calm, not breathe too heavily, but it's dark, and he doesn't like the dark. He doesn't fear what may lie in the dark, he knows there's a monster down the hall that will come if he angers it. In truth that monster is the most terrifying he has to face, even more so than the ones he sees in his dreams. Those? They attack and he wakes up, a sting of phantom pain for a moment, but it's gone before he even blinks his eyes again. When this monster attacks, the pain lasts and never seems to end, and if he acknowledges it, the monster becomes angrier and may hurt him again.

He's taken to telling people all kinds of lies to convince them that he's okay. The class clown persona helps with that, as he can play the role of a clutz.

"Where did that bruise come from?" they might ask.

"I ran into a door." he'd lie.

"Why are you limping?" they'd worry.

"Guess I slept wrong." he'd shrug it off.

"Why do you have a bandage on your nose?"

"I cut myself making breakfast." he came up with lies and learned to come up with them quickly to sound believable. Perhaps one day he might even make a great actor.

Time passes as he lies there, listening to the ticking of the clock, and, upon hearing no sound coming from down the hall, lets out a silent sigh of relief, and prays the monster falls asleep and decides to focus on what he had just dreamed. *The light?* he thinks. *How did he know about the light?* It couldn't be true, could it? He just had to focus his eyes and see...

He lifts his paw from beneath the covers and holds it out in front of his face. "If what he was saying is true, then I just need to focus and the glow will appear." He stares at it, straining his eyes to make it out in the dim light of his bedroom. He tries focusing on it intently, squinting, crossing his eyes, or letting his vision go blurry. He tried everything he could think of, but it was no use, no matter what he did, he just couldn't get that green shine from earlier to reappear. He tries for what feels like hours, and it might even have been hours, as he lost track of time as he tried.

Giving up, he lowers his paw back down and sprawls out across his small bed the best he can. *Magic's not real.* He disappointedly reminds himself, closing his eyes. *If it was, that would have worked, and I wouldn't be here, and mom would...* his thoughts trail off. *But why would he say that to me, get me all worked up over nothing?* And then he remembered, *O-oh, right. He's not real either, he's just a dream. It's just a dream...*

He tries to fall back asleep, but it's no good, he just can't fall back asleep after all that, not that he would need to anyway. Glancing over at his clock, he sees that it's already six in the morning. Soon the monster will be gone, having left for work for the day, and he can get up and just have an early start to his day.

He knew his routine well enough by now, and with the extra time he had gotten after the monster left, he managed to make a halfway decent breakfast, nothing fancy, just some toast and jam, and an overcooked potato he diced up and microwaved. Lute was many things, but a cook was not one of them. If it couldn't go in the microwave or toaster, he hadn't a clue. On his way to school he manages to avoid Randy today, so hey, maybe it's his lucky day for once! He crashes next to Boe in the back of the bus.

"Are you alright? You look... tired," she said, taking note of the small bags under his eyes.

"I can't be too tired." Lute responded, "After all, I'm not a bike."

"That's not what I mean and you know it! You're gonna get in trouble for sleeping in Mrs. Fairgrove's class again you know. She'll throw the book at you!"

"Oh cool, I hope it's a bedtime story, those always help me catch even more sleep."

"Maybe it'll help you learn something for once," Boe grumbles before going back to her phone. Lute meanwhile begins drifting off to sleep again, usually, he waits until class, but he is extra tired this morning, and figured Boe would watch him and wake him when they arrived. Thankfully he was right, and after arriving in class and staying awake long enough for attendance, he went fully back to sleep.

Immediately he awoke in Culania's bedroom... in particular, in his bed, despite remembering having last sat on the floor. "Hey! You're back already!" Culania was there, smiling, watching over him. "You had me worried when you suddenly woke up like that and didn't come back!"

Lute sits up in the bed. "Yeah well, it's your fault for waking me like that," he grumbles. "Don't be surprised if it happens again, I'm supposed to be in class right now."

"Oh, then why are you asleep? We can play tonight or something." he shakes his head. "You should go back now."

"Hah! I can't if I wanted to. Thanks to you I woke up early and didn't get any real sleep last night. I'm exhausted." he laughs. How *can he be exhausted in a dream?*

"Oh, sorry," Culania says, as a frown crosses his face. "Let me take care of that for you."

"What do you?" Before he can respond, Culania places a paw on Lute's forehead and he suddenly awakens in class. It's still the Fogish lesson, and no one seems to have noticed his sudden start. He looks around, everything seems fine and he feels... good? Great in fact! Like he does right after lunch and he's in the playground. He's full of energy and in a good mood.

At least the mood started good anyway. He stays awake and alert for the entire class, sure, but his mind does still drift as he tries to figure out WHAT has just happened. *How can a dream, no matter how good, make him feel so energetic in less than a half-hour?* Class continues as normal, though the teacher does notice Lute's extra attentiveness, she just assumes he's decided to try harder today, or he got better sleep last night.

Lunch came, and Boe had to ask why Lute seemed so energetic all of a sudden. "Just this morning you were sleeping on the bus, and now you look like you're going to run a marathon during recess!" She wasn't wrong either, that's exactly how he felt, and even considered doing so. "Be honest with me Lute, are you taking something?"

"No! What? Boe, come on, you know me. I always get more energetic after lunch."

"Yeah, but usually you sleep through class!"

He shrugs, "I dunno man. Maybe it's like, my second wind or something? Isn't that a thing?"

Boe just sighs and finishes her lunch. "I mean I guess. Just... don't do anything stupid. ESPECIALLY after that trick, you pulled yesterday." Speaking of yesterday, lunch ended, and it was time for recess, everyone was gathered by the slide when he arrived. It seems that they had all seen Lute's jump yesterday and wanted to try it for themselves. Some were more successful than others and managed to reach the fence, one even managed to grab near the top of it as Lute had. But it was an unspoken rule that you can't climb up the fence for their game, so they would just climb back down to try again.

Lute couldn't help but laugh at the fact no one had tried that before or thought to try it before. Not that he could care less, Randy was busy over there with the rest of the "tough" kids trying their luck, so Lute didn't have to worry about him today and could instead focus on his training. He has all that extra energy today, so it was a good time as any to work out. With the extra pep in his step, he managed an additional two laps around the playground. He also thinks he manages to jump a bit higher than he normally would, but that could just be his mind playing a trick on him because of everyone else's jumping.

Classes resumed soon enough, and it was in music class again that he noticed something odd. While it wasn't the shine and glow that he had seen yesterday, he could have sworn that while he was playing, he could see just a faint sparkle of light dancing around the class. It moved rhythmically as he played, keeping its dance in time with his music, rising high and falling low with the change of notes. The song they were playing as a class was a slow nursery rhyme, and it danced slowly, performing what might be called ballet. Of course, it's really hard to say exactly what type of dance a cluster of flying sparkles of light is performing, but that was the only thing that came to Lute's mind as he watched.

When the song ended, the lights faded and were soon gone, as if they had never existed. He shrugs it off, and the class helps clean up the room, before he knew it, it was time to go home! And bonus, he managed to avoid detention. At least, that was a bonus for Boe and would have been a bonus for just about anyone else. Lute, however, was disappointed it meant he had to go home with less practice time.

Boe walked home with him. The two talked about their next possible group project, as there hasn't been one all year yet, and they knew they were due for one.

"Also, I'm surprised at you, you managed to go a whole day without detention! What, did you finally get bored with it?"

"Nah," Lute smiled, as he played with a pencil in his paws, "I just forgot to goof off today, maybe tomorrow

I'll flip over my desk or climb the fence again, something that will get me detention for like a month."

"Why do you even want detention? Seriously, it's like, the most boring thing. I like learning and all, but even I don't want to stay in school after it's over." she sighed as they rounded the corner to their street.

"I mean, you're not wrong, but that's because you have things that you could do instead. Mrs. Fairgrove wouldn't let you keep your cell phone, but I ain't got one of those." he sticks the pencil back in his pocket and begins to list other things. "You've got a tv with like, a gazillion channels, and your own flute, and a video game console, and a computer..." he stops counting and starts laughing. "Meanwhile I've just got public access! Least at school, I can play the recorder for a bit."

She just looked at him like he was some kind of alien. "Well if that's the case, then why are you so happy about it?"

He took a breath and smiled wide. "Cuz', I don't need all that stuff. I mean sure, I'd like my own instrument, and sure, I'd like to see some new movies, but I'm happy with what I have and can make my own fun." he says as he hums a little song to himself, he then hops down to his house, right next door to Boe's. He waves goodbye to her and heads inside.

As he flipped on the TV, his mind started to wander again, back to his strange dream, and his imaginary friend. He would need to remember this for the next time they meet, and ask just what the heck he had done. Regardless, he found himself enthralled by the TV, a movie marathon on his channel of old Destiny movies. Well, old in general, but to him, several of them were new, and being new, made him forget about keeping an eye on the time and world around him. He fell in love with these 'new' movies, the animation, the jokes, and most especially the songs. One, in particular, about a goat who found a lamp that contained a djinni. They became friends, and the djinni could grant his every wish. If only he could have a magical friend like that. He couldn't stop watching, but that would end up being his downfall.

Eyes still transfixed on the TV, his ears twitched and heart sank when he heard the front door opening. He fumbled with the remote, but the battery had died, and he couldn't shut it off. He threw it down onto the chair and jumped up to turn it off by paw, just as he did, however, he heard a terrible, horrible sound.

"What do you think you're doing?" It was gruff, and short, and very angry, with each syllable it reeked a stench similar to paw sanitizer, or the bottle of burning liquid the school nurse would use on students that got cuts. Turning to face his fear, the first thing he saw was the puffs of smoke emanating from its mouth, as if it were some fire breathing dragon, then came the horrible sight of his uniform and scruffy, unkempt appearance. The bloodshot eyes and perpetually unkempt fur gave him an appearance of having given up, yet made him look nonetheless intimidating.

The monster was home.

The Monster:

"I said, what do you think you're doing?" it grunted out again, as it took a solitary step forward. The monster was short, barely five feet tall, but it might as well have been five hundred feet tall since either way he towered over Lute.

"I was just-" Lute tried to defend himself, but was interrupted by the monster.

"I was just blah blah..." it said in a shrill mocking tone to further condemn Lute as it took another step forward while Lue shrank backward, pressing up against the wall behind him. "You know you're not supposed to be watching TV." it cracks its knuckles, "TV costs money and drains power that costs more money. Do you have that kind of money boy?"

"N-no, but Da-!"

"No buts! You know the rules, or at least I thought you did, you little punk." Another step, now not even the monster's chair was between the two. "It looks to me that you need another lesson."

Lute tried to calm himself, tried to figure a way out of this, or how to prevent what was about to happen, he could try to run, there's a gap to the right of the monster, if he was fast enough, he could make it to his room and barricade the door... He'd need to distract it first.

"Look!" he shouts, pointing to the left behind the monster, "A distraction!" by some minor miracle, perhaps because of how drunk the monster was, but it turned its head to look, and Lute dashed off towards his room.

"HEY! Get back here now or I'm going to give you such a beating!" it shouted as it gave chase as if it wasn't always going to beat Lute. He ran down the hall, nearly to his bedroom door, if he could just make it inside... "GOTCHA!" But it was too late, the monster grabbed him by the back of his overalls, and then in his other paw, grabbed Lute's ears so he couldn't struggle or try to break free without hurting himself. "You think you're hot shit, don't you?" it gives Lute's ears a hard tug, making him fall to his knees. "Well, we'll fix that."

Lute had to try something else, he couldn't just let it end there. There was one thing, but he doubted it would work now. That song... the one that made his teacher cry, and he was so reluctant to write down the notes of. For whatever reason, that song makes people cry, and feel sadness, dread, and all manner of unpleasant thoughts. They just break down upon hearing it. And he knew it was effective against the monster for he had used it against the monster before! He didn't even need an instrument, he just had to hum the notes. He doesn't know why but it seems to always work.

He tries to hum it out, but all he can let out is a whine after the first note, for the monster hits him hard in the ribs. "Shut up," it growled before punching him a second time. "You think everything is easy don't you?" it asks as it tosses him into the wall before grabbing him again. "You think it's all gonna be okay. Don't you?" It punches Lute in the face with all the fury of a car on the road. "This is all YOUR fault!" it screams as it knocks him down.

Lute just lays there, he doesn't try to fight, or to run, or to sing and try and make it stop, he was in too much pain to do anything other than cry and grab at his chest and face. Why did he have to be here? Couldn't he be anywhere else? It's just not right.

The monster spits on him. "I'm gonna make sure you pay for what you've done," it growls as it picks him up by his left arm. "You're never going to forget this, you hear me? I'll make sure you know to obey me!"

"N-no! P-p-please, stop!" Lute cried as the monster put its second paw on Lute's arm.

It hissed. "Tell anyone, and you're dead." And with a quick shove and twist it broke Lute's arm clean in half!

"AAAAAAAAAAAAAAAAAAAA!" Lute screamed at the top of his lungs as the monster did, tears running down his face. The monster let him go and seemingly lost interest in the crying child curled up on its floor and wandered off to fall asleep in its chair despite the sobs and wails that overtime became quieter and quieter.

Slowly, but surely, still filled with pain, his arm flailing about, he knew he couldn't stay there, he had to get out and get help. But what would he say? He couldn't tell the truth, and he couldn't come back to the monster if he did. Regardless, it didn't matter. He picked himself up, one arm in his other, and began making his way to the front door. The monster wouldn't wake up after that, so he easily managed to get outside.

The hospital would help him first, and ask questions later. Maybe he'd get really lucky and not have to say a thing, and just act like he didn't know anything. But it was late and dark, and the streets weren't safe, and he knew it. He made it to the end of the street before collapsing again from the pain.

"C'mon, I can't stop here." he whispers to himself, "Just gotta keep moving forward..."

"Oh my god! Lute!" a familiar voice came up from behind him as a porch light was turned on. Looking up, he saw he had managed to collapse right in front of Boe's house who ran out to him. Boe helped him up while her mother came over and got both of them into her car.

"Hang on, we'll get you patched up real soon." Boe's mom said as she ignored all decent road rules to quickly get them to the hospital.

"We heard the scream." Boe admitted, "was that you?"

Lute just sniffles and nods sadly.

"What happened?"

He doesn't respond. What could he say? No one would believe whatever lie he could come up with, and the truth could get him killed.

"Boe..." her mom said, not taking her eyes off the road as she ran a stop sign. "Maybe it's best not to ask such a question right now. Let's just worry about getting him fixed up."

Boe's a clever girl, and hearing what her Mom just said, she knew what had happened and understood why she couldn't say anything. So instead she just hugged him tight and said they'll figure something out.

They arrived at the hospital, and Mrs. P carried Lute into the emergency room. She received a surprised look from the receptionist as she carried him right past the desk and to her office up in the pediatric ward. She sat him down on a counter and went to gather the supplies she needed to set his arm. "I'll be just a second," she said, before leaving the two kids alone.

The office is cold and smells damp, yet strongly of antiseptic and old medicine. The walls are brightly painted to keep the children that come in for their check-ups in a positive mood before the almost inevitable inoculation and vaccination they're due for. There's an analog clock on the wall that ticks loudly as each second passes, seemingly in time with the pulsations of pain that emanate in waves from Lute's arm throughout the rest of his body. The air is heavy and silent as if there was an unseen force preventing any sound from being made.

"Lute... you know you can tell me anything, right?" Boe finally broke the oppressive silence as she placed a paw on Lute's unbroken arm. "I'm your friend. I promise you're safe to tell me anything you need to say."

"..." Lute just sighed and grabbed his paw; he couldn't think of a good lie, so he decided on a lousy half-truth. "A monster broke it," he admitted.

"A monster?" Boe asked, half annoyed and half concerned.

"Yeah, I was home alone, and this giant burst through my front door, it broke my arm, and I managed to run out before it could finish me off."

"I... see." she looks down at his broken arm. "And this monster... is it gonna..." before she could finish, Mrs. P returned, and Boe hopped down from the table so the doctor could set his arm and put him in a smart cast. There was a good half hour or so of them moving between this office to a nearby X-ray chamber, getting Lute some child painkillers, a cast, and applying the harder outer layer of the cast to prevent him from moving his arm too much.

"Try not to move your fingers; it's going to hurt whenever you do. Also, it's probably going to itch while in there, and you're going to need to wrap it in plastic before you bathe." Mrs. P sighs, "I can't believe he did this..." she muttered.

"He didn't do this!" Lute panicked and tried to deny the truth, reflexively twitching his arm and getting a fresh jolt of pain as his reward. "It was some kinda monster that broke down the front door."

"Look, kid-"

"Lute," Boe told her.

"Lute." She sat down next to him on the table, petting his head and holding his paw. "Look, I know you're afraid, but you can't just make up stories like that. You know what happened, I know what happened, Boe knows what happened. We all know what happened, and we want to help you okay?" something about her words was calming, Lute felt like he could trust her. "You've gotta be honest with me though. I promise I won't let anything happen to you."

"That's right!" Boe said, a fire burning in her eyes, "Nobody deserves treatment like that! We'll keep you safe!" she bleated out.

Lute was silent. He wanted to believe them and felt like they were being honest, he wanted to trust them, but the pain was still fresh, and the monster's words filled his head. "Tell anyone and you're dead!" it shouted as it rang through his ears, and he winced.

Mrs. P glanced up at the clock and shook her head, "It's late. Why don't you have a sleepover with Boe tonight? I'll take you both to school in the morning, and we can figure all of this..." she gestures to Lute's broken arm, "out."

He nodded, and within a few minutes, they were back in the car on the way back to Boe's house. Nobody says anything on the ride home, Lute still in pain and worried about what will come next, Mrs. P figuring out what she should do to resolve this issue, and Boe wondering how to help her friend. Faint sounds of thunder are on the horizon, it's supposed to rain in the morning.

Soon enough they arrive home, Mrs. P lays Lute out on the couch, gives him a spare pillow and blanket, and a drink of water. "Try your best to get some sleep okay?" she says as she pets his head, and takes Boe off to bed. Lute lies there on the couch, trying his best to fall asleep, the pain does eventually fade, and he adjusts to the new lack of mobility. He hums a quiet melody to himself as he tries to stop his tears, and not long after he starts, he finally collapses, exhausted from all that has happened today, and falls into a strange, though not dreamless sleep.

It was curious, darkness surrounded him as he felt like he was falling through an endless void. Nothing around him was visible, but at the same time, he still felt the recognizable sensation of falling. As he fell down down down, he heard a voice, or was it a voice? It was quiet, whatever it was, sounding like a whisper of hot breath breathing down the back of his neck, and there was a strange tonality to it as if it was a hushed song. It quietly sang strange notes and words into Lute's mind as he fell.

I cry out to the empty void, hatred born from a lie. To take revenge for what was destroyed, a kiss with darkness, and so I die.

He sees the ground approach suddenly, and just as he hits it, he awakens. The words linger in his mind, he'll never forget them, nor the strange musical tone they had when spoken to him. He couldn't forget. The words fit his sorrow filled song too well.

Somehow, even more tired, if that was even possible at this point, his nose is immediately met by the smell of rich pancakes and fresh fruit Mrs. P made for the four of them, Mr. P having just returned from another night shift, but wanting to see the truth with his own eyes before going to bed. He can hear them talking from the kitchen, "I can't believe he would do this to the kid." Mr. P's lower voice sounded, "What are we going to do about this Mary?"

"I'll tell you one thing, we're not sending him back home. We're just lucky that the bone didn't pierce his skin, and that Lute managed to get as far as our house without going into shock."

"I say we call the cops on him. Child protective services maybe. Get him out of there asap."

"Couldn't agree more, I'll drive the two of them to school, and then make my way to the station downtown. You get some rest, you've been up longer than me."

"Right right." he sighs, "I'm taking the night off, we can make sure he's safe ourselves if we have to."

Lute heard enough, and got up and walked over to the kitchen.

"Oh!" Mr. P, a gruff-looking billy goat that had a reputation in the hospital for being the 'toughest nursing director the hospital had ever seen', said upon seeing the small child. "Good morning!" In truth, both of the Ps had been considered some of the kindest staff the hospital had ever had, they were loved by most if not all of the patients, and made sure the other doctors and nurses kept in line.

"Mornin'" Lute responded as he rubbed his eyes with his one good paw.

"Come, come, take your seat, Boe should be down soon. How did you sleep?" Mrs. P asked.

"Not great," Lute admitted, doing as he was told. Mrs. P served him a bowl of fruit and two of the largest and fluffiest pancakes he had ever seen. He stared at them for a moment.

"Well, go on." Mr. P said, "There's plenty to go around, and you need your strength after yesterday."

He started eating, and true to Mrs. P's word, Boe joined them at the table and began eating her breakfast. "Will you be alright with going to school today?" Mrs. P asked, "I understand if you don't want to." She tried to comfort him.

"I-it's fine," Lute said groggily. "I'm gonna have to go back sooner or later, aren't I?" he half-heartedly laughs. "Just 'cuz I broke a bone doesn't mean Mrs. Fairgrove's not gonna give me a tonna work." He chews his pancake for a moment and reaches for a strawberry, "a skele-ton." He chuckles, while Boe just lets out an exasperated sigh.

"Least h- the monster," she corrects herself, "didn't break your sense of humor." she rolls her eyes.

"Yeah, you could even say I still have my... funny bone!" he half-smiles at that one, but accidentally twitches his fingers and another wave of pain shoots up his arm. "I'll go."

The parents nod, and breakfast is finished, a kiss from his wife and Mr. P is off to bed. A quick bathroom trip later and the kids are ushered back into Mrs. P's car. Much to Lute's horror, it seems Boe usually takes the bus because of how terrible a driver Mrs. P is. Her record is spotless mind you, never having gotten a ticket or angered a cop, but she makes such overly sharp turns and speeds through every light and stop-sign on the way to the school, that they arrive well before the bus does. She gives them each a packed lunch she prepared and speeds off to her errand at the police station.

Before class starts, the duo head inside, and Mrs. Fairgrove is shocked to see them. "Huh, what are-?" she stands up from her desk as she gasps at the sight of Lute. The eye his father punched was bruised and blackened, and the broken arm was obvious. "Oh no, Lute! What happened?! Who did this to you?" She runs over and grabs the small rabbit.

"Mrs. Fairgrove," Boe said. "I think he doesn't want to talk about it." she tries to pull her attention off of the subject. "There was a monster you see, that entered his home and broke his arm." She shot the teacher a knowing glance, that was well understood and received.

"I... see," she said, not letting go of her grip on Lute's shoulders. "I'm sorry this happened. If you need anything..." she's at a loss for words to say in all of this. "Look, I know you must be tired, why don't the two of you take the seats in the back of the classroom today, and you can just sleep, okay?" She crouches down and hugs Lute, he doesn't respond, just stares blankly, feeling all in all kinda numb.

What happened next, at least from Lute's perspective, was sort of a blur. Despite his earlier jokes, he felt strange. That numbness didn't leave him, nor did it just start. It was as if it had been the only thing he could feel since he woke up. Maybe it was the leftover effect of the painkillers from last night or the creepy words from his dream, but it felt like he had just shut off. He went to the back of the class, and following Mrs. Fairgrove's advice, he immediately fell asleep. Some students shot him weird or concerned looks or whispered among themselves, not that Lute was awake enough to hear them, but none of them bothered him. Even Randy, the big tough bully that he was, just took one look at Lute's broken arm and decided to pick on some other kid for the time being.

It was as if the students all had a silent code about them that whatever had happened was best ignored, or left to Mrs. Fairgrove or Boe to deal with. Lute had woken up, just in time for lunch with the usual burst of energy he would get at this time of day, but with his emotions still in their numb-locked state. He and Boe were allowed to eat lunch in the classroom, and even spend recess there as well, which was great because Lute felt like doing absolutely nothing. Probably what made the rest of the class the most concerned, if they bothered to think about Lute too much, was that during Music time, he didn't try to play. Didn't help set up the classroom, nor clean it when music time was over.

He just sat at his desk with this strange look in his eye, like he was feeling his first genuine emotion all day. What that emotion was, nobody could quite put their finger on, but one thing was for sure, and that's while Boe wasn't looking, he used his one good paw to write down something on a piece of paper and stash it in the pocket on the front of his overalls.

Class ended, and Lute was back asleep, deciding to stay asleep until the time detention would be over, Mrs. Fairgrove giving her blessing to this, as Boe kept a sharp eye out on the parking lot, hoping her mother would come and pick them up. It was time to go, and unfortunately, she never came. Boe received a quick text from her mom, they were being held up at the station and wouldn't be home for a few hours. Shaking her head, she helped wake Lute up, and the two of them started heading home.

The clouds had started to roll in, a bit late in the year, but Orange Bay usually does get some daily rain during the evening in late summer and early fall. It doesn't usually start until after the sun sets, however, so the kids knew they'd be fine on their walk home, though the low distant rumbles of thunder let them know it was set to be a rough night.

Lute led the way home, a different route than the one they had gone the day before, much longer in fact, twisting and turning around several streets and past some private homes and the small local play park. Boe wondered why they were going this way, but chalked it up to Lute not wanting to be near his home just yet.

They get back to Boe's home, but before they can go in, Lute speaks up. "Hey. I want to go home and get some things," he said in a slow monotone.

Upon hearing these words, her blood ran cold. "A-are you sure that's a good idea? I mean, we could wait for Mom and Dad to get home, and I'm sure that they'd be happy to help you get your stuff." she offered as she began looking up and down the street, partially in search of her parent's cars, and partially in search of the monster's.

"I'll be quick, and it'll be fine." Lute said, "I don't have much, but there is one thing I really want in there. Please." he responded, still in that dry monotone.

Boe felt a lump in her throat, she hated this weird voice Lute was doing, hated the idea of him going back to where the monster could be and hated the fact that there was no one around to help them in case this all went sideways. "Alright, just please be quick and be safe, okay?"

With those words, Boe heads inside and grabs the phone before heading over to the kitchen window that overlooks the street and Lute's house next door, at the first sign of trouble, she'd call the cops. Lute meanwhile turns and marches his way into his own home, that strange look still in his eye.

Inside, he doesn't go far, just into the hall the monster broke his arm in, and he turns the light out. He doesn't go to his room, he doesn't have anything there. He doesn't go into the kitchen for food or the bathroom for his toothbrush, he doesn't usually plan things ahead. Instead, he just crouches down low in the hall, drops the note, and waits.

The tension is heavy between the two houses, each second ticking by in perfect unison with the heartbeats of the two children, both of them waiting and fearing what was to come next, but both of them also filled with determination to see their end goals. A low rumbling sound comes up from down the road, and Boe quickly runs to the other window to see what it was.

Her heart sank when she saw the monster's car.

It pulled up and parked right in front of its house, just as Boe arrived back at her post. "C'mon Lute, get out of there..." she said under her breath, afraid the monster might hear her from the other side of the wall.

The monster shambled out of its car and went inside. It lurched in its seemingly ever-present stupor past the hall where the small rabbit laid in waiting and took its seat in the uncomfortable chair. After turning on the TV, it heard strange music that didn't sound like it fit with what the news was broadcasting. At no point did it try to lift itself from its chair, nor did it take its eyes off the terrible things its station kept playing.

The song was beautiful. Melancholy, and morbid, a dirge by all accounts, the type of music one would find at funerals or memorial services. It was haunting as the notes, though low, pierced its skull and reverberated in the black abyss that was once the monster's soul. Tears welled up in the monster's eyes as it listened closer and closer, and it even began to sob and weep, tuning out the rest of the world around it aside from the beautiful melody.

The singer stood behind him, a mix of fear, determination, and pure hatred fueling his tiny body as he kept humming the melody for what felt like hours, though in truth it was only a few minutes before the final verse came.

"I cry out to the empty void, hatred born from a lie~" the singer's voice, now not limited by the tonal range of humming, proved to be a wonderful soprano that any chorus teacher would consider to be their top student. The monster fished out its tool from between the cushions of its chair as it heard these final notes.

"To take revenge for what was destroyed~" the monster lifts the tool to its head, the cold metal of the tool pressed against its temple.

"A kiss with darkness, and so I die~"

Bang!

Runaway:

The aftermath of what occurred was not pretty, nor entirely necessary to go into great detail on. Suffice to say the sound was enough for Boe to call the cops on, and not long after they arrived, the good doctors in tow. They comforted their daughter as the monster's body was carted away.

"Suicide," the cops shrugged. "His car is full of beer bottles and pills, chances are he has had issues for a while now."

A note was found in the hallway nearby. It was crudely written and crumpled. "Goodbye, I'm sorry, don't look for me." was all that it had written on it. The search for the lost child began immediately, but before the cops could scramble and get places shut down, Lute had already made his way back to the school. Soon after, he found himself further north than he had ever been before, at the Orange Bay Bus Station.

It wasn't long after that he had convinced the stationmaster that he was heading to his grandmother's up north, and after giving over all the small amount of money he had, he found himself on a one-way bus heading out of Orange Bay, and up to Horse Country. It was set to be a long twelve-hour drive, and there were to be several stops on the way there. Exhausted after what had just happened,

Lute took his seat at the back of the nearly empty bus and slept.

It was another nightmare, but nothing out of the norm for Lute. The only real change from his standard is that the giant looming shadow of a monster was nowhere to be found. No piercing red eyes or grabbing claws, but still he ran and hid and felt like he was moments away from death.

Morning came as the bus arrived at the station, and all the passengers were ushered out. Lute made his way to the public bathroom, and despite the size difference between him and the enlarged furniture common in Horse Country, he managed to make it work. This however was just one of the problems he encountered here. EVERYTHING was bigger in Horse Country, not just the bathrooms, the people as well were huge, some of the tallest Eaglelanders in fact. Your average bunny like Lute would grow four to five feet in height, but a full-grown stallion could average to six or even seven feet tall. As such, they had a hard time noticing someone as small as Lute.

Perhaps that was a blessing in disguise, however, as it meant he was less likely to be found or turned over to the police. He gathers his thoughts in the lobby, trying to figure out what to do next. The TVs were playing a mix of news and travel advertisements as he sat on one of the large benches. He couldn't go back home, not after what he did, and he didn't have any other family he could live with.

Maybe this was a mistake. He begins to think. *Maybe I should just turn myself in and say I don't know how I ended up here. They'll never be able to blame his death on me, right? He...* his thoughts begin to wander as he realizes what he did. *He shot himself. And... And I made him do it with a song! Wh-what kind of...? This can't be real, right? It has to just be another nightmare.* He tries to deny it, tries to push it out of his mind, but the truth remains. *I killed my dad.* He nearly vomits in his mouth but manages to swallow it down.

I killed him, and no one can pin it on me. And... I feel so awful. I just... He begins tearing up again, like all his repressed emotions of the past day just hit him at once. All the pain and sorrow that's the inevitable aftermath of the rage and hate he felt the day before. *What am I going to do?*

A song. Beautiful, operatic, sung as if by an angel, full of words of hope and kindness and life after loss fills Lute's ears. He looks around for the source and sees it on the travel channel. "... And don't forget to visit the Anima Theater on Broadway right in the heart of downtown Big Apple," the invisible reporter talks over the singer on the screen's performance. "This is truly one of the best places for any aspiring musician to find their big break and become a star. If you can make it here, you can make it anywhere!"

Big Apple? Lute wonders. *That song was beautiful. I wonder...* He wipes the tears from his eyes. *If I have a song that makes people die, if it's so beautiful and sad they kill themselves, then maybe I could make another song? Something happy?* His stomach growls, he hasn't eaten since lunch yesterday. *I can't go back. I don't want to die. If*

I don't find a way to get money or food, I'm going to starve. The guilt of his murder still fresh in his mind, he makes a resolution. He stands and begins walking out of the station. *I won't use that song on anyone else, never again. I refuse to kill anyone, even someone like dad. I'm going to Big Apple, I'm going to become a famous singer, and I'm going to use my music to help people!*

The look in his eye from the night before was back, but his emotions still flared and he looked less dead inside, in fact, he was positively *glowing* his fur shining a bright emerald green he could spot out the corner of his eyes. The name for that strange emotion finally hit him.

Determination.

The glow faded as he stepped outside and was immediately greeted by the chilly northern air, his fur returning to the normal white color in his eyes. Having lived his entire life in the near-endless summer of Orange Bay, he was not adapted for life in the cold nor properly dressed, and a chill ran up his spine. While it wasn't that cold out being only in early September, it was still much colder than down south. *First thing's first*, he decides, *I need food.*

And while not the most book smart student, Lute had seen enough movies to know what to do when you're a musician in need of cash. He found a piece of cardboard and a pen in a nearby trashcan and wrote the word "TIPS" in big bold font on it. He then took off his hat, tossed the cardboard in, and proceeded to the crowded park across the street. Finding a busy area he sets it down and begins to sing.

About an hour passes, maybe longer, with Lute just singing away. He only sang his mother's happy song, since it was the only complex one he knew that *that wouldn't kill people.* Occasionally one of the passing horses on their morning jogs or heading off to work would drop in a dollar or some change not bothering to stop and ask why a child with a broken arm was singing on the side of the street and asking for money as opposed to being in school. A few dollars richer, he finds a fast food joint nearby, McDanny's, and proceeds to chow down until he is full.

The restaurant is mostly empty, still too early to be busy, so aside from the service staff, he was one of the only people in the entire place. He hops up to reach the counter a couple of times to order and paw over his money. "One Hula Burger combo meal please!"

The cashier was puzzled, "Aren't you a bit young to be here by yourself kid?"

"I'm not a kid!" Lute lied.

"Really? Is that how tall rabbits grow then?"

"I kid you not!" he laughs.

"Heh, you must save a lot of money on clothes then, just shop in the colt section." the cashier whinnies.

"Sometimes, other times it costs an arm and a leg." Lute jokes back, showing off his cast. It felt good to laugh again, things are starting to look up. Soon enough he has his meal and finds a seat in one of the corners of the restaurant. Some TVs were hanging from the ceiling, playing various news stations, though he didn't care, just more excited to finally get some food.

I should go back to the bus stop and see how much a ticket to Big Apple is. He thinks as he shovels down mouthfuls of fries. *Then I'll be able to go back to the park and keep singing until I have enough money for a ticket, and maybe another meal or two.* He laughs at himself. When did he get so good at planning? Satisfied he gets ready to leave only for something to catch the corner of his eye. A news story just started, showing his picture.

"Disturbing events rocked downtown Orange Bay last night," the reporter starts, "when local resident Har P. Rabbit was found dead in his home. Police have already ruled the case as a suicide, but the search has begun now for his son one Lute T. Rabbit, as seen here, who went missing after his father's death. A note was found at the scene indicating the child wasn't kidnapped, but rather ran away, police say out of fear of his father. Lute, an eleven-year-old boy with a broken arm, was last seen leaving school with a classmate and neighbor..."

Lute stopped watching, not wanting to see the faces of Boe's family. *Well then, the police will be looking for me now.* It was at this moment he noticed he was getting a suspicious look from the friendly cashier from before, another worker making a phone call in the back and glancing out at him. *Time to go!* As he gets up to leave, the cashier tries to stop him.

"Oh, sir! I just realized you're our 1 millionth customer! Would you mind meeting with our manager? He'd love to give you a special prize of a $100 gift card!"

"Give it to the next guy," Lute says as he tries to make for the door.

"Are you sure sir?" the cashier asks as he follows him, "It's a rare opportunity you know," he says as he tries to get between Lute and the door.

"I'm good!" Lute says as he quickly runs out the door before he can be stopped, and starts hopping down the street.

I'm in trouble, there's no way I can outrun an adult, let alone a horse. Looks like the bus ticket out the window. He thinks as he hops down a back alley. *I can't just stand in a park all day where people can see me and call the cops. I really don't want to have to walk all the way, but I may have no other choice.*

He comes to a stop a few streets away and hides from the road proper by ducking behind a dumpster. *I don't know where Big Apple is, or how to get there from here, all I know is that it's north of here. If I get to the north end of town, I can follow one of the roads out of town and then keep following it north. With any luck, I should get there, or at least some other town, and maybe try my song and dance again there to save up for a map or something.* Agreeing with himself on his plan, he begins making his way across town, dodging behind trash cans and parked cars whenever he sees a cop. It was early afternoon by the time he had managed to get to the north end because of his slow travel method. The good news is, this gave him plenty of time to think.

It's only been one day, and I'm already hungry. He says as his stomach roars again. *I should have brought food with me, but I guess it's too late now. When I go along the roads, I'm going to have to stay far enough inside the bushes and trees not to be seen by cops driving past. Maybe roads aren't the way to go then? That's it! Trains!* The idea hits him like a bolt of lightning. *If I follow train tracks, then there won't be any cops, and I'll definitely arrive in Big Apple, 'cause of Grand Central Station! I just need to find the station in this town, and check the rail map!*

Lady luck was feeling kind today, so he managed to find it just as the sun began to set. Heading inside, he was relieved to see that while there was a cop in here, they hadn't noticed him yet. He ducked behind a bench and began to inspect the room around him. That's when he noticed it, next to the ticket booth was a large map showing all the major lines and destinations across Eagleland that the trains in this station go to. Scurrying over while the cop wasn't looking. He was even more delighted when he noticed a small stack of pamphlets nestled into the side of the map. Miniature replicas of the map, perfect for someone like him! He pockets one and begins studying the larger map.

Alright, so if I go down the C-line, I can take the first right path, and that should get me started towards Big Apple. If I take these turns one at a time, then I should be able to make it there. He nods, now more pumped up than ever, though it was a short-lived celebration as the pain from his broken arm shot through him again, and he nearly buckled under. *Grrr, I can't stop here. I'll deal with the pain and keep going!* He shakes it off and starts moving. It was going to be a long walk.

After a glance at the tracks to figure out which way he'll need to go first, he leaves the station and begins walking alongside the tracks heading north. It was at sunset that he found himself walking on the unpaved ground outside the city borders, and not long after he was surrounded on both sides by trees and bushes, only the rumbling and hums of the city behind him, and the quiet path of the train tracks ahead.

After an hour of walking, he finds a small clearing to the side of the tracks and decides that's a good place to rest for the night. *I may not have traveled far today, but at least I know where I'm going now.* He thinks as he sprawls out in the middle of the clearing, another tinge of pain and another growl of hunger overtakes him as he grabs his stomach.

...What am I even doing out here?

He stares up at the branches and leaves above, and beyond them the approaching stars in the dark night sky. Pinpoints of light half-shaded out by the overgrowth above. *I'm going to die out here. I... I'm just a kid! I'm never going to make it to Big Apple! And what am I even going to do there? I just...* tears begin to well up in his eyes again. *Why did I keep going? Why didn't I give up? I keep saying everything is going to be fine, but will it?* Thoughts of fear and despair wash through his mind. He's not used to feeling like this. The world seems to fall away as he just dissociates into space.

"Oats and beans and barley grow~" he starts to sing again, this time to the tune of his mother's song. Maybe this would cheer him up.

"As you and I and anyone know~" the leaves in the trees seem to sway a bit as he sings.

"As you and I and anyone know~" he doesn't notice as they keep swaying rhythmically.

"Oats and beans and barley grow~"

Thud.

"Hmm?" Lute sits up and turns around, something landed near his head. He turns and spies an apple lying on the ground. "Oh? Now where did you come from?" he says, picking it up. It's small, and a bit lumpy, but he doesn't care. "No one's around, so might as well~" he rubs it on his shirt and takes a bite. It's a bit bitter, but at least it's edible.

"Heh, that's a bit better I guess," he says before returning to his song, now hitting the notes a bit more proper, and singing a bit louder. "Waiting for a partner, waiting for a partner~"

Thud.

He stops again and picks up the second apple. "...Okay, that's weird. Is anyone there?" he asks as he gets up, only to receive no response. A thought crosses his head, but it's a silly thought. *That can't be the case. No way. But dad did... was he right?* He takes care to make these next few notes land on key and in perfect sync.

"Open the way and take one in, waiting for a partner~"

Thud.

Sure enough, another apple. Lute's heart skips a beat as his eyes shine and he puts two and two together. *Magic.*

He continues the song, as he does the apples keep coming, growing better looking or larger, he tries dancing as best he can with one arm, and as he moves the apples continue to change. Moving in time with the music made them appear shinier while moving against it made them lumpier. By the time he finished the second round of his song, he had a small pile of apples. He tested them as he feasted, the shinier and prettier ones were sweeter as well, and the lumpier ones had a more bitter taste.

I have no idea how this works. He thinks as tears run down his cheeks as he consumes one apple after another. *But I don't care! This is amazing!*

Full and satisfied, he looks over the cores of the apples, proof that his meal was real. "Culania wasn't lying," he says to himself. "Magic IS real."

Suddenly the bushes shake and rustle. "Hello?" Lute turns and faces the source, "Is somebody there?"

The noise moves from bush to bush, something is there, and it's circling Lute. He backs up into the center of the clearing. *Oh no, is it an alligator!? Or maybe a big lizard?* He suddenly realizes how helpless he is out here. He's not super strong, even with both arms, and the best he can do is sing at whatever could attack him.

A voice, slightly high pitched, but lower than Lute's rings out, it sounds almost deathlike, no real emotions, and yet an underlying sense of confident coyness. "Do it again."

"What?" Lute asks.

"Make the food appear again." the voice demands.

"O-oh." Lute gulps down his fear and sings the first verse again. Sure enough, another apple falls.

"So it was you." the voice confirms with itself. "You tiny mortal."

"M-mortal? What are you, some kind of monster?" Lute asks, taking a step back from where the voice last came from, only to hear it from behind him now.

"Me? A monster? Yes... and no." the voice contradicts itself. "I am... like you," it says, taking long pauses to think through its words. "You ran away to be out this far on your own, yes?"

"...Yes." Lute admits, for what would be gained from lying to this monster about that.

"I ran away too, from my prison, and now I seek my future. Fame, wealth, power, glory! It will all be mine! And you, my small mortal, are going to help me with that."

"W-why should I help you?! You just admitted you're a monster! I know your kind, you're gonna suck my blood or bite me or something!"

"Hahahahaha!" the voice cackles. "Man, I don't know what monsters you've been hanging out with, but they sound awesome! Also gross. As for why you'll help me, well because I can help you. I see you've got a broken arm there mortal, how about I fix that for you?"

Lute grabs his cast, "And what, you're just gonna do this out of the kindness of your heart?"

"Heh, no. We'll make a deal, I have to make a deal to heal it anyway. What to take, what to take. They always say to highball these things, so how about your soul? Ah, no, then you couldn't make food anymore..."

Lute feels something run across the back of his neck, he turns and the voice has moved again. "Ehhh screw it. And them! I'm hungry and I know exactly what I want."

Lute tries to stand tall and find out where the voice was coming from now, in the darkness he lost it. "A-are you gonna eat me?"

"Uhg, so many mortals only see the small picture. What good would eating you do when you can **make** food? No no, I want your loyalty. I'll fix your arm, and in exchange, whenever I ask it of you, you have to make food like that. Yes, yes! That is a fair deal, isn't it?"

Lute ponders for a moment as he wipes away the cold sweat and tries to brush off his fear. *My arm, for serving him? He wouldn't eat me if I served him, and if he needs me for food, then when he gets better food he might just let me go right? And until then, he'll probably keep me safe right? At least safer than being alone...*

He knows it's stupid, but he agrees. "A-alright, so how do we do this?"

"Look up."

Sitting on a low branch above Lute's head is a small raven. His black feathers blend in with the night sky, but Lute can see his red shirt and green shorts. His purple eyes are a stark contrast from Lute's orange ones, and his grin takes up the entirety of his beak. He hops down and spreads his wings wide to slow down his fall, and lands right in front of Lute revealing the most bizarre part of this whole thing.

He was another child, couldn't have been more than a year or two older than Lute, barely a few inches taller too. "My name is Edgar," he says, "Shake my wing and say your name," he commands as he outstretches his wing.

"Lute," he says as he shakes the bird's wing.

A purple light shoots out from where they meet, and it surrounds the duo, a wild wind billowing up around them. Lute's eyes dart around rapidly as he tries to take it all in, but Edgar's grasp doesn't let him go, his eyes locked firmly on Lute's face. The beams of light form ribbons that wrap around the cast. He feels the pain from the injury quickly fade and vanish, the bindings releasing and soon he's able to move it around again with no pain at all. He examines his paw in awe and wonder as the lights settle and the wind dies down.

"It's as if it was never broken," Lute admits feeling better than he had in the past few days.

"Of course it does. That's what real magic can do." Edgar clears his throat. "Now then, as I said, I'm hungry. Sing for me."

Danse Macabre:

And so the two slept that night. While not feeling the safest, Lute was exhausted from his long journey and grateful for the chance to rest. When they woke up in the morning, Edgar gave Lute the chance to relieve himself in a nearby bush before making him dance for their breakfast. "Hop to it bunny boy," he said. "And you better perform well too!"

As Lute finished the song and dance, the apples began to fall, large and shiny. Edgar quickly grabbed them all up and began dividing them out, naturally he kept the larger ones to himself. "You know," Lute began, looking over his pile, "you could stand to be a little more polite. I have a name."

"Polite?" Edgar asks between beakfuls of apples. "And I know you have a name, I literally can't forget it because of our contract." He swallows and narrows his eyes. "What does that word mean?"

"Contract? The deal?" he shakes it off, "And what do you mean you don't know what 'polite' means? You know, like manners, saying 'please', and 'thank you'." He takes a bite and swallows before continuing. "Didn't your parents teach you that stuff?"

"Bah! Parents." Edgar tosses his cores away. "He taught me magic and nothing more. 'Please' and 'thank you'? You have a lot of strange words, don't you."

"Uhg." Lute sighs and tries to explain as he finishes his meal. "Okay, so you say please when you want something, thank you when you get something, you chew with your beak closed, and don't make a mess with your food. That's what being polite is, you're being nice to those around you."

"Sounds pretty dumb." Edgar laughs. "If I want something, I either take it or make a deal for it. When I get something, I've either earned it, or someone has tried to hurt me in our deal. Being 'nice' gets you nowhere."

Lute rolls his eyes as he gathers the cores to bury them. "Right, well whatever you've got to tell yourself." he quietly finishes burying them in a small hole. "Well, thank you for fixing my arm, it's been nice and all, but I'm heading out. Cya around!" he says as he tries to begin following the tracks north again.

Edgar quickly moves in front of him. "And just where do you think you're going?"

"Big Apple, now stand aside, unless you want to come with."

"Hah! I don't think so. See, you made a deal with me, a verbal 'contract'. This is some powerful dark magic you know. Try to break it and I'm afraid your arm will break all over again, and this time you won't even have a cast!" he grins, but it quickly fades. Lute takes a step back and winces as he grabs his arm. "Look, I don't know you, you haven't done anything to me. I don't even really want your arm to break again. But those are the rules of the spell."

He comes over and grabs Lute's shoulders. "But the truth is, you're on a timer. See, your arm would normally heal in what? Three? Four months? After that then my contract won't affect you and you're free to break it! No more singing and dancing for me." He lets go and takes a few steps down the track. "But if you try to leave me, I'll ask the wind itself for you to dance, and when you fail to hear it, your arm will break, and then it's all over."

"Grr." Lute spits. "And suppose I break your beak so you can't ask me to?"

"You couldn't even if you wanted to!" Edgar laughs again. "Trust me, I've got more spells than you could handle. Tell you what, you come with me, and I'll teach you about magic. Free of charge, no contract on this one!"

Learn magic? Lute thought. *I mean, I know the food song and the other one.* He shivers, even Edgar didn't deserve that. *But if I could learn more? I wonder how useful that could be?* "...Alright." He says.

"Wonderful! Now then, let's get moving!" Edgar says returning them to the north path.

Lute was caught off guard by this. "Wait, if we're heading north anyway, why did you stop me?"

"I knew you were probably going a different way than me eventually. There's a split up ahead," Edgar explains, "I was there last night when I sensed you. I came from the right, and was heading left!"

"Left?" Lute asks as he pulls out the map. "What's out that way?"

"Spectacle City!" Edgar's eyes sparkle as he gestures wildly with his wings. "It's the perfect place for mages to go! ...As long as you don't mind the fact you can't trust anyone there, and they're liable to stab you at any moment."

"Isn't that the movie place? I think my teacher went there once... Why do you wanna go there?"

"Mages gather there! Anyone sensitive enough to magic can feel them from here! It's a perfect hiding place, AND we can make it rich there!"

"Yeah, okay, I guess if we used our magic we could probably do good in the movies." Lute laughs, "You could even say we'd be A-MAGE-ing."

"Oh, my shadow stop!" Edgar chirps angrily.

Lute just smirks, "What? Can't handle any PUN-ishment?"

"ALL OF MY HATE!" Edgar cries.

"Hehe, I'll stop for now. But seriously though, that's on the other side of Eagleland. You can't honestly expect to walk the whole way there?"

"Well, I may not have a day ago, but now with you and all the food I can eat, yes!"

"You did not plan this through, did you?"

"Did you?"

"Heh, fair enough, what is your story anyway?" Lute finally asks. But for whatever reason, this causes Edgar's expression to drop cold. He seems less animated and even falls quiet.

"I'm not gonna tell you that," he says flat out as he pulls something out of his pocket and begins to fiddle with it in his wings.

"Oh?" Lute asks, now even more curious. "Don't trust me yet I take it? Eh, that's fine." He says as they make it to the split. "I'll tell you mine first if you want to hear it," he says as he takes the left path.

"...Alright." Edgar says, still playing with the thing in his wings.

And so Lute began to tell the tale you've already read up to this point. He omits certain parts and embellishes others as children are want to do. No need to talk about his imaginary best friend or the boring lessons in class. But the incident with Randy went from jumping off the slide to jumping off of Randy's face. And he didn't tell about what he did to his father, instead just saying he snuck out of the hospital.

"That's about it I guess." he laughs. "You know it's kinda nice to actually tell someone about all this," he admits as the two park themselves on the side of the tracks for a chance to eat some lunch and better plan out the route ahead. "Phew, we've come quite a long way, haven't we?"

"Maybe, what does the map say?" Edgar says, taking a seat and pocketing the thing he was playing with. Lute opened it up and placed it between them, the network of train tracks spread out far and wide in an intricate net across all of Eagleland. Starting in Horse Country on the East Coast, the kids will have to travel through the Stone Mountains, and the deserts surrounding the Native Lands before they'll arrive at Spectacle City. "Uhh, it's so far away. How long is this gonna take anyway?"

"Could be weeks... or months? I don't know. There's a bunch of different ways there, we just have to pick the right tracks."

"Bleh, we'll deal with that later, I'm hungry. Dance for me!"

Lute sighs and stands, and before he starts he speaks, "It wouldn't kill you to say please you know." And, with no further hesitations, he begins to perform. However, unlike this past morning, apples did not fall, wild plums did instead. "Huh, I wasn't expecting that." He says as he picks one up.

"Well, that could be a problem." Edgar sighs as he begins grabbing the rest. "I was hoping your song made apples, but no it looks like it just causes plants to grow fast."

"I mean, we should still be fine, right? As long as we've got fruit trees or wild veggies right?"

"Yeah, until we get to the mountains or desert where those things don't grow."

"Crud, I hadn't thought of that... What about towns? These tracks connect towns, so if we follow them, we could get food in towns right?"

"Even then, will we be able to make it from town to town? Especially in the deserts. Hot sun, no food or water..." he shivers a bit. "We'd need a plan. Or some better spells." Edgar takes note of. "Which means we're gonna need some practice."

"Yeah..." Lute says as he hears the whistle of a distant, yet approaching train. "I'm sorta... new to all of this. Like just discovered it yesterday new," he admits as he pinches his nose. "Please, anything you could tell me would be really helpful."

"Great. My first minion and he only knows one spell." Edgar grumbles. "Let's go with the basics. Do you know about altered sight? You focus just right, and you can see the auras of people, their magical potential, and what magic they're best at."

Lute thinks back, recalling the strange glimmer. "Yeah, I think I had it once. I was in class and started humming a tune, hmmm hmmm..." he starts humming the same tune, as he does so the green glimmer overcomes his fur. Edgar, however, seemed unchanged. Maybe his feathers were a bit darker, but overall, he seemed normal. Lute stopped humming and the glimmer faded and fizzled out. "Huh, guess I know how to do that. It makes me all green."

Edgar nods, "Yeah, that's right, you have a green aura, which means you work best with earth magic. That explains the food song." He sighs, and the two finish eating as the train passes by them. They don't talk, as the sound is deafening, and they have to steady themselves and hold tight to Lute's hat and their map to prevent them from flying from the gusts the train kicks up. Once it's passed, Lute gets an idea, singing and dancing again, he manages to get a few more wild plums, the kids pocketing them in the case where they make camp for the night doesn't have edible food.

Walking along the tracks once more Edgar pulls the thing out of his pocket again and begins fiddling with it more. "What's that you've got there?" Lute asks.

"Hmm? Oh, this is a piece of quartz." Edgar explains holding up a smooth purple stone. "In particular, it's Amethyst. My old home was a mining town, and when I was allowed outside, I would go over to the mine behind my house and grab some loose rocks the miners dropped. Quartz is really good for magic. Have the right color quartz, and it can enhance that element of magic. Purple to darkness, green to earth."

"Huh. How does that work?"

"The best way I can describe it is that the quartz can store magic in it, and when you cast a spell you can use the magic in the quartz to make your final effect 'stronger'." He says with air quotes.

"What you don't know?" Lute laughs.

"No," Edgar sighs, "My family didn't teach much? Like they taught me spells, but not how they work. And words are... hard," he winces. "I know enough, but more... big words I've had to learn on my own, mainly overhearing them. So trying to describe big things with small words doesn't... fit." he tries to explain.

"I think I understand," Lute says as he balances himself on the side of the tracks. "So what you're saying is that you don't know what you're doing either!" he laughs.

Edgar takes offense and tries to comment, but silences himself and focuses on his quartz. "I can't argue," he admits. "But I do know a few things! Like how quartz makes magic stronger, and how you can make quartz stronger by cutting and polishing it, hence why I'm grinding this," he says as he shows Lute his wings. They're glowing a deep purple color around the ends. "As I rub it with magic, it smooths out and becomes round, which is great for enchanting!"

"Enchanting?" Lute questions, "Like cursing a spinning wheel to make someone prick their finger on it and die?"

"Ooooh!" Edgar grins, "Never heard of that, but sounds fun! How do I do it?!"

"Erm," Lute catches himself, "I don't know. I just saw it in a movie once."

"Movie?" Edgar tilts his head before shaking it off, if his servant wanted to talk in nonsense words, then so be it. "Either way, I suppose so. Magic has several forms you see. I work best with enchanting, and I'm willing to bet you can only use it when you sing!" Edgar teases.

"What? That can't be true, what kinda sense does that make?" Lute pouts.

"Oh? You don't believe me? Well then bunny boy, why don't you show me what you can do with your mouth shut!" he says, pocketing his stone. A clever plan. If Lute succeeds, Edgar learns of another power he has and can use later. If Lute fails, then he knows Lute's limits and how to work around him. Lute has only demonstrated the two spells, surely though, there has to be more.

"Uh..." Lute hesitates, "Okay, do you have anything in particular in mind?" he asks, trying to find a way to gain a new spell from Edgar.

This manages to make Edgar fall silent for a small while as the two continue their walk. The trees and shrubs of the groves around Horse Country come to an abrupt end and give way to open fields and small rivers as they enter the farmlands between the major cities and the much smaller towns. The sun starts to paint the sky orange as it hangs ever lower in the sky, and with the whistle of another oncoming train, the duo decides to make camp for the night, finding a singular tree on a hill a few yards away from the tracks.

Thankfully, this is farm country, so Lute goes over to a nearby crop field and grabs a couple of cabbages as Edgar begins building a small circle of stones, in the center of the stones he places a chunk of bright red quartz. Carnelian as it's commonly known. He then looks up at the tree and finds one branch that stands out. It's small, with few leaves on it, and he spreads his wings wide. "SLICE!" he shouts as he claps them together. As he does so, a small wave of dark energy seems to emerge from them. It fades into nothing just as it hits the branch, but manages to do the job, cutting it off of the tree.

"Heh." Edgar huffs out as he gasps for breath. "Impressed?" he tries to boast in front of Lute who saw the whole thing.

"Very!" Lute admits as he sets the cabbages down. "Nice work!"

"..." Edgar doesn't know how to respond.

"Something wrong? Are you okay? You seem out of breath."

"I'm... fine," Edgar says. "Why are you asking?"

"Because I'm worried about you?" Lute says, "Like, I'd still have a broken arm if it weren't for you. You're kinda rude and all, but like, I'm grateful for that."

"...Thank you, Lute."

"Hey! I gotcha to say thanks! That wasn't so hard now was it?" Lute laughs as he playfully pushes Edgar's shoulder.

He rubs it and laughs back, "Heh, well. Anyway, how about we try a new spell for you? I'll set up these sticks here." he says as he picks up the branch and starts breaking it into pieces, tossing them into the ring. "And you light them with magic!"

"Cool! How do I do it?"

"Y-you don't know?" Edgar asks crestfallen. "Okay... uh, fire magic, just think of really hot things and focus it on the sticks."

"That's it, really?"

"That's what I do with my dark magic, I just think and it happens." Edgar shrugs.

"Lucky," Lute says as he turns to the pit. He concentrates on the sticks, eyes them intently, focuses with all his brainpower, and strains his body to try and make them ignite. *Fire, the Sun, volcanoes, lava...* he lists off every hot thing he can think of as he does so, trying to feel the warmth and perhaps pass it through him as he moves it into the sticks.

"...GAH! I can't do it!" he cries as he grabs his head. "This is dumb! How does it work for you and not me!"

"Heh, I knew you couldn't do it." Edgar grins. "Eh, I wasn't expecting you to do so anyway."

Lute hangs his head as he waits for Edgar to start it, only to suddenly get an idea. "Hang on, let me try once more." He says.

"Knock yourself out," Edgar says, taking a step back.

He picked up two sticks of relatively equal size and began dancing. The movements were rigid, calculated, very much unlike his normal way of movement. While it was clear he was in complete control, the stiffness somehow also seemed wild, rhythmic, like the pulsations of flames in a fireplace, or the beating of one's heart. He moved fast, keeping in time with his own heartbeat as a metronome, twirling the sticks around him in near hypnotic fashion, taking care to make sure the tips never contacted him nor Edgar. His ball cap fell off his head and landed at Edgar's boots as Lute kept the pace of his dance, beads of sweat forming on his forehead, and rolling down his cheeks.

This is so strange. He thought as he danced. *I've never done this before, yet it feels like I know exactly what to do. It's strange, like the dance itself is guiding me. Is this like the voice from my dream? Should I trust it? That voice... I hate that voice.* his anger flows through him as he thinks about that voice. *If it weren't for that, then I wouldn't be here! I'd still be back in Orange Bay, and living with Boe, and... no. I need to focus on the dance. If I let go, then this could be bad. I can't go back! I don't need to.* Heat radiates from his body, sweat turns into steam and fizzles off of his white fur. With one final growl, he slams the tips of the sticks together, and suddenly, they ignite!

He begins huffing, standing there, lit torches in each paw. The entire dance has left him hot, and exhausted like he could collapse and fall asleep right then and there.

"Woah! You did it!" Edgar cheers. "That's impressive! ...Lute? You gonna toss those in the fire?"

"Oh crap!" Lute says as the sticks start to burn to the point the fire nearly reaches his fur. He quickly tosses them into the pit, and thankfully they ignite the rest of the twigs. And with that, he falls down and collapses next to the fire. "Can I have my hat back please?"

"Thank you," he says as Edgar gives it back.

"Well, that works. Though man, it looks like it took everything out of you!"

"Yeah, I don't think I've ever felt this tired after dancing... ever!" he sits up and begins nibbling on his cabbage. "Gah, not even the dance I do for food is that hard. What's up with that?"

"It's called Magic drain." Edgar tries to explain. "The more you use magic, the more tired you get. The more you practice the less tired you get, and the more you practice certain spells, the easier it is to cast them."

"Huh. I guess that makes sense." Lute laughs, "So if that's the case, the more I use the food song, the better the food we'll get too right? Since I won't get as tired and get better at the spell."

"Right! Which is why you should practice at least three times a day!"

"You're just saying that 'cuz it means you'll get free food!" Lute laughs.

"Guilty!" Edgar admits as he stares into the fire. "Actually, I wonder." He fishes around in his pocket for a moment before pulling out another stone, bright green."This stone..." he says. "Aventurine..."

"Pretty." Lute half-heartedly says as he finishes his cabbage.

"Yes, the green color means it's good for earth magic. If I can cut and polish this just right, then maybe..." he pockets it. "Eh, we'll save that for later. I'm tired." he shrugs and sprawls out on the grass. "How far away is the next town?"

"If I saw the map right, we should get there by tomorrow afternoon, why?" Lute asks, lying down next to Edgar.

"Cuz maybe we can get some stuff there. Like, water bottles and backpacks."

"Heh, with what money?"

"The heck is money?"

"You're hopeless, aren't you? Just, get some rest, alright?"

And with that, the two runaways drift off to sleep. Many questions still linger on Lute's mind as he drifts off. Who really is Edgar? Where did he come from? Why does he know so much about magic? He's such a strange bird. He can't be much older than Lute. Questions of magic in general flood his mind as well. Why is he only learning about this now? Why doesn't anyone else use magic? He's just started to use it and has already learned how to start fires and grow food. Why wouldn't everyone be using this stuff?

Perhaps he can get some answers out of Edgar in the morning, but for now, it's Friday night, which means he's lined up to meet his best friend and hopefully figure some of this out.

Recital:

"Hey, you made it! Good evening sleepyhead!" Culania teased Lute who found himself 'waking' up in his bed again. "Hope that energy I gave you back on Tuesday came through for you in the end, heh." He laughs, but then he gets a closer look at his friend. "H-hey," he asks as he tilts his head frowning, "Is everything alright?"

Lute shot up quickly. Maybe it was the heat from the dance and the fire, maybe it was just the weight of everything from these past few days finally crashing down on him, but for whatever reason, he felt anger, sorrow, and immense relief that he was able to just hug his small friend again. "No," he admits as he nearly crushes the prince in his arms. "No, it's not. A lot of bad stuff has happened and now... I don't know what to do!"

"Oh, dear," Culania responds as he hugs Lute back, "It's okay, just tell me what happened, I'll see what I can do to help," he says as he tries to comfort Lute.

"Okay." Dream Lute agrees as he wipes his nose. "Dad broke my arm."

"What?! That's horrible! Why would he do that!" he asks as he looks at the bunny's arms.

"Because he hates me, so I ran away."

"By yourself?! But isn't Eagleland like, really dangerous? And you've got a broken arm, Lute, you should go back home. Maybe tell someone about your dad-"

"I can't go back." Lute interrupts. "And I'm not alone either. I made a... I met someone. His name is Edgar, he's a Raven and has magic. Culania, he fixed my arm by shaking my paw." He says this as he instinctively grabs that arm. "I still can't believe he did it to tell you the truth. And now I know what you mean, magic is real."

"I... see." Culania hesitates. "And Edgar, is he a kid like you?"

"Yeah, he's maybe an inch or two taller than me, and can't fly, so those are good giveaways. I... I have a song and dance when I use it, plants grow! And another one I did before falling asleep. When I did it, I made some sticks light on fire. Magic is real." he takes a step away from his friend. "Culania, what is this place? Who are you really? You're not just some figment of my imagination. What *are* you?"

The young prince hesitates, but upon summoning his courage, he decides to tell the truth. "We have many names," he begins. "This place is my home, that much is true, it's where people go when they sleep. Oneiros, Dream Weavers... Dad and I, we make dreams for everyone and keep this place in shape for people to have good dreams. I told you a few months ago that I'm just starting out, which is why I helped you," he beams. "You were in a bad spot with a nightmare, and well, I save people from them!"

Lute just smiles and shakes his head. "I should have figured that you weren't gonna tell me anything bad. Reckon if ya were, you'd have already done whatever bad thing you do to people." He takes a moment to laugh, at least some things can stay consistent in his life right now. "So, think you can help save me from another nightmare?"

"Another one?" Culania tilts his head and looks around. "Where?"

"Real life! Nah, but seriously, I'll take whatever help you can give us since it's just Edgar and me out in the woods on our own."

"Right. Right..." Culania says as he shakes his head and tries to formulate a plan. "I... don't know how I could help you. I can only really do stuff for you when you're asleep, which isn't gonna help you too much in Eagleland."

"You know what I could really use though?" Lute asks. "A spell that like... brushes my teeth or makes soap or toilet paper appear!" He laughs some more. "Because I've never been camping before, and already miss that stuff!"

"A hygiene spell?" Culania asks. "Hmm. We might have something on that in the library. Of course, you won't be able to read it, but I can read it for you. C'mon!" he says, opening the door. "Let's see if we can't find anything!"

Despite being a dream, Lute can sense many things about the castle as he's traveling through it. Sure, the sudden chill could just be their fire going out in the waking world. Not really a problem in August, but as they keep traveling they'll have to keep it in mind so they don't freeze as winter comes in. The sensations don't stop there, however, as he can practically smell the dust and musty odor of the old books that line the library's high walls.

Culania begins his search, a few volumes seem to be missing, and others are spread out on the large table in the center of the room, someone else has been reading them recently but left not too long ago. Lute attempts to read one, but as stated before, people can't read while asleep, instead, the pages being filled with incomprehensible text. Random letters and numbers and foreign characters are haphazardly splashed across the pages looking more like a printer threw up as opposed to someone trying to write something down.

After searching for a while, Culania comes down off a ladder he used to reach the top shelves, a large volume in his paws, nearly as big as him and covered in dust. "This one's a bit old, but it might do the trick!" he says, as he lays it on the table and begins flipping through.

"Aha! Here's one, an old healing spell, maybe you could use this. '*Si offendi obumbratio...*' Ah, it's in mage's script, let me translate it to Fogish for you. Alright, repeat after me." He clears his throat and reads the passage out loud.

"If we shadows have offended, think but this, and all is mended. That you have but slumbered here, while these visions did appear; And this weak and idle theme, no more yielding but a dream, Gentles, do not reprehend. If you pardon, we will mend."

"..." Lute hesitated, "Uh, buddy? That's a nice poem and all, but my magic only seems to work in song and dance form. Like, I sing for food, or dance for fire, I don't think some old poems will work."

"Oh? Well, beans then." he taps his paw. "Ah! I know! There should be..." he flips through the book again until he comes to a page he seems happy with. "Here! This poem is a piece of a much larger play and is supposed to be accompanied by some music. If you say it in time with the music, you could sing it right?"

"Worth a shot." Lute shrugs, "How's it go?"

Culania places his paws on the pages and the song billows up and outward from it. Musical notes dancing in the air as the melody fills Lute's mind, sounding like an entire orchestra was seated and playing in the library. The backing of the music is very fast, much too fast for one to logically place lyrics into, while the fore is very dynamic in its own right. While it wouldn't be impossible for Lute to match words to the music, or at least part of the music, the melody would require him to embellish and repeat several words to make it a more fitting tune.

"Is this... Ballet?" Lute asks.

"Yeah, it's an Overtrue."

"Overture," Lute says. "It's the intro song to an opera or play, and often gets the main themes across in it. While the dance goes on, the music will call back to the overture many times. It's like a table of contents in a book." he ponders how he can make use of this. "Really starting to wish I had taken a recorder from the school. Then I could just play this, but instead, I need to figure out how to incorporate your spell into it. Could you play it again, maybe make it repeat?"

"Sure thing!" Culania says as he sets the book up the notes now continuously pouring out and cycling around the room. "What are you gonna do?"

"The only thing I can do," Lute admits. "Practice! C'mon, you're filling in for Edgar in this dance, I'll lead."

And so the two began to dance the remainder of the night away in Lute's dream. The same song on repeat, Lute didn't trouble himself with singing the spell or even trying to find a spot to fit it in. Instead, he focused more on the dance, trying to find the right movements for the right parts of the song, a turn here, a jump there, step, twist, step, lock, roll. This dance needed to be as calculated as the fire dance if not more so. With a fire dance, the stiffness and calculations are needed for personal safety, but the wilder the dance, the more passionate it becomes, and in turn the better the performance. Here however ballet is the dance of restraint, of perfect movements and precision marks. One could spend years of their lives mastering just one ballet dance and still be seen as not as good as another performer.

Lute's dance didn't need to be perfect (nor was it, as his partner was much too small for him, even with Lute leading, the two of them tripping over themselves for the first few run-throughs). *If this is a healing spell,* Lute rationalized. *Then a perfect dance might have been able to heal my arm, though I wouldn't have been able to do it with a broken arm. I just need it to be good enough to prevent us from getting sick and help us wash the dirt off.* His thoughts focus on ideas of cleaning and health as he dances, the habitual washing and scrubbing he would do back home to prevent it from becoming an utter stye.

The sun begins to rise through the library's windows, and Culania calls off the dance. "It's time for you to wake up." He says. "Morning's come."

"Can I return tomorrow night to keep practicing?" Lute asks.

"I don't think that's a good idea," Culania admits. "I only bring you here so often because this place doesn't let you rest as well as a non-magical dream," he laughs, "doubly so when you dance the entire dream."

"Then you can use that boost thing you gave me the other day right? The energy you gave me?"

"Even then we could only do this every other night." Culania laughs, "I'm still in training myself you know!"

"I'll take what I can get." Lute smiles, "You said it yourself, I need help."

"Yeah, I suppose you're right." Culania's tail wags as the delight dawned on him how it meant he could spend more time with his friend. "See you tomorrow night then!" He says before putting a paw on Lute's chest, causing him to suddenly wake.

Eyes still closed, he yawns and stretches, feeling refreshed, "Man, I don't think I'll ever get used to that." He laughs as he opens his eyes, only to be greeted by a large brown bull in a flannel shirt and blue jeans, sporting a straw cap, sitting on the nearby fence.

"No, I don't reckon you will." he grins.

"Uh... Edgar." Lute says, shaking his still asleep ally, "There's someone here."

"Mmm, wha-?" he bolts up. "What?!" And immediately notices the guest.

"Howdy," he says. "Mind telling me what y'all are doing on my farm here?"

"Uh..." Edgar doesn't know what to say and tries to think of something fast.

"Sorry, Mister!" Lute beats him to the punch, "We weren't trying to cause any trouble, we just wanted to go camping and found this nice hill out here and figured it'd be a good place to spend the night."

"Is that so?" The bull snorts. "So then, where are ya from?"

"Horse Country!" Lute quickly responds, "We followed the train tracks to find someplace good to camp." He remembers that the best lies have a grain of truth in them.

"Right right, camping." the bull snorts again, unamused. "So then, where are your supplies?"

"S-supplies?" Lute stammers out as his deception is broken.

"Mhm, y'all's food or water, or tent."

"Who needs a tent..." Edgar says trying to assist Lute's lie, as he casually backs up to the fire pit to recover his stone. "And we've got water right here, see?" He says producing a never before seen canteen out from behind his back. Something seemed off about it to Lute, and he wondered why Edgar never showed it before if he had it this entire time.

"And your food?" The bull grinned wider.

"We ate it all?" Lute says half-heartedly, "We were only going out for one night..."

Surprisingly he seems to buy this, or at least accept it. "Well then that covers it up I suppose. Ya'll must be hungry this morning then," but before either of them could lie, their grumbling stomachs gave them away. "Why don't you two come on over to my barn and I'll give ya a nice breakfast, maybe a ride back to town if'n y'all want."

Lute hesitates, but Edgar sees an opportunity and agrees. "Yes... please?" he says, hoping to have used the new word right. Lute's eyes widened but the bull just shrugged and ordered the kids to follow behind him. As they walk through the rows of cabbages behind the absolute giant, they begin to whisper back and forth.

"Edgar, are you crazy? What if he's some kinda monster?"

"Then we can take him on with our magic. It's two on one."

"Yeah, two kids, against a giant! And where did you get that bottle?"

"I don't have one," Edgar admits, pulling the Amethyst out of his pocket from the day before. "I used an illusion spell on this gem to make him think I have one. Transmogrify is one of my better spells." he smiles.

Lute stifles a laugh, "Well, at least I'm not the only one with new tricks. When we get back on the road, you better tell me everything you can do."

"Maybe." Edgar slyly responded.

Approaching the barn, they notice that aside from the lone dirt road running parallel to the field of cabbages the barn is surrounded by large fields of amber-tinted corn. The barn itself at first seems like your classic style of a barn that is expected in farmlands. Brown roof, red exterior walls, and white shutters, but upon closer examination, one can spot the peculiar parts that don't seem to mesh. The front porch's roof is held up by columns that appear to be made of marble, and the walls are coated with trellises covered in grapevines. The air smells sweet of grapes and pomegranates, yet it also feels oddly heavy, like pressure is building.

Still, the giant bull welcomes the kids inside, "I'll start cookin', y'all head on upstairs and wash up in the bathroom, ya hear?" he tells them. While not wanting to go deeper inside, Lute doesn't want to be separated from Edgar and is glad for the chance to use a real toilet again, so they go together.

"This is crazy," Lute says to Edgar in the bathroom.

"Hmmph," Edgar just huffs, "You need to trust me when I tell you we'll be fine. Just don't do anything stupid, and maybe we can even get some money and won't have to walk to Spectacle City."

I've gotta admit, I hadn't thought of that. Lute thinks. *But still, this whole thing is... unsettling. It's like something is just OFF about this whole place.* "Okay." He eventually says. "I trust you."

Feeling refreshed, if a bit uneasy, they return to the kitchen, just as the Bull finishes making breakfast. Corn and rice. The trio begins to dig in, though it seems Edgar has a bit of trouble with his fork, taking a minute to see how Lute and the bull handle it. "Thanks for the food Mr..." Lute fishes for his name.

"Talos." The bull grins and snorts. "And don't mention it, kid, I used to be like y'all, I know how it goes. It's kinda a tradition in my family to guard things, we each pick something to guard, and well, I chose to protect whoever comes here."

"Huh, that's interesting," Edgar says, more interested in his food.

"Yeah, I suppose it is." Talos' smile quickly begins to fade. "Though to tell ya the truth, I ain't nothin' special. And tradition can sometimes be a bad thing," he says as he stops eating.

"Tell me about it." Edgar moans under his breath.

"Is something wrong Mr. Talos?" Lute asks as he finishes his meal.

"Yeah... I need y'all, to be honest with me. Y'all are mages right?" The kids stop, their eyes widen as they glance at each other, giving away the whole story. "I'll take that as a yeah. Heh, don't worry about it, I'm magic ma' self." Talos grins again, "All us bulls are. We're descendants of Minotaur, guardian of Marbleland!" he laughs a deep bellowing laugh. "Bwahaha!"

"Really?!" Lute's eyes sparkle. "That's so cool! Oh! Can you teach us anything about magic."

Talos snorts. "Fraid, not kiddo, us bulls are magic, but we've got limits. We can't use fancy magic like y'all, but we can sense where everyone and everything is on our property, we've got the best sense of direction this side of the world, an' if yer talking strength, well look at me. The phrase isn't "Strong as an Ox" for nothing! Bwahaha!"

Edgar crosses his arms. "So why tell us all this if you can't help us?"

Talos grins, "Well first as I said, I used to be like you. Figured I could get by on my own, running away from all my problems. I know y'all ain't from Horse Country, an' givin' the way you were going, y'all soon be in the mountains." His grin fades again, "Fair warning, turn back now and go back to wherever y'all are from. The mountains are dangerous, especially this time of year."

"Oh yeah?" Edgar angrily questions as he stands in the chair. "And what would you know?"

He snorts again. "Because I know what's in those mountains! Look, kid, there's something old and bad in those mountains. And it's **hungry**. Have yall ever heard of something called a Wendigo?"

A chill runs down Lute's spine as he hears the name, he's not sure why either. He's never heard of it before, and yet the sound is so alien and terrible that he can't help but feel afraid at the name. "N-no," he admits. "What's that?"

"A mage gone bad. So hungry for power and control, that they sacrifice themselves to the quest for power. Their hunger consumes them as they grow so thin that y'all might think it could be knocked over in the breeze, yet it's much stronger than it appears. That same hunger gives them an insatiable lust for blood and flesh, and it'll eat anyone that comes near. Most of the year they lie asleep but come the fall they get rowdy and start to wake up. They hunt all winter long and go back to sleep in the spring."

"Why do they do this?" Lute asks, "How does eating people help them if they want power?!"

"Let me tell you, something kid. Everyone is magic. Everyone has and can use magic to some degree. When birds grow up, they use wind magic to fly. When the foxes and cats do, they use dark magic to see at night as clear as day. The Wendigo? It knows this and can gain the magic of anyone it eats, increasing its power. It will eat anyone to gain even a drop of power."

"...What do they look like?" Edgar asks.

Talos crosses his arms. "You don't want to see them. They have these big antlers, like a deer, and I already told you about how thin it is. Its head looks more like a skull, with giant eyes that go so deep into the sockets, you'd swear there weren't any at all. Long spindly arms and legs, makes 'em about as big as me, but with no real muscle there."

"And how do we fight them?" Edgar demands.

"You don't, you go back to where you came from." Talos retorts.

"That's not happening!" Edgar says. "I refuse to EVER go back there. I won't go back! I can't go back! Not to those monsters!" He says this as he kicks the empty plate off the table, panic in his eyes, and a note of fear in his mad voice. Talos, however, doesn't get angry at this gesture. Especially when he sees the large number six emblazoned on the bottom of Edgar's boot. A mixture of the number and the sudden outburst told him everything he needed to know about where Edgar came from.

He looks away from his houseguests, he knows they won't go back, and he can't stop them from going forward. He briefly considers taking them across the mountains in his pickup truck, but a loud, deep vibration soon fills the room, confirming to him at least this would be impossible.

"The heck was that?!" Lute panics.

"Don't mind that none, that was just Ma, out in the cornfield. She does that from time to time." Talos tries to brush it off, but it's clear based on the look on Lute's face that this didn't help. He rubs the back of his neck and flicks his tail a couple of times. "Don't be afraid of her." He tries to comfort them.

Something was wrong about this place. They hadn't felt it last night, but the air wasn't quite right. It was thick with tension and heavy like before a big storm. Perhaps it was different when they made camp last night, but the tension had been growing since they first met Talos and had only gotten thicker over breakfast.

"They don't like bright lights." He snorts. "The Wendigo, that is. In fact, sunlight can kill 'em from what some of the native eagles have told me. Heat is also an issue for 'em. For them to live even without food, they let ice magic take over their body. Fire will burn them up quickly, of course, that's the issue. Sure, sunlight and fire work, but getting close is the issue. They stay up in the mountains most of the year cuz of all the snow to keep 'em cold, and they only hunt at night, comin' out of caves and abandoned shacks they've made their homes up in. Travel by day, and y'all might be alright."

Edgar crosses his wings as he sits back down. "Good enough for me. Lute, get ready, we'll get as close to the mountains as we can, and find someplace to make camp. We'll just have to be quick and get through them fast!" The loud rumbling sounds through the house again, Edgar's anger giving way to a bit of fear of his own as this one seems louder and closer than before.

"No. I wonder if y'all will." Talos admits. "Ya'll have stayed too long it seems." He lets out a deep sigh. "Darn it, kids, why'd ya'll have to go and eat the dang cabbages?"

"W-what?!" Lute stammers out, "How'd you know about that?!"

"I told ya, we bulls know where everything on our property is. Y'all were lucky when you got here last night, Ma was already asleep. So she didn't notice the theft until just now."

"I didn't steal them! I regrew them instantly!" Lute tried to defend himself.

"You an' I both know that, but to her, it doesn't matter. She chose to protect the farm, y'all damaged it, and now she's comin' for you." Talos stands as another even louder rumble can be heard, this one a clear howl of anger from a deep voice growing closer by the second.

"THIEEEEEVES!" It bellows out, as Talos makes his way to the back door and opens it.

"C'mon kids, I can't stop her," he laughs, "she's stronger than me, and well, I just can't hurt my Ma', I'm sure y'all can understand." Had it been the father, perhaps they couldn't understand, yet the mother was a different story. Lute knew his mother and knew she was a good woman, and if given the chance would do anything to have her back. Edgar's understanding was similar yet different enough.

"Go through the corn maze," Talos says, pointing to the clearing between two rows of corn. "You can get out of the farm from there and circle back around to the train tracks you came from." he sighs as pounding can be heard from the front door. "Go quickly."

The kids don't hesitate any longer, they run as fast as they can into the corn maze. The last they see of Talos is him giving a small gesture with his fingers. *Keep to the left.* They indicate, just before he shuts the door. "Howdy Ma!" he tries to stall her for a time while the two sprint across into the maize.

A-maze-ing Grace:

They sprinted and ran as fast as their tiny legs could carry them, Lute leading them, hugging the left wall as they spiraled through the twists and turns of the maze. "Can't you fly us out of here Edgar?!" Lute demands, trying to think of a smarter way of doing this.

"Heck no! I'm not old enough to fly! And even if I was, you'd be too heavy for me! C'mon, let's just cut our way through..." Edgar says as he starts to charge up his spell.

"Stop!" Lute cries and smacks his wing. "Don't be stupid. She's after us because we ate TWO CABBAGES! Think how mad she'd be if we cut down a ton of corn!"

The ground begins to shake as the two come to a stop at a dead-end, they quiet down and try to whisper to one another, hoping to keep safe. Lute lifts his ears to try and hear her approach better. "Hiding isn't going to work!" Edgar scolds. "They know where everything on their property is remember? We can't just stop. She could just charge right in here through the corn and grab us!"

"Shhh-!" Lute scolds. "Listen, look." The growling she had been doing moments before went quiet, the frantic sound of hooves on cobblestones and packed mud from outside the maze went quiet, replaced instead by the rhythmic thumping as she proceeded to slowly stomp her way through the maze. Through the stalks, they could see a bright flash of red, only for a second or two. It's high enough up to be her hair, and far enough back in the maze that it might take her a few minutes to catch up, but it was sign enough they had to get moving again.

Edgar began to lead now, following Lute's example of hugging the left wall from earlier. "I don't get it," he whispers, "she's stomping around, but so slowly, if she's so mad at us, why isn't she just charging us as I said?"

Lute tries to think of a solution and comes up with one that, while not perfect, maybe all they need to survive this. "She's following maze rules." He offers as they round another corner and manage to avoid walking down a long dead-end, able to spot it even from a distance.

"Maze... rules?" Edgar asks, baffled. "What kinda rules?"

"Well, back when Mom was alive, every Halloween we went to this farm down in Orange Bay that was also run by some bulls right? They had some games, hayrides, a haunted house, we would go trick-or-treating in this mini-town thing they set up with the other nearby farmers..." he smiles, remembering the happier times he had with his parents, looking back, he thinks he now understands why his dad always shot him such dirty looks. He would raise his fists around Lute, but the second that his mom looked over, his dad would hide them.

"Anyway, one of the attractions they had was 'The A-maze-ing cornfield'," Lute explains, as they come to a split and choose left. They were moving faster than her, so one might assume it was enough to keep them far enough away from her, that her stomping would soon quiet and maybe even fade away entirely, but the erratic structure of the maze made that impossible. At one point, the twist turned them back to the right for so far, they arrived at a long corridor next to the one she was in.

They got a good enough glimpse of her through the five or so stalks of corn that separated them. The top of her head, covered in long red hair stuck out just above the corn. She was wearing a red flannel shirt and blue jeans, just like Talos. It looked tight on her, perhaps because of a large udder she no doubt had under the clothes, but to the kids, it looked more like a muscular gut under those clothes. She spots them back through the corn, and snorts, her voice is deep, yet distinctly higher than Talos'.

"Just wait till I get my paws on you kids! I'll teach ya twice from thinking about stealin' from me!" She says, not slowing, not stopping, just stomping the ground so hard that it throws the two off-balance as she passes.

"Less talky, more runny!" Edgar says as he helps Lute up and practically drags him down the remainder of that path to the next turn. They run for a good five minutes, putting some distance between them and the bull, but need to take a small break to catch their breath.

Panting heavily for a minute before they continue walking again, Lute has a chance to continue his story. "The maze rules," he huffs out, "are simple. Number one is you can't break the maze, no cutting, burning, whatever. Number two is no cheating. You can't jump up or fly up to look around or just shove your way through the corn."

"I see." Edgar says, "So if she's bound to these rules, why don't we cheat?"

"I don't wanna risk it!" Lute shouts. "She might stop following the rules if we stop following them.

"That's... a good point," Edgar admits. "Hadn't thought of that. Fine then, Mr. Smart Guy, what do we do then?" His humility quickly gives way to grumpy pouting.

"Well, another rule," Lute adds, "Is that there has to be an exit and a way to that exit, look over there." He says pointing to the wall on his left. "It's the barn, can you see it through the corn?"

"Yeah, I think so... gah! This is so annoying! It's like we haven't made any progress!"

"You're right, it does feel like we haven't. But, here's a question for you, can you tell directions without a compass?"

"The hell's a compass?!"

"Hah!" Lute laughs, taking a moment to calm down from the intense panic he feels about the bull chasing them down, an idea forming in his head. "It's still morning, so the sun is in the east, got it? And it's behind us right now." He says just before rounding a corner the barn now behind them. "Which means the east is now to the right, south is behind us, and north is the way off of the farm. Hehe, Thanks, Billy Nye!"

"So we need to head north to get out of the maze?" Edgar tries to understand as he starts grinding another rock, trying to prepare in case they fail and have to get into a fight.

"Mmm, it's more we need to find a spot on the north end of the maze that's close to the woods, and we can get off the property, then she can't find us, and we can sneak around."

"But she's like really fast, I hate to tell you this, but we did pass by a spot like that a couple of times, the treeline is pretty far away still. I thought you said we had to follow these rules?"

Lute grins, "Ah, but the final rule is the best. The layout of the maze can change! In the one I went to, they would change the maze every year as they grew new corn, and one adult would dress up as a large bush to block off paths temporarily to make it seem like the maze was shifting around us."

"So you're gonna shift the maze for us to escape? And how do you plan to get away with that crazy idea?"

"I'll tell you once we get to a good spot. Just help me keep a lookout for it. It needs to be right on the edge of the maze. And just in case, she can't be too close, got it?"

"...Alright. I trust you." He says, and so their new game begins. They keep following the maze, either they get to the end and escape that way, or they get to the perfect spot for their new method. This latter plan of action is probably what's more likely to happen, as this maze has been going on for so long now, they're beginning to believe that most of the entire farm is this corn maze.

It twists and turns, and they keep putting more distance between them and the only passage the mother can come from. At least they hope they are anyway, as while they move fast, she knows the way, so she doesn't get tripped up by things like dead ends or crossroads. They start to find some parts on the north end of the field, and weigh their options, but decide it's best not to stop and try here. Either there's a row closer that they can see through the stalks, or they can either hear or see her through the corn.

At one point when she's close enough, Lute tries apologizing. "Would it help if I said we're sorry? We were just really hungry! And I figured it wouldn't matter if I just regrew it..."

She just bellows back, "Son, it's not about what you did, it's about the principal. I'm gonna teach you a lesson you won't forget. This is how things work around here. It's traditional."

"Screw tradition!" Edgar shouts back. "Tradition sucks! It's caused me nothing but trouble! Don't you try to talk to me about tradition!" He picks up a pebble and throws it over the corn at her. It misses, and she ignores it, just continuing to stomp forward through her maze to catch them. "Don't you ignore me you jerk!" Edgar attempts to run towards her but is caught by Lute.

"C'mon man, you know you can't take her. I think I see our spot up ahead." he tries to comfort his friend.

"Feh, fine. But this isn't over." He says as they continue their trek. "Adults man. They come up with the dumbest traditions. Starving kids on your doorstep steal some food and replace it? Better chase them through a maze to beat them up! Oh, you want something? Well, better practice your dark contracts so you can earn it with some stupid deal. That tradition will teach you how to mess people up to make it weigh in your favor." He rants and raves. "Sure, it's good power but there's no way for you to learn how to just freaking heal someone's injury! You HAVE to make them your slave!"

"Edgar..."

"And don't even get me started on stupid names, and brandings, and teeny tiny rooms you have to be shoveled into with bars on the window because it's 'Traditional'," he says with the biggest air quotes, "Let alone how you need to have some big jerkwad watching over you so you don't 'get hurt'... WHEN HE'S MORE LIABLE TO BEAT YOU UP THAN ANYONE ELSE! GAH!" he shouts as his feathers get all ruffled.

"Edgar! Breathe!"

"I... I..." he takes a deep breath and clams himself. "You're right. I can't get distracted now." He looks over at Lute. "Thanks... right? That's the right word, yes?"

Lute smiles. "Yeah, it is. C'mon, there's a spot just at the end of this hall." He says as he runs on over to the end ahead of his friend. "This is a lot of corn, it's gonna take some time."

"What is?" Edgar asks.

"I'm gonna make the corn move! In the meantime, do me a favor, guard the passage back!"

"Heh, sure. Why not?!" Edgar laughs as he charges up his magic into his wings. His normal incantations, while not as strong as his enchantments, might be able to slow her down if she approaches too suddenly and quickly.

And with that, Lute begins his dance. "Oats and beans and barley grow~" he begins the song again. In truth, he's already so used to this song after a day of singing it for the power that his mind begins to wander. He sang it so many times without effect that he knows the words by heart. And it's this that his mind focuses on as he sings. *Why wasn't there an effect in the past?* He's had to have sung this same song so many times. *Talos said everyone uses magic, but they don't realize it? Is that even possible? If it is, then why don't people know they're using magic? Has it all just been a coincidence?*

The stalks around him begin to sway as Edgar seems to be forming a large shadow, the footsteps are getting louder and closer as Lute just keeps dancing and trying to figure this out. *I sang this at home and school... There are no plants at home, or in the classroom. But what about outside? I've had to have sung it at least a few times while walking home. Wouldn't the grass have grown or danced if it heard this song?* He wasn't wrong to think this, and the realization hit him.

Wind. I always wondered why... it wasn't windy, but sometimes, while walking home, I'd be humming, and the trees and leaves would bend in the wind, but I couldn't feel it. Because there was no wind! He almost lets out a chuckle, but can't stop singing, or else all of this will be over. *If I don't focus it on specific plants, then grass and tree leaves will dance and shake. But if I do, those plants will move as I need them to, while others nearby won't at all.* He thinks, taking note of the stalks surrounding his bunch, still standing as tall and rigid as soldiers at attention. *And look at Edgar. He's concentrating on his shadow, and it's growing. Is that the key?*

Perhaps that is the solution. People have access to it, but write off the actions of magic as coincidence because they don't realize what they're doing. And when they are doing something, it's so minor because not only are they untrained, but also because they're not focusing their power on anything in particular! It's power with no control and very little power at that.

Ah, but let's not forget Edgar's part in all of this. It's hard to describe his actions as anything other than 'charging' like some kind of SciFi ray gun, he's been holding his wings out in front of him and channeling the same purple colored energy he used for the cutting spell the night prior into an orb. Though to call it an orb is a bit of a misnomer, it looks more akin to a bullet, standing up on its edge, pointed skywards, as dark as a shadow.

The corn was now in full dance, swaying back and forth in time with Lute's dance moves, and not a moment too soon. At the far end of their corridor enters the bull. *You know, Talos never did tell us her name.* Lute shrugs it off. He'll have to ask if they ever come back.

"And just what do you think you're doing?!" She snorts, and yet, not speeding up in her approach.

"Changing the game!" Lute shouts, "Edgar! Get ready to jump!"

Edgar backs up so he's next to Lute, "Right! Are you sure this is gonna work?"

"I have no idea!" Lute laughs. "Now jump!" And on his command, the two of them jump through the stalks of corn that move out of their way. This causes her to finally speed up and charge them, crashing right through Edgar's shadow, sure, but this does seem to slow her down a bit, her steps become out of sync and are softer on the ground.

"W-what?" she asks as she stumbles over, the corn standing tall once more. "What's this feeling? It's like I'm...."

"Drunk!" Edgar laughs as he sticks his tongue out of his beak to taunt her. "Haha! That's what you get! Enjoy the next eight hours as everything shifts and changes around you!"

"Edgar! Don't taunt her! C'mon, we need to keep moving."

"C-cheaters!" She slurs out as she tries to give chase, but the boys both being small, relatively quick, and able to walk in a straight line, manage to make for the tree line and, once they were sure they were out of sight, began their long walk around the outskirts of the barn.

They do decide to take a small break to catch their breath and drink some water from the river first, just happy to be out of the maze and see something other than corn. They had to have spent hours in there, as it's already afternoon, and soon it's even well past dinner time before they make it to the tracks. Only to be greeted by a surprising face.

"Glad to see y'all survived." Talos smiles at them.

"Barely," Edgar huffs, exhausted. "No thanks to you! I thought you said you 'protected' anyone who came by!"

"Yer alive, ain'tcha?" Talos laughs back. "Sides, I brought y'all some things that will help ya on the road." He says showing a backpack he's carrying. "I can't go with ya, cuz I gotta watch the farm, and can't take ya nowhere, otherwise Ma will get mad at me." He shrugs, swatting his tail a few times at some nosey flies. "And well, after that stunt, I'm pretty sure ya'll don't wanna stay here. So consider it the best I can give, bwahaha!"

He unzips the pack and shows it to the boys. "I've gotcha a couple of water bottles, be sure to fill them every chance you get, especially when you make it to the mountains. Y'all can melt some snow for quick water." He begins to list off. "Speaking of, a nice big blanket for the two of y'all to share. Sleep together to preserve body heat, especially when winter rolls around. I also gave ya some of our famous corn and cabbage seeds. Figuring a good couple mages in trainin' like y'all can find a way to make 'em grow fast for some instant meals. Save a kernel from each ear or cut the tops off of the cabbages and you can get more seeds."

He laughs again as he tosses the bag over to Edgar. "Shame this didn't work out, a spell like that song and dance of yours woulda made us a fortune, bunny boy!" He sighs, "Awe, I guess that's just life. Heh, if the whole magic thing doesn't work out for y'all, you should consider becoming farmers! Bwahaha!"

Edgar, still mad, chose not to say anything and just accept the supplies, Lute however was more grateful. "Thanks for all your help, Mr. Talos."

"Don't mention it, kid, now, y'all better skedaddle before Ma figures out you're over here. And hey, if y'all ever make it big, remember to buy Golden Bull Farm products! I'll make a deal for mages like y'all, bwahaha!" He lets out one final bellow of laughter before turning and heading back to his farm.

The kids likewise began their journey across the tracks once more the air is still, and the evening is quiet. They can't have made it too far before the sun was about to set once more, and, reluctantly, they decide to make camp, not much closer to their goal than they were the day before.

Unfortunately, There's not a large clearing for the boys to make camp in, nor is there anywhere that looks particularly safe. Thankfully, Edgar has an idea. Using the blanket they had received from Talos earlier, he ties it tight between two trees in a rough hammock shape. "Beats trying to sleep in a bush." He laughs as Lute begins piling wood and stones to make another fire.

"I don't think I've got enough in me today for another fire dance." He reluctantly admits.

"Ah, then let me show you what I can do." Edgar beams as he pulls out the carnelian from the night before. It's rough and jagged, but shining slightly in the dim light. "Remind me to start polishing this one more tomorrow, I wanna give it a disc shape." He holds it in his wings, closing his eyes and focuses on it for a minute or two, and then he shouts. "BADA BOOM!" A sark shoots out of the stone, it's big, a bit too big perhaps, as it knocks Edgar back in the recoil, but it manages to light the twigs and branches on fire. "Haha! It worked!" He says as he sits up and tosses the rock into the fire.

"Woah!" Lute gasps, "Edgar, how'd you do that?!"

"Heh, it's all in the Quartz. I told you how it's good with magic and the color decides which magic right? Well, this one's red, so it goes with fire magic, the best way to charge it is by tossing it in a fire. So you charged it last night, and now it can charge itself so long as I put it in the fire I make with it."

"Makes sense," Lute says as he pulls the plums he grew a few days ago out of his pockets. They're a bit bruised but still edible, so the two decide to eat those for dinner. "Seems a bit... explosive though."

"Yeah, that's why I want to polish and smooth it. If I can get it into a cylinder, then I can cut a hole in the center and make it into a ring. Magic rings are great. Easy to control and direct, no real knockback... it'll be great!" He laughs, which in turn causes Lute to laugh. They spend some time just eating and laughing, occasionally making fun of the bull lady, or Lute telling some lame puns, it's a good way to destress after the crazy day they had.

"That spell of yours back there was crazy! Like, you made her drunk? How's that work?"

"Illusions! I cast that shadow thing, right? It was a trap sigil. A type of magic that stays in place until someone steps on it. This one made your eyes go all shaky. It's not really becoming drunk, but it makes the ground look like it's moving around you. Besides, she would have caught us eventually, it only lasts so long. You were pretty smart back there thinking to use your song to make the corn get out of our way!"

"Well, **shucks**, Edgar I was just tired of getting lost in there."

"You know what? I'm letting that one slide because you got us out of there."

"What's the matter, to **corn**-y?"

"Don't push it."

"Heh, fair enough." Lute stares into the fire for a bit, not wanting the conversation to end yet, trying to figure out what he can say- "Edgar. What you said back there, about traditions, what did you mean by that? Bars on the windows, and brandings, and all that."

Edgar's good mood quickly fades and turns sour. "I... I was just making stuff up." he lies.

"All that? Made up on the spot while you're in an angry rage?"

"...Uhuh." He tries to lie again and looks away. It's so strange, never in a million years would Lute have ever thought that he would become the Boe Peep of the friend group. But here he was, Edgar lying to him and not wanting to talk about the obvious truth.

Lute sighs and decides not to press the issue. *He'll talk when he's ready I guess.* "Alright then. I trust you." He laughs, those words do manage to put a small smile on Edgar's face, "Though I know that whole contract thing is true," he adds. "Kinda hard for it to not be after the deal we made and all."

"Oh. Right, that." Edgar sighs as he rubs the back of his head. "Yeah, I guess the word to use is 'sorry' right? That's the one you said earlier. I don't like those contracts too much. It always ends poorly for the other person, but I can't take too little, or it won't work... wish I could though. They always say, 'Go for the soul Edgar, that one always works,' bah."

"Hey, one year of making food for my friend on demand seems like a good trade-off for a fixed arm," Lute says, trying to lift the mood.

"Fuh-rend?" Edgar tilts his head. "What's that?"

"Seriously dude? You don't know what friends are? They're like people who care about you and watch your back when you're in trouble. They're there for you when things go wrong, and help you make them right. Like... back in the corn maze, you trusted me to dance right to get us out of there, and I trusted you to hold her back while I did." Lute tries to explain, though it's evident he's not the best at describing it. "Friends help each other, comfort each other, make things better, you know?"

Edgar's blank look gives away the fact he doesn't truly understand what Lute's trying to say. Annoyed, Lute finally turns to his friend and hugs him tight. "You know, we're kind to each other, like brothers, but not." Edgar doesn't know where to put his wings and just holds them out until Lute lets go.

"So... you want to hit me?" Edgar asks.

"What? No! Why would I?!"

"Cuz that's what they all did."

"That's... jeez, I'm sorry Edgar. Just... I like you. We're friends. I'll have your back and you have mine, got it?"

"I... think so?" He says tearing up, he wipes the tears away, looking at his wet feathers on his wings. "I feel... weird. You're so strange. I... now I think I'm even more sorry for cursing you."

"I've already forgiven you." Lute laughs, "C'mon, let's get some rest, we've got a long way to go in the morning."

And with that, the two of them climbed into their new blanket hammock and fell asleep under the starry night sky.

Entry of the Gladiators:

The next few days were for the most part, uneventful. The duo quickly adapted to their new accommodations while traveling, and have managed to learn a bit more about one another. For instance, neither of them particularly like the rain, something they learned fast and hard when they ran into a storm and were fortunate enough to find a small outcropping where they could hunker down for the day. Overall though nearly two weeks had gone by without much trouble.

Lute finally managed to convince Edgar to tell him, "Most of what I can do."

"Most? Why not all?"

"Heh, what's the point in showing off everything I've got? Just means I can't show off later!" Edgar boasts. That said, there's not much more that he hasn't told Lute. There's his grinding spell, the cut spell, and the 'drunk' spell of course. Then there's the "Rocks Spells" as Lute has taken to calling them. Spells Edgar needs quartz to use.

"Like the firestarter." Edgar explains as he polishes it in the cave, grinding it down more and more, "I can use it to make that fire-burst when I have it, but without the carnelian, I couldn't even make a spark."

"So what all do you have?" Lute asks, and much to his surprise, Edgar pulls out a collection of about ten stones. The Carnelian in his wings, the Aventurine, four pieces of various sized Amethyst, a colorless one, and "Citrine, Blue Quartz, and Milky Quartz." He says as he displays his rainbow-colored collection.

"Wow, when you said you were carrying a bunch of rocks on you, I thought you meant like... three." He laughs, "So, what do they do?"

Edgar shrugs, "Aside from the Amethysts being good in general for me, and this one is the fire starter, but the rest I haven't figured out what to do with yet. Figured it'd be good to have them as I go through, in case I figure out other elements of magic."

"Lame." Lute teases. "Just make them something good, alright?"

"Duh!" Edgar laughs back.

"So, anything else?"

"Well there is one, but I don't think now would be a good time to show it." He explains. "It's big and powerful, but also really dangerous, so not something I'd be willing to use on someone like you."

"Now I'm even more curious." Lute laughs some more, "C'mon, won't you at least tell me what it does?"

"No. You'll see if I ever have to use it." Edgar sighs as the two get ready to hunker down for the night. It would seem the rain has no intention of letting up until morning, so it would be best to stay put for now, much to both of their dismay. They've agreed that if they're going through the mountains, going before winter hits would be for the best if it meant being less likely to run into the Wendigo.

The nights have become equally formulaic for Lute, as he falls asleep quickly and alternates between his traditional nightmares, and dreams of training with Culania. In the few nights of training he's gotten, he's gotten strong enough with the hygiene spell to use it... well enough on the duo while awake. It's not as good as a shower in his opinion, but it does the job.

Of course, to every cycle, a change will eventually come, and while this journey has been nothing but changes for them, this one seemed a bit more... magical.

Upon waking a smell quickly drifted over to their little outcropping. Sweet and savory, a myriad of different foods with a distinctly deep-fried flavor to them. As the kids get up and pack their bag before going to explore and find the source of the smell, they also begin to hear the sounds of musical piping. There is a calliope and the sounds of bells and an organ, someone's giving a spiel to draw the attention of anyone nearby.

"Step right up folks, step right up!" The voice shouts from somewhere. Edgar pulls back some leaves of a bush and they see it. A circus has set itself up, seemingly overnight. There's a train pulled off to the back, and several large tents spread out between it and the kids, the largest of which is in the center. Several booths are also scattered around, many of which seem to be food stalls where the smell is coming from.

"Huh. Did not expect that." Lute admits.

"What... what is this?" Edgar asks, confused.

"It's a circus! I mean... I guess it is kinda a thing for people who run away to find or join a circus, but I wasn't intending on finding one." He shrugs. "I'm guessing you've never been. Wanna check it out? They're a lotta fun!"

"I'd rather keep moving..." he tries to protest, then thinks better about it, "though actually, this might be a good way to get more ready for Spectacle City."

"Oh yeah, I've heard that place is like... a circus but more intense. Not to mention super freaking big. So this is probably a good prep place for that."

"Fine, we can visit, but we're not staying!"

"Don't think we could anyway, most of the stuff down there costs money, and we're broke." Lute laughs some more, "Though it'll be fun just to see some sights."

They agree and head right on over to the front gate, taking a moment to read over the sign. "Low-Key Circus." Edgar reads. "See the most amazing sights from across the Nine Realms. Wonder what that means."

"It means," the barker starts up his spiel again, taking note of the children, "You'll see some amazing sights if you come on in." He grins, the kids getting a good look at him. There's this... serpentine quality to him. He's an arctic fox, but his eyes are slit, and he's strangely flexible like his spine is not normal. He's got a white suit and red vest on and seems rather full of himself. "And you're in luck too! Kids under 13 can come in for free." he grins a toothy smile at them.

"Yes sir, we have some of the finest oddities from across the globe and even far beyond it! We've got all kinds of strange and mysterious objects, creatures, and not to mention the wonderful acts and shows we perform all day long here, at the Low-Key Circus!" The gruff fox continues. "It's so great, you may never want to leave!" he laughs.

The kids look at one another, then back to the barker, they shrug, though instinctively they know something's not quite right about this guy. At first, Lute looks behind him at the bushes and hills they emerged from and considers going back. Before he can, Edgar grabs his paw and starts heading inside. Walking past him, they take a moment to throw out some ideas. "Think this is some kind of trap?" Lute whispers to Edgar.

"I'm willing to guess, though I can't be certain. Maybe we're just being paranoid after the whole Talos Farm thing." Edgar tries to defend.

"Dude, he laughed evilly after saying 'we'll never want to leave', I'm pretty sure I've seen a movie with something like this in it."

"Yeah, okay, this is a trap."

"Then why didn't we walk away?"

"Because if I know anything about traps like this," he shudders, "if you don't go in, there's a worse trap waiting outside. Just keep sharp, and don't eat anything, okay?"

Lute takes a deep breath and nods his head. It's a shame that they won't be able to really enjoy this place, but he knows right now, survival is more important. So they begin looking around for a way out, unfortunately, the tents and booths are tightly packed together with large wooden fences in the few gaps between them that form a large ring around the outside of the entire circus. Had it not been for the strangely similar looking attendants at the various booths, they may have tried to break a fence or climb over one, but any such acts may result in repercussions for them.

Leaving through the entrance is also not advised, at least not right now, not with the barker still standing there, they would need to wait at least a small while before they could reasonably leave that way. One thing they agreed on quickly was to not go into the big top. If there was a trap here, that's where it would be sprung.

That left them with few options, but Edgar thought of one that might work. "We know there's probably a trap right? Then what if we try to outthink it? If we can outthink the trap in here, then we can just walk out."

"How are we supposed to do that exactly?" Lute tilts his head, "We don't know what it is, and while we think it might be in that tent, it could also not be. Heck, there could be multiple traps."

"Ah! And that's how we'll outthink it! If there are multiple traps, then if we spring a small one, and manage to get out of it, then we have an idea how the rest will work."

"That's a brilliant idea!" Lute cheers. "Alright, alright, where should we start?"

"Not with food," Edgar thinks, "and it has to be something simple so we can hopefully outsmart it." He looks around and manages to spot something, a smaller tent, with a sign out front, surrounded by small white and yellow flowers. "Hall of Mirrors... Well, guess we can start there. A bunch of glass can't be too hard right?"

Walking over to the entrance, they notice just how short the 'hall' is. There can't be more than maybe six mirrors, and they're lined up against one wall with about a foot of distance between them. They all have some minor decorations around them, and the final mirror has more of those yellow and white flowers at the top of it. "So how do we do this?" Lute asks.

"We'll go one at a time, if you go through and something happens, then I'll know how to free you. If nothing happens, then it means there's no trap here, and maybe we're overreacting."

Lute nods, "Yeah, that makes sense... wait, why do I gotta go first!"

Edgar beams, "Cuz I said so!"

"Jerk! Fine, but you do the next one first," he says as he stomps down his foot.

"Deal! Now get going!"

Swallowing whatever fear he had, Lute heads inside and parks himself in front of the first mirror. He turns to face it and sees... a distorted and rather silly reflection of himself that causes him to burst out in immediate laughter. "Bwaha! I look so fat!" He says as he points and laughs at his reflection. "Haha... okay, so not that one." he laughs as he wipes a tear from his eye.

Heading over to the next one, this one distorts his image to be tall and lanky, he bursts out into more laughter. "Hahaha! These things are so dumb." He shouts over to Edgar. "Unless the trap is to make me die from laughter, I think I'll be fine." He says before turning to finish the hall. The next three repeat the formula, see a mirror, laugh, continue to the next. Just one mirror was left.

He turns to face it. But he doesn't start laughing. In fact, he barely speaks or moves at all. "Lute? Lute! What's going on down there!" Edgar calls over.

"So..." Lute mumbles under his breath as he reaches out a paw towards the mirror. "So... beautiful...." Edgar can just barely hear Lute's voice. Deciding the trap's been sprung, he charges down the hall, "Hang on, I'm coming!" he shouts. *Dang it, these mirrors are cursed! I knew it! I've just gotta not look at them.* Immediately, he is met by an invisible barrier just after the first mirror.

"Mmph! Let me through, you stupid-!" He tries banging against the strange force but finds it futile. He looks around, trying to find anything he could do to get past, and accidentally glances at the mirror. His heart skips a beat as he sees another bird. It's not his reflection, it's not a distortion. It's someone else, someone he **knows**. Before he can even squeak out a note of shock, the mirror explodes outward, shattering in hot gas.

He wants to just sit there, accept what he saw and beg for mercy, or cry out why, and how did they find him. But he picks himself up. *They might take me, but I'm saving him first!* He pushes against the force again, only to find with the shattering of the mirror, it was gone. Lute's still sitting there, just staring at his reflection, so Edgar runs at him only to run into another wall. *So I have to face the mirror? Is that the trick?*

Reluctant, Edgar tries this theory and glances over. The mirror instantly shatters, but in the fraction of a second he could see into it, he saw an abomination. It had parts of him mixed with long tentacles of an octopus, and leathery wings sprouting from the back, where its tail should have been, the feathers were replaced with a scorpion's stinger. Just a glance made him feel as if he was drowning in the ocean itself.

Gasping for air, he puts a wing out towards Lute, and unfortunately (for Edgar, not Lute), the force was gone, and Edgar knew what saving him would mean. The next mirror didn't immediately shatter when he looked at it, instead, it was just coated in darkness. As he stared into it, the mirror began fracturing into more and more tiny slivers but never fell or fully shattered. By the time it was done it was as if it had returned to being sand, still pure black in the frame. Suddenly, a single point of bright light came from somewhere in the mirror, and it blew away in the wind.

The fourth is quicker by far, as it seems to shatter without Edgar even looking at it, the sounds of broken glass and angry screams ring through his skull as he panics and remembers just why he had to leave. He drops to his knees as he tries to get a hold of himself and block it out so he can finish this whole mess. He gathers his thoughts and breath, he's seen the worst of it now, surely right?

The fifth sends a chill down his spine, it's as if winter had come early as he stares into it, his reflection a tall figure wearing a distorted crown and some creature writhing at his talons. He screams at the face in the mirror that's grinning back at him, darkness envelops the mirror before it finally shatters like snowflakes. The glass pooling under Edgar, he charges at Lute and tackles him.

He manages to knock Lute out of the hall, and he snaps to, but the force from before prevents Edgar from leaving himself. "H-huh?" Lute asks, "Edgar? What happened?" But alas, Edgar didn't respond. He curls himself upon his knees and places his wings on his head, trying so hard to figure out a way out without looking at the mirror. *There's only one thing that could be in that.* He rationalizes.

He closes his eyes as he stands, "Lute. Am I facing you?" he asks.

"Y-yes! Edgar, are you okay?"

"I got you out of the trap. Now to get me out of it." He says and immediately begins walking backward. He takes maybe four steps but feels the same force from before now solidly behind his back. He's stuck.

"Hang on! Let me try something!" Lute shouts as he finds a small rock. He tosses it with all his strength at the mirror, but it doesn't even scratch the thing. "Crap. Hang on! Let me find a bigger rock!"

"No," Edgar says. "Breaking it will work, but your way won't. I gotta look." He winces at his own words and turns to face the mirror. "Look away, Lute!" Edgar orders, and after giving him a minute to do so, he opens his eyes.

It's him.

Just him.

His reflection, and nothing more.

The mirror doesn't break or shatter, it doesn't enchant him to stare deeper into it, it works just as any other mirror would. Or does it? After all, it's just Edgar in the mirror. Perhaps he should feel relief, let out his breath, or drop his guard as he only sees himself staring back, but he doesn't. Instead, he just holds his breath and quickly walks outside before he finally exhales.

"I don't know what happened," Lute says, putting a paw on Edgar's shoulder, "but it doesn't matter. Edgar, are you okay?"

"Yeah," he lies as he takes some deep breaths, "I'm gonna be okay. Just... those enchantments were messed up. At least..." he looks back into the hall, "I hope they were just enchanted." He straightened himself up. "Right, I'm done with this circus business. We need to get out."

"I'm all ears for any good ideas," Lute says.

"You're mostly ears anyway," Edgar snickers as he looks around, "so now we know most if not everything here is trapped."

"Rigged." Lute suddenly has an epiphany, "The games are all rigged! This means if we want to get out, we need to cheat!" He spots something nearby and has an idea. "Look there, see that tent with the green and yellow stripes? See that thing next to it? I'm guessing you've never seen a carousel before." He says pointing at the spinning contraption adorned with ceramic dragons that twist around it.

The machine is quite intricate and impressive, especially for Edgar who Lute was correct to assume never saw one before. Brightly colored and covered in glowing balls of lights, the top looked like a tent held up by a central column and the poles that ran up through the dragon statues. All the statues were also intricately carved, no two looking quite the same, and all of them saddled and so detailed, one might mistake them for being alive.

"It's a type of ride." Lute explains, "And if you'll notice, that sign says it's free. I think I know what the trap might be, which means we could break it."

"I see." Edgar says, "Quick question, how will that get us out of here?"

"They want us to stay, right? Then why don't we make them not want us to stay? If we break enough of their traps, they'll want us gone."

"Or dead," Edgar says, shattering Lute's plan. "Look, after that whole mirror thing just now, I just want to get out, eat something, and go to bed."

"I... yeah, you're right. Let's just get out of here." He says as the two begin to walk back towards the entrance. "You know, it's funny. I guess by making us want to solve the traps, that would be a way of making us 'never want to leave', considering how much there is here."

"Heh, yeah... maybe that was the big trap. Just get us obsessed with everything else here. Now come... on?" He stops and looks around. "Hang on, wasn't the entrance here earlier? Yeah, it was! The orange tent was across from the blue stall."

"Hang on, we probably just got turned around in the mirror hall. Look, We'll just follow the outer ring and arrive at the entrance, okay?" He tries to brush it off, and they begin their large circle, they pass by the hall of mirrors, the train, oddities museum, and arrive back at the carousel. "...Where's the exit?"

"That's what I was saying! The exit's gone!"

"Well... crap. I guess we'll have to try breaking down the walls now." Lute offers.

"I wouldn't try that dearie..." a voice says from a nearby tent.

"Oh yeah?" Edgar growls as he turns to face it. "And why's that?!"

The tent he faces is striped purple and deep blue, lavender smoke pours out of it, and a blue sphere sits on the sign up above. Standing in the door is an elderly woman, a lioness, and despite her silvered mane, she wasn't wrinkled and had a strange elegance about her that spoke to her age. She carried herself well, while it was clear her steps were a bit slow she was clearly still capable, perhaps in her day she was a fine warrior.

"Because," she responds, not even bothered by Edgar's tantrum, "the walls are enchanted, and any damage done to them will just cause damage to you. This entire place is cursed for people like you."

"Gee, you think? We figured that out already!"

"We considered not coming in, but figured that might be worse."

"Then you are clever." She grins, "The barker would have thrown the two of you in if he needed to. Please, won't the two of you come in? My friends and I are enjoying a cup of tea, and we would love to have you."

"And how can we trust you?" Edgar demands.

"Because, if you stay out here, you'll get lost in the circus, tire, and die. Inside it is safe... for now." she laughs as she turns and heads inside herself.

Lute looks over at Edgar. "Looks like we don't have much of a choice."

"I'm still in favor of destroying the walls, maybe this whole place as well."

"Just... c'mon, maybe we can figure out how to get out once we go inside."

They head inside, and something seems immediately off about the tent. The ground is strangely carpeted, something you wouldn't expect to see in a traveling tent. Deep purple to match the fabric walls, and there's a strong smell of incense that hangs in the air.

However, the truly strange part is the sheer size. The exterior seemed smaller than the hall of mirrors and even smaller than some of the nearby food stands, but inside there had to be at least three rooms separated by wooden poles and flaps of fabric, and the central room they find themselves in is bigger alone than the exterior would make one believe.

In the center of the room, a small circular table with a blue cloth draped over the top sits, five chairs sat around it in a star. There is a kettle and several cups and sweet cakes at the table being eaten by the people sitting there. Two of the chairs were already occupied. To the left was a snowy lynx with long golden hair and deep brown eyes, she's smiling and listening intently to the tale of the lady to the right. She wears a white gown and a curiously glowing necklace.

The right lady was a bat, wearing a dark black dress, her hair was slightly less long than her companion's but had light blue highlights, clearly dyed, she seemed to have this otherworldly air about her. "...and so I told her, 'Sis, I know you think you know what's best for me, but I love him and he loves me.' And she was all, 'No no, Persephone, he kidnapped you!' And I got so fed up with her I spilled the beans. 'He didn't kidnap me! I asked him to come grab me and take me away from that crazy perv you hang out with!'" She laughs.

"Persephone, Freya, the kids I told you about are here." The old lady says as she sits in the chair between the two.

"Huh. You weren't kidding about the future vision thing, were you Ishtar?" Persephone says looking the two of them over. "Hello, kids!"

"So, how about those lottery numbers?" Freya teases. "Take a seat, you're among friends here," she tells the kids.

They do so, taking the two free seats, and Persephone pours each of them a cup of tea. "So..." Lute starts. "You knew we were coming?"

"Of course," Ishtar says, "I may be catching on in years, but I still have some of my older tricks. I knew you kids would run away from home before you were born, and I knew you'd end up here, and I knew we had to be here to help you."

Persephone's eyes sparkle as she lets out a quick gasp. "Ishtar! You didn't tell us we got to help people with a quest!" she's bubbling over with giddy excitement, convincing herself of whatever's going through her head. "I haven't done that in like... two thousand years!"

Freya sets down her cup, "Well, maybe you haven't but I've been keeping busy. Think you can keep up with me?" She laughs at her friend.

"Of course I can!" Persephone pouts. "Now you two, c'mon, you've gotta tell me what your quest is!"

"Quest?" Edgar asks.

"Two thousand years?" Lute questions. "Not to be rude, but what are you three on about? How can you be over two thousand years old?"

"He's such a flatterer!" Persephone teases as she gives him a cookie. "I know I've managed to keep my good looks for this long. Oh but Ishtar, now she's got the real looks." She leans in close to the kids and whispers, "Psst, she's actually FOUR thousand years old!"

"Persephone!" Ishtar scolds. "You're not supposed to tell someone a woman's age! As for your questions..." She stands and holds her paws up, several objects around the room begin to float, including the table, chairs, teacups, and even Edgar and Lute. Her eyes shine with a blinding yellow light, and yet despite all of this, Freya and Persephone take it all in stride. Lute was freaking out and wondering if this was another trap, while Edgar was mentally preparing himself for a fight.

"WE ARE LEGENDS!" her voice booms and bellows about the tent. "Guardians of the world, and heroes of our times! In our day, people once considered us gods!"

"In truth," Freya says, "We are just very powerful magic users. Legends are born or made, and then their stories are told and retold as time moves on, and stories have a power all of their own."

"Some legends are born into power, others are given it by an object or another legend, regardless as to how we gain many boons, one of those including immortality." Persephone giggles.

"W-what does that have to do with us?!" Lute asks as Ishtar lets them back down, the light fading from her eyes.

"It means, we saw you coming and decided to help you. We have powers and abilities far beyond the average magi and plan to help you get stronger so you won't die anytime soon."

"AND! And, if you do die, I promise my husband and I will take good care of you in the underworld." Persephone offers.

"Not helping Persephone," Freya remarks.

"Agreed, your hospitality is welcome, but we need them alive for now."

"What do you mean you need us?" Edgar demands. "We're not your servants, lady!"

"I know that." Ishtar scoffs, "I have no use for more servants, no. I need you alive. That's the price for these lessons. Consider it similar to your contracts." As she says this, she grabs a crystal ball off a nearby table and shines her light into it, figures dance and come to life within the orb as it floats through the air, projecting them about the room. "I have no doubt you haven't heard of us small hatchling, but prey tell Lute, have you heard of any of us?"

"I don't think so..." Lute admits, taking a bite from his cookie. "Though Freya does ring a bell."

Freya grins and pulls something out of her gown, "And this ladies is why adapting with the market is so important." She sets it down on the table, it's a comic book. It depicts the superhero Thor on its cover, a red-headed polar bear with a mighty electrical hammer, teaming up with the Amazing Spiderham to battle against... a familiar-looking arctic fox.

Lute's eyes sparkle and he immediately goes into rapid-fire question mode. "Wait. THAT'S THE BARKER! If he's real, is Thor real? Freya... YOU'RE THOR'S MOTHER! HOW? I mean... how are you real? Are other superheroes real? Can I meet Spiderham!?"

"Settle, settle." Freya calms him. "Sorry kiddo, the superheroes aren't real. We were just around before the comics, and well... we funded them to help spread our stories." She laughs. "When you get to be like us you learn the value of keeping your story alive. Just people knowing your name can help deal with a lot of problems, especially nowadays."

"The heck is a superhero?" Edgar tilts his head at the book.

"Okay, seriously dude, I don't know the details but I know your home life sucked and all, but we HAVE to get you caught up on superheroes. They're so cool!" Lute gushes as he shakes his friend's wing.

"I think we're getting off-topic here." Ishtar interrupts. "The point we're trying to make here kids is this. We've been around for thousands of years, and we have our own goals and desires. You don't need to know what those are, at least not yet, we're willing to help you on your journey, and in turn, you're going to help us down the road."

"We've done this for many heroes and mages in the past," Persephone explains. "These often become legends in their own right. Sometimes they ascend as high as us, and other times they don't, but they always end up able to accomplish their destiny." As she says this, the figures show various depictions of heroes from across time. Hercules wrestling Cerberus, Persephone cheering in the background. Ishtar granting a blessing on a strange-looking character that appears neither male nor female. Freya fighting in battle against frost giants to save a wounded warrior. Images of their pasts.

Edgar scoffs, but nobody pays attention to him. "I wondered why Ishtar brought Persephone with her to visit me." Freya adds, "If this had been any other magi, I could have gotten you out on my own. She sees something in you two if she's getting involved. What, I do not know, but hey, I'm willing to go with it for now."

"So what would we have to do?" Lute asks.

"You'll spend a week with us here, and we'll train you how to better use your powers. There will be one final test, and should you pass, you'll be free to leave the circus and will be capable of crossing the mountain. It won't be safe, but you're more likely to survive this way."

Edgar squirms in his seat. "A... a week huh?" He glances at the door, "Is there any way we could speed it up a little?"

Ishtar laughs. "Don't worry kid, you're safe-ish here. Don't trust anyone else, they're all the barker, screw it, he's Loki and he's using his magic to make him look like everyone else here. The rides and attractions are also traps he made to catch mages like you. You'll see what we mean in the final test. Go crazy with the darkness, Loki and Persephone are legends of darkness, and Freya and I are legends of light, we've drowned out your signals."

"Remind me to add that skill to the training list." Freya remarks.

"Oh-oh! Tell me what elements you kids use, I'll make sure we start formulating spells in those groups!"

Noticing his friend, Lute speaks up. "Could you give us a minute?" He says grabbing Edgar and heading outside. "Alright, I'm giving you your space and all, but I need some details. Why are you freaking out, this sounds good, doesn't it?"

"It does, it's just..."

"Just what? If you want to leave now, we can get out of this circus and turn back, maybe go to Big Apple instead where we don't have to fight some ice demon in the mountains."

"No!" Edgar stomps. "We can't stay here, and we can't go that way! They'll find me!" He catches himself and slides down on his talons. "They'll find me if I stay there. They're always after me. I know they are. They'll do anything to get me, and when they do..." he falls silent.

Lute takes a deep breath. "Alright. Alright, that's all I need for now. Heh, you should have told me this, I would have picked up the pace earlier." he lets out a sigh, placing a paw on Edgar's shoulder. "They say we're safe, they can't find you, and these guys are really strong, right? Then even if your family could find you here, there's no way they could beat all three of them."

"Y-yeah, you might be right." Edgar calms down. "This is our best shot to get to safety. To get power." He nods. "We're going to need more power to protect ourselves. Let's do this."

They return into the tent, Lute looks up at the three legends. "So, have you decided?" Ishtar grins as she asks.

"We have, we accept your deal Ishtar!" Lute responds.

Eye of the Tiger:

And so with that, training began. Their first lesson would start that afternoon after a small chance for the two of them to rest, recover, and eat some food the legends provided them.

"Alright," Freya began, leading them outside to find a good target, "what can you kids do?"

"Hmph!" Edgar scoffs, "You guys knew we were coming, why don't you tell us?"

"I did not know you were coming." Freya corrects as she spots her mark, "Ishtar can see the future, not I nor Persephone."

"It's not like we need to anyway." Persephone laughs, bringing up the rear as the group makes its way to the classic circus attraction, a strength tester. The bell sits high above their heads, a large mallet laid casually across the plank.

"Well, Edgar here has a spell that cuts things, and I can make plants grow with a song and dance..." Lute says.

"Shut up! No way! Plants are like, totally my thing!" Persephone beams. "Oh-oh! I know! I just need the right seed..." she fishes in her dress and pulls out some tiny brown seeds, and scatters them around the tester. "Let me show you what you can do!"

She snaps her fingers and raises her paw high, vines erupt from the ground around the game and snatch up the mallet. She holds her paws backward, mirroring the grip of the vines as if the mallet were in her paws. She throws her arms forward and down, the vines following as they bring the hammer down on the plank, shooting the ringer right up to the bell, sounding it with a loud "DING!"

Lute stood there flabbergasted at the sight in front of him. She was so much better at his skill than he could ever hope to be. She goes down on her knees, touching her paws to the ground, as she does so the vines recede and vanish, she pockets her seeds and smiles. "Your turn!" She tells him.

"Um..." He tries to think fast and remembers the corn seeds that Talos gave them. He quickly took a few and scattered them about. He begins to dance to convince them to grow, "Oats and beans and barley grow~" he sings. Soon enough, (a few minutes later), the corn stalks have grown to full size and are shaking back and forth with him. It's clear however that this much has already made him pretty exhausted.

"Stop," Freya commands, and Lute thankfully collapses, the corn stalks standing at attention. Edgar goes to Lute's side to help him up while Persephone reverts the corn to its seeds. "It's clear you are not strong enough for this yet. Let's try your partner instead." As she says this, she points to another nearby booth.

Approaching, they find it's a shooting gallery. Red and white targets move sideways, up and down, in circular patterns, or are blocked by other objects. "We shall try your powers here." She tells Edgar as she picks up the game rifle. In about ten seconds, she manages to hit every target knocking them back.

"Hang on! What does shooting a gun have to do with magic?!" Edgar demands.

"Who said you were shooting a gun?" Freya remarks as she breaks it over her knee. "Shoot it with your cut spell."

Edgar faces the range, gulps and charges... and charges, and charges... After about a minute, he finally has enough charge and lets a blast out of his wings. "Cut!" he shouts as the energy shoots out smacking a target dead-on, carving it in two. Edgar lets out a huff. "How was that?"

"Better than your friend," Freya notes. She kneels down and gets on eye level with Edgar, "But I sense something greater in you. Why are you holding back?"

"I'm not holding back!" Edgar protests. "W-why would you think that?"

"A true warrior knows when someone is holding back," she says. "I can sense the power inside of you. Show me," she demands.

"No!" Edgar responds, taking a step back. He knows the power she's talking about, his ultimate spell. Sure, the cut spell is good, but he can't move while charging it, and he has to charge it for a while to slice through anything. The drunk spell? It's an even longer charge. And the rocks, well, they're useful for sure, but aside from a quick illusionary object or spark of fire, they don't have a purpose.

This spell was different. Quick, strong, and dangerous. Not to Edgar, no, it was actually super easy for him to cast, and probably the only thing to ever give him reprieve back at home, as aside from the contracts, it was the spell he had practiced most.

"So you are holding back." Freya laughs. "Let me tell you something. Where you're going there's going to be trouble. You'll need to defend yourselves, and you won't always have the luxury of holding back. The two of you need to be able to go full power. So stop holding back, and show me what you can really do!"

Edgar goes quiet and looks down. *She wants to see my full power? Fine then, I'll show it to her.* He takes a few steps away from her, Freya seemed annoyed that it seemed he wasn't going to show her what he could do. He takes the precaution of standing between her and Lute and Persephone, Freya had angered him, not those two. He stands halfway between them, his back turned to Freya.

"Be afraid." He whispers. The words are spoken softly and quietly, yet with so much tense energy behind them that they seem almost deafening, silencing all the nearby rides and music. The dark energy pours out of his body like a fiery aura of darkness. Imagine if you would a roaring fire suddenly catching and consuming Edgar, but instead of warmth and light, it's cold, seemingly removing heat from the nearby air. Further still, while fire would give off light, this one seemed to absorb it, as if a black hole appeared in space around Edgar.

"Be very afraid!" Edgar shouts at the top of his lungs as he turns, the shadowy aura erupts from him taking the shape of a giant melting bird that shoots up above him. Its face has a look of pure malice on it as it grins down at

Freya. It's as if she immediately realizes her mistake when it comes crashing down over her, washing over her body like a wave on the beach.

Maniacal laughter filled the air around her, and she began to use her energy to try and repel it, but sadly the **thing** just kept attacking her, poking holes in the light that shrouded her body. She tried to attack it, to fight back, to just get a handle on it, to do something, ANYTHING to stop it! It just laughed more at her as it began tearing apart the nearby carnival grounds. It spread out further, not only attacking her but destroying stalls, and rides and games, it attacked Persephone and Lute and even Edgar, the power was too much for him to control as it exploded outward like a bomb.

She conjured up weapons of light and began attacking the darkness, now the only thing in front of her and in every direction, her aura glows brightly as she does so, but it doesn't repel the shadow, merely work as a beacon calling it to swallow up the ground and sky around her before crashing down again and again and again. Never relenting, never showing signs of damage or pain, just a relentless endless force.

Her light began to fade until only darkness remained, and with that, she held her head and screamed in true terror, unable to do anything, unable to fight back, and watch as it attacked her once more.

"Freya!" Persephone's voice snapped her back to reality. She looked around, the nearby circus had been damaged, but only by her weapons scattered about. Swords and spears and axes logged in nearby stalls between the scattering of stray arrows and bullets of pure light. Persephone has erected a shield of pale blue lilies and darkly colored thorn-covered vines around her and the huddling children.

As she surveyed the damage, Freya realized she had transmuted her dress into her battle armor, harder than steel, the armor looked fitting for ancient Viking raiders, with a winged crown on her head, and a thick breastplate of glowing light. "W-what?" she asked as she allowed the armor and weapons to dissipate and evaporate away as if they were made of smoke.

"What just happened?" She asks, approaching Persephone's cage. Persephone lowers it, giving Edgar the chance to respond.

"I warned you," he says, "That's the power you wanted to see. Fear. My ultimate spell."

"I..." Freya looks over the damage, thinking her words carefully. "See. That's... impressive." She half-heartedly smiles, as she takes a knee to catch her breath. The spell still seems to be lingering, and fear still weighs on her mind, but she's able to force herself to smile at the child. "Good job kid."

"So..." Persephone says, "Good spell, love the darkness, remind me to show you how to use it a bit better, but uh... we're not gonna use that one again in training. Kay?" She tries to laugh off the situation.

Lute however was more horrified by what he just saw. In truth, the above visions of darkness and destruction, and the growing shadow were seen only by Freya. To the onlookers, Edgar's shadow had simply washed over her once and then faded away as she went quiet. A look of fear slowly grew across her face as no one could get her attention. This look quickly intensified as she began pulling more and more weapons of increasing complexity out of the air and attacking in random directions.

Edgar has this kind of power. He realizes and tries to rationalize. *He has this kind of power and didn't use it on Talos' mom? And he didn't want to use it until she made him. Is he afraid of it? I... my other song...*

"Persephone, can I ask you a question?"

"You just did. What's up?"

"What... what kind of magic was that?"

"A dark illusion," Edgar responds. "I'm good at enchanting and illusion, and well, I use dark magic."

"Dark magic..." Lute parrots back. "What separates dark magic from other magics?"

"The element." Persephone answers, "Like, Freya uses light magic and ice magic, I prefer darkness and earth magic... which makes me the perfect teacher for the two of you I suppose." she laughs.

"Does all dark magic do stuff like that? Like, mess with people's heads and make them do stuff?"

"No," Edgar and Persephone respond at the same time, Edgar continues, "My cut spell is also dark magic."

"Plus other elemental magics can mess with people's heads. Each element has a different emotion tied to it." Persephone finishes.

"Wh-which element is tied to sadness?" Lute asks.

Persephone looks over to Freya, they lock eyes, unsure what to say. "That's... a good question. How sad are we talking here exactly?"

He goes quiet and looks down. *I... I can't just tell her can I? Certainly not Edgar, I really...* he swallows his fear and gestures for her to lean down. She folds her wings over him, keeping Edgar just far enough away so he can't hear. Lute whispers the question to her. "Sad enough to die."

Her face goes somber as she realizes what he means. "That's... that's advanced magic. Though I suppose that Edgar's spell might be similar. That fear spell was very strong, so either he's been training every single day, or he's tapped into a very advanced power source..." she starts to ramble before catching herself.

"We call it Madness, it's a fusion of Darkness and Water magic." she finally answers.

"Madness..."

"Looks, I think Freya needs a moment after that-"

"No! I am perfectly fine." She responds as she quickly stands.

"Uh Huh. Well, I'm sure you need to recover after your dance. We'll work on powering that up next, but for now, why don't we break for dinner?" Persephone offers. They all agree and head back to the Fortune teller's tent where Ishtar is waiting, having already gotten dinner ready. As they eat, Lute notices Persephone pull out a cellphone.

Baffled, Lute asks the obvious question. "Hang on, you guys have really advanced magic, but still use cell phones?"

"Of course," Ishtar says. "Kid, I've lived since before writing was a thing, magic is great and all, but sometimes it can be a pain in the butt to use. Modern technology is absolutely amazing. If you told me back when I first started that eventually, I'd have a magic rock that would allow me to talk to anyone in the world, look up and learn anything I wanted to, and write down messages and reminders, I would have thought you were insane."

Persephone seems to be deep in a text message conversation with someone on the other end and doesn't notice the conversation, so Freya picks up next. "Which sounds easier to you? Writing a letter, stamping it with a seal, burning it, and then repeating it on the other side, or just texting someone a quick two sentences?"

"Fair enough," Lute responds between bites of food. "Actually, that's another question, if you've lived this long, how come no one has noticed?"

"YES! That's what I've wanted to know!" Edgar slams his wing on the table. "Four thousand years, and what, you live in a tent? I'd want a palace or something!"

Freya and Ishtar just laugh. "We do!" Freya responds, "This tent is just for keeping an eye on Loki right now. Heh, I live in a gigantic palace of wood and gold and silver, high above the clouds!"

"W-wouldn't that appear on maps and things then?" Lute asks, "I mean, people can fly, not just birds, but like, airplanes and things. And satellites! We have like, photos of Earth from space down to street levels. Wouldn't everyone see your palace?"

"I told you he was the clever one," Ishtar comments, causing Edgar to lob a carrot at her, only for Ishtar to quickly dodge out of the way. "And he's the angry one."

"You're right, and that's why we create 'new homes'. Each legend chooses how to hide their own home. Some choose to live in nature, others stay in modern luxury, some go into other dimensions to live as Persephone and I do."

"I just use the whole 'Bigger on the Inside' trick," Ishtar comments, "I've got a nice penthouse apartment over in Marbleland, but the inside is a giant palace full of the best luxuries of both magic and technology I can get my paws on."

Freya pulls out her cellphone to show the kids. "The dwarves made this for me," she says, showing them an app called 'Bifrost' with a rainbow for an icon. "Just a tap of a button and I can teleport home from wherever in the world I am, as well as teleport out to anywhere else."

"That's so cool!" Lute's eyes sparkle as he sees the app. "When can I learn a spell like that?!"

"Heh, maybe when you're older." Freya laughs as she pockets her phone. Persephone meanwhile finally seems to finish her conversation and pockets hers as well, a distraught expression crosses her face as she glances over at Lute.

"I wonder how powerful the two of you truly are," she admits.

"You want another demonstration?" Edgar beams.

"No!" Freya commands. "N-no. That spell is great, but using it on me is enough. Using it on Ishtar might be just about the worst idea I've ever heard."

Edgar pouts, something in his gut let him know that she wasn't wrong. Neither of the kids has heard of Ishtar before, but it seemed that both Freya and Persephone respected her, and maybe even feared her. Making her go berserk would probably result in a lot of pain for all of them.

"For now," Ishtar says, "Let's get your magic sense up to snuff. It's something that will help you stay safe. Just by being able to sense where magic users and creatures are, you'll know the best way to avoid them."

"Mainly, going in the other direction." Persephone laughs.

"Sounds good to me," Lute admits. "Can't say I'm looking forward to the idea of battling some kinda monster in the mountain."

"Then let's not waste time." Ishtar orders as she stands, follow me outside so we may begin." Returning outside, they immediately notice the damage is already cleaned and cleared from earlier.

"Woah, it's like she never shot up the place." Lute comments.

"Mmm. Loki's trickery no doubt." Ishtar replies. "He must be preparing for a new capture, and wants this place to look good. Now, focus on me." She commands, standing tall before the two. "I'm going to release so much power that anyone will be able to sense it, brace yourselves."

Capture? Lute wonders, *what does she mean by capture?* Setting that aside for now he turned his attention to the legend before him. He takes a stance he once saw in a kung fu movie, which caused Edgar to laugh at him, he doesn't care though since he's pretty sure it looks cool, (but that's up to interpretation).

Regardless, Ishtar begins glowing brightly, the air around her seems to blow and billow outwards from her body like a dust storm forming around her. Pure white light shoots out from the top of her head in a column of energy straight into the sky. The gusts are so strong, they knock both the kids off their feet.

On the ground, eyes closed and one paw on his hat, Lute can't feel anything other than the strong winds, is that what he's supposed to feel? Wind? "I can feel it!" Edgar's voice calls out to him. "Lute? Try clearing your mind!"

"What does that even mean?!" Lute calls back, but Edgar has gone quiet. He decides to try and steady himself, getting up on his feet, he manages to catch his balance despite the winds. *What does that even mean?* He continues to wonder. *How am I supposed to sense her if I can't even see her, this wind... the wind is coming from her. That means she's in the direction the wind is coming from.*

As if a drop of the light from her head dropped down and entered into Lute's mind, he suddenly realized where she was. His ears flapped behind his head as he turned to face her, eyes still closed. The wind was the guide.

Soon, the wind started to die down, but as it did, she began to move. "Follow me, do not lose track, and do not open your eyes," Ishtar commands. And so the children do until the gusts become a breeze, the breeze becomes a whisper, and the whisper fades all together into the background wind of the cool afternoon. And yet, despite them unable to see her, they still follow her perfectly.

She grins as she tells them "you may open your eyes now." And pets them as she tells them the first lesson is done. "Congratulations. Now you should be able to sense all magical sources, all you need to do is concentrate."

"Anything?" Edgar questions and closes his eyes. He takes a deep breath. "The tent is magic, the circus is magic... Freya and Persephone are sitting at the table in the tent. There's a strong force near the carousel."

"That's probably Loki?" Lute offers. "It feels different than Ishtar."

"You're correct. That's dark energy you're feeling. I use light."

"So in the tent, Persephone is on the left, and Freya is on the right because of how the elements line up?"

"Now you're getting it!"

"In the Big tent, there's a lot of magic. A LOT of magic." Edgar frowns.

"Loki's trophies from this circus of his." Ishtar comments. "That will be explained later. What else do you sense."

"I can sense some weird stuff on the rides..." Lute comments.

"The sources of the traps!" Edgar realizes. "We can figure out how the traps work easier now!"

"Can you sense each other?" Ishtar asks outright.

"I... can't," Edgar admits.

"I can though." Lute reveals, "Perhaps it's because Edgar's stronger?"

"My my, you are clever. Yes, the stronger you are, the easier you are to sense, and the further away you can be sensed from. With the right training, you can suppress your magic so others can not sense you. The best part is that it doesn't use any mana, so you won't get tired just using it all the time."

"That's so cool!" Lute cheers. "So what's next? A new skill, a new spell? Oh! Can you teach me something cool? Like flying!"

"I want to fly too!" Edgar says, "I'm tired of waiting to grow into my wings."

"Settle down children." Ishtar coos as they return to the tent. "Those spells will come with time as you become stronger. Trying to use them now would probably be too much for you." She coughs into her paw. "Whooh, I'm getting too old for this. As for now, I'm afraid I can't help the two of you too much. Especially you Edgar."

She pats his head. "Darkness and I are old enemies. Light and darkness can not mix, and while I can not teach you, Persephone is equipped for both of you."

"So THAT'S why you brought me!" Persephone laughs as they re-enter the tent. "And here I was thinking you just wanted to say 'Hi' and maybe get a drink at Dionysus' place."

Freya just shakes her head and sighs. "So that's why you brought her. Well, the more the merrier. Better than being left alone here with Loki and two kids... Odin knows

I would probably castrate him for trying to harm these two."

"What about that snake poison thing?" Persephone offers.

"Ehhh, that's more your husband's department. And he got out of the last one anyway, so it's not even worth it."

"Uhhh..." Lute tries to interrupt.

"Hmm? Oh, sorry. Just reminiscing." Freya laughs. "Right, so given what we've seen, it seems that both of you are complete crap."

"Rude!" Lute pouts. "I'm number one, not number two!"

"Sorry, but she's right, you know. It took you a half hour to grow corn stalks from seeds, and by the time you were done, you looked like you were gonna collapse right there!" Persephone scolds.

"What about me?" Edgar asks. "Or do I need to give you another taste." He teases Freya.

"That spell is great. You've learned it well, and it'll take you far." Freya admits, "But relying on one spell for everything is dangerous, since if it fails, then you're defenseless."

"...Fair," he reluctantly admits, "So what would you suggest then?"

"If that spell can't scare them away or distract them enough to take them down," Ishtar begins, "then nothing really will. Illusions are nice, and I strongly suggest you keep practicing them on your own. Your cut spell is best for direct combat."

"While I can't help you with darkness itself, I can show you how to hone elemental energy into a blade, like my weapons from before," Freya says, "That way you can hopefully bypass the charging time."

"Well then, what are we waiting for, let's get started!" Edgar says more pumped than ever.

And so it began, the training and dancing, the magic and chanting, the spell-slinging and the singing. The boys practiced well into the evening and late into the night taking only short breaks here or there for water or the bathroom, the three legends showing them the best ways to enhance their skills. As the moon rose high in the sky, the stars came out and began their nightly dance across the heavens. It was time for bed and they retreated into the fortune teller's tent. They were warned not to go outside without one of the legends to protect them from Loki and given a few pillows to help them sleep.

"This tent is enchanted so Loki can not enter. You'll be safe so long as you don't go outside. Now get some sleep." Ishtar tells them before heading with her friends into the other room.

It was hard for either of them to quickly fall asleep, they tossed and turned on the floor as they tried to drift off. Their bodies were exhausted, so it should be easy, but something was holding them back. Lute turned on his side to face Edgar, and after they were sure the legends were asleep or couldn't hear them, they began to whisper.

"This turned out to be a lucky break, doncha think?" Lute asks.

"I'm not so certain," Edgar admits, a thought stuck out in the back of his mind. "They mentioned something earlier that has me... worried. They said Loki is 'capturing' things in this circus."

"That explains why he wanted us to come in then." Lute tries to brush it off.

"Yeah, but why? Why go through all this trouble to capture magical creatures and items and mages and all that. What does he get out of it?"

"That's a good question. If he's anything like in the comics and movies though, it's because he's evil and is doing it for the laughs."

"How foolish." Edgar scolds. "Evil people don't do evil things for no reason. There's always a reason to do something like this."

"Maybe he wants to take over the world? Or maybe he's trying to make himself stronger somehow like he has the power that the Wendigo has to steal magic from others?"

"Maybe..." Edgar's mind races, the fact that Loki's doing all this isn't the only thing weighing on his mind. The mirrors from earlier were also still messing with his head. He closes his eyes and concentrates. This entire circus is flooded with dark magic. Loki's handiwork all over the place. He can't tell any source in here apart from any other source, it's all too evenly spaced or enhanced as if it were one large blanket of pure dark energy over the entire circus. The only things he can feel that aren't dark in here are Freya and Ishtar. And in this darkness, he feels the same he felt back home. He feels alone.

Intermission:

Darkness. Hatred, pain, and misery. In the far north of Eagleland, even further north than Big Apple and Witch City where the infamous trials of old were held, there's an abandoned town. Once, it was on the maps, a quiet mining town deep enough inland that the only sea one was likely to encounter there was the endless forest of birch trees. Yet even back then few were brave enough to approach the town, let alone do business there.

These were dark days indeed across the world, where the ideas of magic were seen as evil, and many different species were hunted down by governments and monarchs that feared their power or hated their hides. As such, many found their only recourse and escape was to run and hide in such tiny corners of the world.

Because of this, while the town may or may not have been rich in iron and less precious gems, it did not prosper, and the poor villagers either starved or moved away in an attempt to find greener pastures.

In these days it was expected to give a reason as to why certain places should be avoided, and many would cite the practice of dark magic by the residents or the curious dimmer light the sun seems to radiate here. As time went on, and more people left, the buildings fell into disrepair, enlarged and swollen tombs for the few that remained.

Fifty families founded this town, and one by one they all died off either within or without of it. Only one family remains there to this day, and they are the only ones to acknowledge it by the name it once held. Perhaps if one were to get lost in the north, they might fly over it or drive their car near enough to see the abandoned husk of Dunwich.

Ashes, dust, dirt, and black feathers are scattered about the town and the empty buildings, the contents of which have long since been hijacked and carted off to the only living residence. These ancient and decrepit homes have braved heavy endless snowfall every winter, and countless powerful storms every summer, and perhaps soon the few that still stand will collapse in on themselves, leaving no token behind of the village that once stood here.

The few that still know of it claim it to be haunted, or otherwise malicious to those who enter, and most still avoid it without going into further details. The land is owned almost entirely by property developers on the other side of the country, yet even then they refuse to build there out of superstition and fear of what they may disturb.

Occasionally, fool-hearty teens and young adults from the neighboring cities and towns will hear about this "ghost town", and bravely venture into it for urban exploration. Those that are lucky enough to return from such outings will often give up this habit, becoming terrified of the woods themselves. These are, of course, the more fortunate, as many who wander into the town, or even the outskirts of it are never seen again.

Perhaps it is fitting then that the place is surrounded by so many birch trees, the markings on their bark resembling crudely carved eyeballs that seem to always watch and always follow those who enter their home. A constant reminder that this place does not care for outsiders and will at any moment find ways to rid itself of them.

When someone goes missing in these woods, the police are called, and a large force is brought in. No civilians ever volunteer, rather it is simply a large number of officers to make sure none of them go missing as well. Such an event was the headline story of the Big Apple Times newspaper about twenty years back, with mentions of the story being heard as far away as Spectacle City.

"Aspiring Actress Lost in Woods!" The title read. The story of how a rising star, one Maria Shelly Hrafn disappeared into the woods alongside three film students who went to shoot a horror movie there. She was a beautiful blackbird who had the voice of an angel, and the body to match. Having climbed up high in stage performance this movie was going to be her big break into the film industry.

Alas, it was not meant to be, for, after two weeks with no one hearing a single word from the crew, the police were called, informed by her manager about the trip to Dunwich, and an investigation proceeded. There are many places akin to Dunwich across the world. Tiny towns that never really caught up with the times or old buildings inhabited only by squatters and cockroaches everyone agrees not to go to.

Such locations seldom see police intervention except in outstanding cases such as these that manage to capture the public interest at large. As such, the officers swallowed their fear, and formed one of the largest recorded search parties in recent history and began to comb the woods. It was only after another two days of no results, that a small group of five ventured into Dunwich itself.

It was January when the investigation took place, the constant grey skies and thick blankets of snow, making the atmosphere all the more dreary on the approach.

There are no real roads in Dunwich, rather while there had been at one time, it was never paved, and any cobblestone markers have long since eroded, the old dirt paths now covered in dead grass and snow. The officers entered the town, on edge, but finding solace in their numbers, for any cop entering this place knew that it had only one resident.

They approached his home, a building that even at the time of its construction had been larger than the rest of the houses of Dunwich. Two stories tall, making it the only multistoried building in the town, the house appeared to fare better than the others, though that was not saying much. Half of the windows were broken, while the other half had bars placed over them, and the roof appeared to be missing most if not all of its shingles. Dunwich had never received electricity or a sewage system, and as such, it was dark inside the home's upper floor, and if it weren't for the puffing smoke and faint glow from one of the windows, they might have assumed it abandoned as well.

Hesitant, the officers scarcely made a single knock on the door before it was flung open wide by the tenant. A gaunt and ugly crow, his body was unnaturally thin and tall, a bulbous head was perched atop, with eyes that were somehow still too big for his skull. He had taken after his father in terms of appearance, as his father before him had. In fact, if one were somehow old enough to have seen this family through the ages, they might assume the son to be a clone of the father for each and every generation.

This creature with its dirty feathers and alien appearance sneered at the police when they asked him if he had seen Maria, and if they may have permission to search the town for traces of her. He quietly croaked out in his ashen voice that they may, only noting to stay out of his family's mine.

To quote the police report, "The mine is old and unstable, I've lived here all my life and never been down there, if she's there, she's already dead." These words are all he bothered to say before standing aside to let the cops search his residence. They moved quickly, for, despite their numerical advantage and weapons, something about this old hermit made all attending officers feel uneasy.

Upon swift discovery that Maria was not to be found there, the quintet quickly left the terrible old crow to his shunned house and began to search the rest of the buildings as best they could.

They had begun early in the morning, and by about four o'clock in the afternoon, they had made their way through all Dunwich had to offer, the only remaining place being the mine. One of the officers suggested it would be a good idea to check as far as the structural stability would allow, and the others begrudgingly agreed. As they approached, a lurking fear grew within them, culminating to a boil when an officer put a single paw on the side of the cave, and it began to rumble.

Hastily agreeing that no good could come from deeper searching and that the hermit had been correct in saying she would not have gone in there (and lived), they quickly returned to their cars and left Dunwich altogether, to meet up with the rest of the search party.

Of course, as any resident of Big Apple who was alive at the start of the new millennium and bothered to keep up with the story will know, Maria was never found, and her case has gone cold to this day. None know what truly became of the once-popular star, and only her friends and family still mourn and sometimes search for her. The common consensus being she had died in those woods.

Of course, that was not entirely true.

The terrible crow smiled as he saw the cops drive off in a hurry.

He waited until he was sure they were gone.

And he went down into the mine.

No stone turned, no wall rumbled or tumbled, it was all solid as the day it was carved out nearly three centuries ago. A simple illusion was enough to keep those imbeciles out of his mine, keep them away from his temple.

His smile only widened as he approached the deepest central chamber. There, surrounded by the corpses of three teenagers and bound to a monolith of stone, Maria Shelly Hrafn stood.

Wings bound above her head, talons bound to the ground itself, she was unconscious as he approached. He laughs with each step closer he takes.

Finally,

It can begin.

Edgar wakes up on the tent floor the next morning. The last thing he heard from that dream was the sounds of Maria's screams.

Sound of Silence:

The next few days were much the same. They would wake up early and begin their training, showing mixed results, but results nonetheless. Edgar seemed to fare better than Lute most days, but Lute was determined. It didn't hurt that some nights he would be able to practice with Culania to gain an extra edge and keep up with Edgar.

However, no matter how hard they tried, Lute was still not strong enough to appear in Edgar's mage sense, which bothered them. If this ability was going to help them, then they would like to be able to know where each other was with it, in case they got separated. Plus it's also a sign of power. If Edgar can sense Lute like Lute can Edgar, then it would put them a bit more at ease when it comes to potentially having to fight.

That said, the training was paying off, Lute could now fully grow a stalk of corn in just three verses, while Edgar could now make vague shapes out of his dark energy. They're not exactly sharp, but they could make for a good cudgel or club, he's ultimately just happy that he can get it to last longer than the few moments the original cut spell could.

The food they ate while staying with the legends was nothing special from an outside perspective, and certainly not healthy. Deep-fried this, and sugar-dusted that, the classic staples of carnival and circus food, but neither of the boys cared. Lute enjoyed having cooked food again, especially food that reminded him of happier times when his mom was still alive, and Edgar...

Edgar could barely contain himself from consuming his meals in just one bite! Never before had the young raven eaten anything so delicious or so wonderful sounding. Sugar? Butter? Cinnamon? These were new concepts to him. It was here at the circus that he managed to also get his first taste of fish, shared with him by Ishtar and Freya. While a large portion of the population is vegetarian, Lute and Persephone included, Edgar and the two cats were not.

On this day, while on break for dinner, Persephone called Lute off to the side. "Hey, there's like, something we need to talk about," she soberly says. "Could you follow me please?"

"Huh?" Lute was caught off guard, for some reason, maybe it was the look on her face or how she spoke quietly, even her normal mannerisms that she had been using for the past few days seemed toned down. "S-sure, is everything alright Ms. Persephone?"

"Just... Come on, okay?" The bat says as she leads him out of the fortune-telling tent and across the circus street, back to the hall of mirrors. "You've been here before, it's a good place for us to talk." She says as she leads him in. Most of the mirrors are still broken, the only one that isn't is the final one. "I know you two broke all these, and honestly I'm impressed," she admits.

Lute nervously chuckles as he glances sideways at the mirror. "Heh, yeah, you can mostly thank Edgar for that. I'm... not quite sure what he did, to tell you the truth." He rubs the back of his head, something feels wrong as he looks over the shards of broken glass and sand and dust on the floor. It felt... bad, a way he couldn't describe, aside from bad. Like a mixture of anger and unsettling. Like he needs to get out, to get away, and Persephone isn't helping that feeling.

"I sort of figured," she admits as she walks over to the final mirror, "this mirror broke too. Do you know what these flowers are at the top?" While asking that, she reaches up and grabs one, just three days ago they were alive, healthy-looking, and bright, but now they were all withered and dried, looking like they had died months ago. At her touch, they seem to fully return to life. "It's called a Narcissus."

"It's pretty I guess." Lute responds, "I'm not exactly that into flowers I mean, I know some of them by name, but they're not my thing."

"Ah, well if you're going to practice earth magic, you may want to learn. Many flowers have magical properties, and I could go on all day listing herbs and flowers like Angelica or Mandrake or Sunflowers and all they can do. Narcissus can draw people's attention, keep their focus on one place. They're named after a young goat who fell in love with himself twenty-two hundred years ago. He died and became the first Narcissus flower."

"O-oh," Lute says nervously, as he glances between her, the mirror, and the flower. "So why were they in the mirror?"

"When they're placed like that and infused with magic, it turns the mirror into a trap to keep people focused on the mirror until they too pass away. With the flowers gone, the mirror is now back to normal. Magic and death often run together you see." Persephone explains.

"Magic and death?" he crosses his arms and tilts his head. "Why death? It's not like my magic causes death to happen, I just grow plants, isn't that the opposite of death?"

She smiles at him and pets his head, it's still a bit of a sad smile like she's trying to break bad news to a child. "That is true I suppose, and while life has its place in magic, death is still ever present. And as such, I need you to do me an important favor, please don't lie to me anymore."

Lute's eyes widened at that statement. "Wh-what do you mean? When did I lie?" his heart races, how could she know about...

"Child, I know what you did. I contacted my husband the other day. Hades, he's a lord of the underworld. He controls the plane where people go when they've been bad enough not to get into a heaven plane, but not bad enough to go to a hell plane. It's a level in purgatory." Persephone's smile fades as she talks about the afterlife, her home for the winter months. That's not to say she doesn't enjoy her home, in fact, she loves it there, she just hopes not to see Lute there someday.

"He had to place a few calls," she continued. "Poke around deeper into hell, and go through a lot of paperwork, but he found someone you know." Her eyes narrow, the glare she gives Lute sends a shiver up his spine. "I'll be frank. It's your father, Lute. And I know that you're the one who killed him."

Tears well up in Lute's eyes as he collapses to his knees. "I... I'm sorry. He was just, I was just..." his crying drowns out his ability to talk. Persephone is not cruel, however, and bends over to embrace Lute, wrapping him tight in her wings.

"I know sweetie, I know, we know everything about him. What he did to you, and trust me, you weren't his only victim," she says trying to comfort him. "But this is what I mean, death and magic go paw in paw." She gives him a moment, things like this, the idea of someone knowing about the bad things you've done, that there's a place after this, that you're being judged, they're heavy things even for adults to handle. Lute is a child. He needs a few minutes before he's even able to hear what she has to say next.

She continues when he eventually calms down. "Now Lute, I didn't come here to scold you... That said, don't do it again." Persephone quickly blurts out, her natural filter failing her. "I brought you here to teach you about magic and death."

Lute rubs his eyes and blows his nose into his sleeve. "W-what about it?"

"Magic... can't kill. Not directly anyway and not without good cause. Nobody has the power to cast a spell that can just kill someone. How do I put this?" she thinks for a moment before settling on an example.

"Alright, say someone was trying to hurt you or kill you, and there's no escape. Now there's a spell you can cast that will cause the wall behind you to shake, and a big rock will fall on them and they die. Magic can do that. But if you try the same spell in the middle of a city against someone you've never met before, it can't."

"Magic is guided. The source of magic in your body is a 'soul'." She makes quotes in the air at that word. "And the soul knows the difference between right and wrong. It won't let you use magic to harm innocent people."

"So what I did..."

"Was an act of self-defense. It was still bad, sure, but it's not like you just wanted someone random to suffer and die. Look," she sighs and tries to pet and comfort him. "I'm teaching you this because what Ishtar told me is going to come up soon. When you get to the mountain, you can't hold back, understand?"

"W-what?" Lute's eyes widened at what he was hearing. "What do you mean, 'don't hold back'?!"

"The Wendigo is a monster," she says flatly. "It's a terrible monster that won't hesitate to eat or kill you both, and none of us can help you with it. You need to cut loose, don't worry about killing it. That thing has been dead for years already."

"But I..." Lute tries to protest but is cut short.

"Don't have to die here. Don't have to die on this mountain with Edgar. But you CAN'T. HOLD. BACK." As she says this, the Narcissus in her wing shrivels and dies, turning to dust in seconds. "I want to help you. I do. But I can't go with you. I'll explain more when the time comes, just... promise me that you'll listen to what I've told you, okay?"

Lute hesitates and thinks. He looks down, and around the tent, back into the mirror to see his reflection, and then when it, unfortunately, doesn't bewitch him, he looks down at his paws. He can't bring himself to look in her eyes as he tries to breathe, but the air in the tent was heavy and he couldn't relax enough to focus.

"I..." he takes a deep breath, he knows deep down, he just can't do it, he won't ever kill anyone again, he won't let anyone die by his paw again. "Promise," he lies.

Persephone looks immediately relieved. "Good," she pats his head. "I'm sorry to have made you go through all this. And I'm sorry to make you cry," she smiles. "Let's go back to the others, alright?" As she stands she offers him her wing to hold, which he does. He may not agree with her about killing, but he admits to himself that he needs someone to hold onto right now.

They return to the tent they call their temporary home and finish off their meal, Lute is unusually quiet throughout the whole thing, something Edgar takes notice of.

"Shall we continue our training now?" Freya offers.

Edgar looks over at the silent Lute, and then a thought crosses his head. "Hang on. I want to know something. Ishtar," his eyes narrow as he looks over at her, something has been eating him for a while now and he wants an answer. "Can you really see the future?"

"Indeed I can," she grins like the cat that swallowed the canary. "Why do you ask?"

Edgar grins back. "You tell me, if you can see the future then you would know why. Do we need to train right now to survive?"

"No, I suppose you don't," she coyly responds, as if reading lines off a script she's memorized a thousand years in advance. "While it might help you become stronger, it is not necessary."

"And are we going to train then?"

"Yes. You have a desire to become strong enough to never go home. To get as far away as possible." Her words are sharp and cutting. Edgar noticeably winces at the truth being told back to him, but Lute finds them hard to accept. *So that's why he doesn't want to go back towards Big Apple.*

"Then I'm not training tonight!" Edgar shouts. "So what do you think about that?"

She shrugs and laughs, "As you wish. The future is always changing after all."

"So you can't see the future!" Edgar chirps triumphantly. "Nobody can, I knew it!" He's standing in his chair now, looking quite pleased with himself. "Future sight is impossible! Destiny is stupid."

"Perhaps," Ishtar laughs, "but if you're not training, I suppose you don't need the three of us. Come on girls, let's go get some air." And with those words, the three get up and leave, leaving the duo alone in the tent.

"Hmmph, coward," Edgar calls after them, though secretly happy that none of them heard his empty boasting.

He quickly turns his attention to Lute. "I don't care what they say, nobody can tell me what I'm gonna do. Fate, Destiny, it's all a bunch of crap!"

Lute looks over at him, tilting his head at the sudden anger about this. "What's eating you? What does destiny have to do with seeing the future?"

"What doesn't it have to do with seeing the future? The whole point of seeing the future is being able to control it. You get that right?"

"Yeah, I suppose. So what? Do you think they're trying to control us? They seem pretty honest about wanting to help us." Lute tries pointing out as the voice of reason.

"Them no. But... alright, let me ask you something. Destiny. What is it? You hear stories about like... ancient heroes that were chosen by some force to fulfill a great destiny and save the world. Some... prophecy set in stone that no matter what they tried, it HAD to come true."

"Ohh. Like that Arthur guy who pulled the sword out of the stone!" Lute catches on.

"Right, it was his 'Destiny' to do that and become a great king. Now, what is fate? It's the same thing, but darker. Someone is fated to die at the wings of their best friend, or they're fated to plunge the world into darkness, or fated to face off against some chosen hero. Fate is a bad destiny."

Lute had never thought about it before, but what Edgar was saying made sense. In the movies, people had destinies to save the world or stop the villain. In those same movies, someone would have the fate to battle or die at the paws of someone else. Heroes get a destiny, villains get a fate.

"And it all comes back to one thing, some kind of prophecy. The fate or destiny is written down somewhere by some old fart and enchanted to make sure it happens."

As Edgar keeps ranting, his feathers become more ruffled and movements become more animated. He flaps his wings up and down as he talks and points and gestures to convince Lute of what he's trying to say, it's actually quite the spectacle.

"Alright so, now the big question, what's the difference between a prophecy and a curse? There isn't one. Your destiny is prophesied, and your fate is cursed. And that's why it's so... dumb." He lets out a deep sigh as he finally calms down and slides back down into his chair. "It's all about perspective."

"Alright..." Lute says as he tries to figure out exactly why this is bothering Edgar. "And this connects to seeing the future... how?"

"As I said, if you try to see the future, you try to control it. It's the same people who say they can 'see the future' that makes all the prophecies and curses. They are the ones who say 'you're going to kill, or die, or save, or destroy'. But no! She can't see the future. No one can! Fate isn't real. It can't be!"

Those words do almost make Lute feel better. If Ishtar can't see the future, then that means Persephone is also wrong, he doesn't need to 'cut loose' he doesn't have to use his powers to kill the Wendigo for them to live. But something about the way Edgar's saying all this. The anger turned calm... perhaps it was even sorrowing near the end the way he seemed to sigh out less in relief, and more in defeat. Then he became more defensive as if trying to assure himself that fate isn't real.

The two just sit there for a moment, an awkward silence washing over the room. Neither of the two know what to say about all that's happened over this one meal. Should Lute say what happened with Persephone? Should he ask why Edgar seems so upset about fate and the future?

Or in turn, should it be Edgar that breaks the silence, asking his friend why he seems so troubled by the conversation with Persephone. Should he tell Lute about his home and why he left? What Ishtar had meant with her earlier statement.

Neither was sure what the right move was. What the right thing to say was. Perhaps there was no right thing to say, and perhaps they both knew it so they sat there in silence as they finished their meal.

*Edgar... what should I do. I can't... I won't kill anything. I won't let anything die. I won't let **him** die.* Lute resolves. *If he won't train to protect himself, then I will!*

He excuses himself from the table. "I'm sorry Edgar, I need... I need to blow off some steam."

"...Okay." Edgar sighs as he begins grinding his quartz again. "You want me to come with you?"

"N-no." he quickly responds, "I think I'm gonna go talk with Ishtar for a bit. Don't wait up for me." He says before quickly leaving the tent. Outside he quickly runs into the legends who were simply waiting for him at the tent across the street.

"Ah. Right on time." Ishtar laughs. "I wondered if you were coming or not."

"Shouldn't you know?" Lute questions. "I'm beginning to think Edgar's right that your future vision's on the fritz."

"I do know what the future holds, and knew you were coming. It's just as I said, the future is always changing." Her tail flicks behind her like a metronome, Persephone and Freya lost in their conversation between themselves, having heard this story already. "Do you know how seeing the future works?"

"I don't... and honestly I don't think I'd want to see the future." Lute winces.

"Haha, do not worry child, I will not give you the power of premonition. You do not need it. No, instead I want to tell you how I see the future. Time is like a tree. Persephone," she turns her attention, "could you raise a treetop for us?"

With a flick of her wings, Persephone does just that, a large trunk sprouts from the ground next to Lute, before splitting off at the end into numerous branches that only grow smaller as they spread out. No leaves form on the tree, giving them a good view of the branches.

"Now this tree, you would say as a whole is pointed one way right?" Ishtar points as Lute nods his response back to her. "Now these branches split off because something happens to the tree as it grows. More and more branches appear and split off as more events happen. The same is true for time."

"I don't follow," Lute admits. "What you're saying sounds like time has many ends."

"That's exactly what I'm saying," Ishtar responds. "Time doesn't 'end'. But it splits like this tree. If you were to say... not brush your teeth in the morning, then that's a change that splits time. But it's so small it doesn't affect the rest of the tree and that branch goes right back into the trunk. But if you were to die, that would be a big change and that branch would stay split off. Do you follow me so far?"

"A bit more... what does this have to do with seeing the future?"

"Because there is no 'ONE' future," she explains. "There are thousands if not millions, and more are created with each 'change'. When someone looks into the future they have to see ALL of these millions of possibilities."

"So it's not accurate. It's like... playing one loud note on an instrument, but not actually using it properly." he starts to rationalize, maybe this would be good news to tell Edgar, a way to make him feel better.

"Ah, but there's the rub. See, that's how most people see into the future. I'm different you see, I'm a legend, I'm much stronger than most when it comes to seeing the future. When I look, I see the end that will come. The only changes I see are unimportant ones."

Lute looks hurt by what she's saying as if he had just caught her in a lie. "So what? The future is set in stone? But what about all the branches? You give this big speech about branches and how anything can happen, but now you're saying it's all... planned out!"

"No. That's not it at all. It's very rude to yell at your elders." Ishtar scolds him. "There are... fixed points in time. Events that just HAVE to happen. Inevitabilities we call them. When and how they happen, that's what we can change."

"This doesn't make any sense! How can anything be possible, and yet some certain points be fixed?"

"You've seen a time travel movie before right? Someone goes back in time to do something, and shenanigans ensue?"

"Like... Back from the Past?"

"Exactly! Now for that movie to work Morty's parents had to get together, or Morty would never have existed, and wouldn't have been able to cause the plot to happen. The parents getting together was 'fixed'. But how they got together changed in the movie. Originally everything was fine, but because Morty went back in time, the events changed. With small changes, ANYTHING is possible."

Lute looks up at the tree, he rubs his temples and clears his head as he tries to better understand all that she's saying. "So... what happens if we do something that outright prevents those fixed points from happening?"

She shrugs, "You can not. The actors will change, the stage will change, but the show will go on."

"But what if it's something really bad?! What if it's..." he glances back at the tent. "What if it's something you can't let happen?"

Ishtar grins and gestures to Persephone to shrink the tree back down to an acorn. "That's not something you can do. You're just a child after all. Preventing such a terrible thing from happening..." she walks past him heading back to the girls, her tail brushes across his cheek as she goes. "That's something that heroes do."

"Heroes? What do you mean by that?" he demands the truth from Ishtar.

"Not all legends are born. Some are made, heh, I remember this one child a couple of thousand years ago, Asushunamir. You remind me of them. I was trapped in a plane of hell, and they managed to save me from it. In doing so, they averted the end of the world that was foretold. They became a hero and a legend in their own right." She reminisces as she takes her seat next to the others. "Ah, they were so cute too! I hope they got back together with Ereshkigal, they deserve to be happy."

"Nope!" Persephone laughs, "and honestly that's probably for the best. Asushunamir is too good for her!"

A look of confusion crosses Lute's face as they continue talking. Not the same confusion one would have at learning something new as he had all afternoon, but rather the look one gets when listening to people talk about someone they don't know.

"So legends can change these 'fixed' points? But wait, you're legends! Can I-" before he can ask he's interrupted.

"We can not fix every problem, even as great as we are." Freya cuts him short, now all three had their attention on the child. "It takes a lot of work to change one of those points, and often magic is not enough to change it."

"Besides," Ishtar adds, "if you follow your current path, then everything will be fine in the end... maybe." She laughs. "Fine for us anyway. After all, if you screw up, it's only you that'll end up hurt."

"I..." he takes a deep breath and gathers himself, "see. I think. But what can I do then? I'm not... I'm not strong like y'all are. I'm just..."

"And that's why we must train," Freya says. "We will keep training until the end of the week, and if you're strong enough then, then you shall survive." Her attention is pulled over to the fortune teller's tent. "As well as clean up the mess you've made."

Lute turned to face the tent, something immediately felt wrong, though he couldn't see anything. It was as if looking at it made the world fall out from under him like something was missing. He rushes over, the legends following close behind, and bursts through the flap. "Edgar?" he calls out to no response.

"Edgar!" he cries again to no avail. "Where are you?"

The Ultimate Show:

It didn't take a genius to know what happened. Edgar wouldn't just up and run away, even if he could, no, with everyone's attention drawn away, Loki had lured him out the back of the tent and took him away. So now Lute is more energized than ever to train even harder to save his friend. And while he trains with the girls, let us take a moment to see Loki's plan in action.

His plan is quite cunning after all, traveling across the world to entrap monsters and budding legends that catch his eye, they'll make a wonderful army of chaos for the ensuing Ragnarok that will come to the world. And what better place to start than Eagleland? It would seem for whatever reason that many new legends are born there every year.

Dark magical constructs clash against the invisible shield of the cage Loki has tossed Edgar into. "Let me out!" Edgar demands as his crude club fizzles out of existence. "You can't keep me here!" he shouts at the arctic fox.

"Let you out? Now, why should I do that?" Loki coyly responds as he crouches down to look Edgar in the face. "You seem to have quite a bit of dormant power in your tiny body. You'll make a fine soldier."

"Like Hell, I will!" Edgar says as he punches the shield again. "Do you have any idea who I am! What I've been through? HOW MANY CAGES I'VE ESCAPED

FROM?!" He punches again. "I'll get out of here, and when I do, I'm going to shove your tail down your throat!"

Growls and moans and the shrill sounds of what can only be described as tv static and goat bleats cry out in all directions around Edgar as he says this, seem's he's not the only thing caged.

"Cocky! I like it." Loki laughs. "Now be a good little pet, and keep quiet in your cage while I work to capture your little friend. It gets so bothersome when the others get worked up."

"Screw you! I'm not letting you anywhere near Lute!"

"Oh you don't have to, and I don't even have to go out to grab him. No, thanks to you, he'll come to me. Really, I should thank you. If you hadn't thrown that little fit of yours, I would have had to wait even longer to capture you. Such a good little bird, managing to find a way to push away all the people who get close to you."

"...What people?" Edgar quietly asks. "Lute's the only one... those women. They just want to use me, like my family."

"And what makes you think he's not just using you?" Loki asks outright, "I mean, and do forgive me if I'm wrong, but if he cared about you, why isn't he here? Surely he would be here right now to free you if that were the case."

Edgar however is having none of it. "Because he's much weaker than you, idiot. Of course, he's not going to come for me now. I'm probably stronger and I couldn't beat you. But when he does come, he'll bring those women with him. And the four of them will kick your butt so hard that what I'll do will seem like mercy!"

Loki's lips betray the trickster, quickly forming a frown for a fraction of a second as he realizes his deception did not affect the child. So he tries another. "Regardless, why would you want to leave? Consider this, if you come with me, you don't have to go up the mountain, you can leave Eagleland, and you'll be in the best place possible once Ragnarok starts."

"Pass." Edgar brushes him off and starts channeling magic into his wings again. "Don't know what that is, and honestly after this cage, I'm more wanting to kick your butt."

"You don't know about Ragnarok? The end of the world? Surely, you've seen Fimbulwinter's effect taking place for the past two years already." Loki asks bemusedly.

"You sure like to make up words, don't you?" Edgar quips trying to get under Loki's fur.

"You mean you haven't noticed how it's been an unnaturally cold and endless winter for the past two and a half years? It's practically frozen the Snowlands! By Odin's beard, do they teach children nothing now?"

Edgar lets out a shot of dark magic against the shield to no positive effect. Other than making him feel tired and causing a ringing note to echo through the cage, it was worthless. "Never heard of 'the Snowlands', and pretty sure something with 'Snow' in the name is already frozen." Edgar huffs out. "Besides, looking outside, it looks more like fall to me."

Loki was usually the one in control of these kinds of situations, the level headed trickster that knew all the right things to say, and yet this *child* was seeing through Loki's words or didn't even understand what he was saying. It was absolutely infuriating.

Edgar sits in the cage to catch his breath. "So," he breathes deeply, "how do you plan to capture him anyway?"

Anger quickly gives way to Loki's greatest flaw, a chance to stroke his ego by boasting about his grand plan. "Ah, well since you asked, I'll tell you. Those three won't be able to stop me from capturing him so long as I follow the old laws of honorable combat. So I shall challenge him to a duel of my people. If he wins, that shield drops and you go free, if I win, he willingly comes with me."

"Great, so you're going to challenge him to something he's never done before and beat the crap out of him." Edgar rolls his eyes. "Talk about fair."

"I said I would challenge him in a duel of my people. I didn't say it was a fight."

"A rap battle?" Lute tilts his head. "What do you mean a rap battle?"

"It's true." Freya smiles as she recalls the days of old. "Thousands of years ago, the citizens of the Snowlands would break out into song and posture similar to modern rap music called 'flyting'. It was mostly done by bards and the more magically inclined to settle petty disputes or for bragging rights."

"So you're telling me, you want me to go up to one of the greatest comic book villains of all time-"

"He's not really a villain or from the comics, he's just very mischievous," Persephone points out as she scatters some seeds for Lute.

"And just... rap my way to victory." he finishes.

Ishtar bursts out into laughter. "Yeah, that's about right. If you think that's bad, I need to tell you about how the people in the Land of Marble made yoyos, computers, and soccer thousands of years ago only to forget about it when their country collapsed."

"Now I know you're pulling my leg." Lute sighs.

"I assure you it's legit." Persephone laughs, "trust me I was THERE!"

"Perhaps we should try that ourselves." Freya offers. "A mock battle between you and me." She walks up to Lute, yet stays a good foot or two away, and faces him. "These battles combine our magic energies allowing for much more powerful than traditional battles. Now you'll need to focus, your words and melody will cause things to happen around you. Dodge my attacks, or deflect them. Focus on me, and focus on insulting me. Oh, and I almost forgot. This will hurt. And usually, the penalty for failure is death."

Lute had to gulp down his fear as he heard that, why did it have to lead to death? "Watch my rhythm and flow, these battles are all about posturing and insulting the opponent. Don't let me get under your fur."

The world seemed to fall quiet as the sounds of the circus faded away. Some returned in a rhythmic melody of piping and beeps from nearby rides in a strange musicality. The air became electric as Freya began her assault.

"Alright little boy, are you ready to fight? Cuz something tells me, you're not very bright!"

The words themselves were nothing special, barely an insult one might see on the playground back at Lute's school. The thing is the words were just part of the fight, a distraction to make the opponent slip up or fall. No, the real danger in these fights arrived right after she finished.

See, as she said this, arrows made of pure light formed in the air above her, they shimmer and glow with the intensity of a fluorescent light bulb, and at the end of the second sentence launch themselves right at Lute. He manages to dodge just in time, the arrows making contact with the ground instead.

"C'mon now kid, you need to fight back. Don't be stupid, launch a counter-attack!" Freya commands as she launches another volley of arrows at Lute. He manages to dodge again but realizes they're getting closer. He needs to say something to insult her.

"You... uh... you think you're really gold? Well, lady, all you are is really old!" He blurts out. Despite his half baked sentence and absolutely terrible pose, flinching like he's going to be punched, his magic carries his slack. Vines erupt from the ground and launch themselves at the lynx, who gets caught in them.

"Old? Well, aren't you a little punk! Class is in session, you're about to flunk!" As she says this an ax appears out of the air and slices through the vines, she grabs it and keeps up her rhymes. "So you want to be a hero? Hate to break it kid but you're just a zero!" She shouts and as she throws the ax it seems to grow as it spins through the air.

Lute manages to duck out of the way, but the ax does cut into his cap. "Dang it! That was my favorite hat! What's wrong with you, you crazy bobcat?!" This time instead of vines it's full-on shrubs that sprout behind her causing Freya to trip up. Anyone else would have fallen, but Freya being a fully skilled warrior quickly flips back up, jumping into the sky. "And of course I know I'm nobody. But hey, at least I'm not some gross harpy!" Lute shouts at her, causing an emaciated tree to erupt under her.

She manages to land on it, dodging the sharpened branches, and then hops over to the carousel. "Not bad kid you've got some game, maybe one day I'll bother to learn your name." These words were ACTUALLY cutting on Lute since he thought that Freya did know his name. The magic seemed to reflect this by launching swords at him instead of arrows. A lot of swords. Like. Too many to dodge swords.

Thinking on his paws, Lute decides to try countering with his magic, but under the pressure, he shouts, "So I may not know about all this mumbo-jumbo, but what do you know you old bimbo!" This caused even more vines to shoot out and the swords got impaled on them as the vines kept rushing Freya, they covered the entire carousel and smashed it, absolutely destroying it in the process.

"Oh no!" He quickly runs over, the light weapons fading out of existence as he goes over to the carousel to check on her. "Please don't be dead..." he keeps repeating as he gets close. "Stupid vines! Get off!" He says as he tugs and pulls at them. However, a blade starts cutting through them, revealing a perfectly fine Freya.

"Heh, good job kid, I think it's safe to say you're ready for Loki." She smiles as the blade fizzles out.

"I'm just glad you're okay." Lute breathes a sigh of relief.

"Oh, it'll take a lot more than that to hurt me." Freya boasts, "Just one quick thing." She smiles as she picks Lute up by the ears and leans in close. "Call me an old bimbo again and I will decapitate you, got that punk?"

"Yes ma'am! Yes ma'am!" Lute pleads and scrambles and tries to break free of her grasp.

Freya drops him. "Good! Oh and word of warning, Loki is a lot better at flyting than fighting. I'm not the best at flyting but can handle myself fine. Also, work on your rhymes. The better they fit, and the more scathing, the better the effects. Hence why your bimbo comment gives you the wall of vines, whereas the harpy one only had that dead tree. It wasn't a good rhyme."

"I think it's safe to say, that's enough for now." Persephone sighs as she begins to clean up the battlefield. "For a first attempt that was surprisingly good though. Many people can barely make waves when they first take flyte."

"Oh come on, that pun was so bad even I'm cringing." Lute laughs, though it's mostly out of the discomfort that just happened. From thinking he accidentally hurt or killed Freya, to being threatened to just the sheer amount of energy that fight took, it was as if there was nothing else he could do but laugh.

"So..." he hesitates to ask the big question burning in his mind.

"No." Ishtar interrupts him.

"W-what?" her words catch him off guard.

"You won't have to kill Loki. In fact, you CAN'T kill Loki. He'll run away before you can."

"O-oh." he smiles upon hearing this. "Thank you, Ms. Ishtar."

She snatches off his hat in one paw before rubbing his head. "Don't thank me yet kid, thank me AFTER you beat Loki tomorrow."

"Wait, tomorrow?!" His eyes widened. "Don't I have more time to train?"

"Nope, after tomorrow, you two need to head up the mountain in the west." She says this as she continues to look over the hat. "Hey, Frigg. Catch!" She tosses it over to Freya.

"I told you to stop calling me that. Literally no one calls me that anymore. Not even my husband." she says as she catches it.

"Yes, and I stopped being Ishtar a long while ago, just fix the hat you cut."

"Heh, fine." She laughs, and with a wave of her paw, the threads in the hat restitch and weave themselves back together making the ballcap just as good as the day Lute got it. "Do yourself a favor, kid. Make sure someone writes down your story so people don't start changing your name in their records."

She offers the hat back to Lute, who accepts it and puts it on. "So wait, if you're not Ishtar, then who are you?"

"I am Ishtar, it's just people slurred my name to the point of it being unrecognizable in modern language." the oldest legend shrugs. "Just call me Ishtar, maybe one day I'll let you know what they call me now."

Persephone lands, now done with the cleanup. "Bad news, I'm pretty sure the carousel is busted for good." She comments as the thing is smoking behind them, the dragon statues cracked to pieces and the whole thing... bent.

"Well... there goes the deposit." Freya sighs. "They're still twelve grand, right?"

"Add another zero and double it, honey." Persephone comments.

"Uhhhhhhhg. You mortals made your own unstoppable force. Inflation."

"I have no idea what that is."

"That's fine, we don't either." Ishtar laughs. "Now come on, you need to rest for tomorrow."

"Right, right," Lute says, and with that, they retreat into their tent. He had a large meal with the legends and went to bed to face his nightmare for the night. He was not the only one with a nightmare, however.

Edgar had a decent meal in his cage, Loki trying to butter him up, and honestly knowing the pain of starvation gave him plenty to eat. But since then Loki has basically left him alone, not even interacting with the young raven.

Edgar got too tired after a while to continue his assault on the cage and decided it was best to stop.

Especially when he heard the sounds coming from the cages around him.

An angry growling sound, like a mix between a crane's honk and the screams of a dying cow coming from above. There was this feeling of being watched and the sound of static whenever he faced left and quickly learned to turn his back to it. Curiously, this one didn't make a sound when not faced. The way he faced now however had earlier been banging and thrashing like he had, only with the mixed roars of a gorilla and bear screaming at the top of their lungs from inside.

Living nightmares all around him, no thoughts of safety, and only his standard night terrors waiting on him when he does fall asleep? *Ah, just like home.* He half-smiles and half-frowns at the thought before curling his talons into his chest and drifting off to sleep.

The morning comes, and the time for battle swiftly approaches. The legends ready Lute with another large meal and escort him to the big top. Immediately stepping inside the first thing to notice is that it's incredibly dark in there. More than should be physically possible as just outside the skies are clear and the sun has fully risen.

Inside, however, it was black as pitch, and not even the light shining in through the open tent flap managed to make it more than a few feet past the entrance. This made Lute a bit more nervous since he knew two important things. One is that Loki uses dark magic, meaning this is probably either him showing off or a clear trap. The other thing he knew is that his magic made plants grow, and plants generally need a lot of light to grow healthy.

Despite his fears, he decided to make Loki go on the defensive immediately and called out, "Show yourself Loki! I want Edgar back!"

Silence fills the tent for a moment before Loki's voice breaks it, "Oh, I'll show myself little rabbit. You'll see your friend again too, but first..." a clunk sound rings out as a spotlight shines down from a ceiling that can't be seen. A set of brightly colored bleachers is shown in its light. "Those three need to sit down for the show to start."

"Geeze, what's his game anyway?" Persephone asks.

"Trust me when I tell you he doesn't have one." Freya sighs. "One time he bet a dwarf his head if the dwarf could make something everyone back home would be amazed by."

"What did the dwarf make?" Ishtar asks.

"Mjolnir," Freya comments as she makes her way to her seat, the other legends following close behind. As they take their seats, another loud clunk and a second spotlight shines down revealing Loki.

"And yet I still have my head!" he laughs and grins, now dressed in a ridiculous circus leader uniform, with a bright red coat and black top hat, he even went to the trouble of getting a cane. He has his arms wide above his head and a wide stance as if he were challenging them to come after him.

"What a shame," Lute responds. "Even with it, you're still crazy. Now, where's Edgar?"

"You think me mad? I'll show you who's crazy!" Loki growls as he points the cane at Lute.

"Relax Loki, it's nothing to lose your head over." he giggles to himself. "And again I ask, where's Edgar?"

Frustration crosses Loki's face as he snaps his fingers, a third spotlight shining down behind him revealing a stack of cages. In the bottom center is Edgar, his wings and beak bound by strips of fabric as he shakes and tries to free himself of the binds. The rest of the cages are somehow still too dark to see into.

"Edgar!" Lute calls out before returning his attention to Loki. "Let him go!"

"Oh, I'll let him go." Loki grins. "I'll let them all go, him, you, the rest of my collection. If you can defeat me in a battle that is. Oh! But if I win, then you have to join my menagerie."

"C-collection?" Lute asks.

If there was a maximum amount of teeth one can put into an evil smile, Loki had found a way to double it. This look of absolute smarm was only highlighted when he snapped his fingers again revealing the other creatures he had captured.

On top, Lute at first thought it to be another bat like Persephone, but upon closer inspection, it was clear that it had wings like a butterfly's and large red eyes like those of a blowfly. It stares back at Lute, tilting its head as if it knows Lute's intentions and that freedom may soon come.

Then on the left of Edgar's cage was what looked like a bear (it even kinda reminded Lute of Randy back home in general appearance), though it was clearly more muscular and had a strange fur pattern that gave it the general appearance of a skunk in nature. It keeps attacking the front of its cage to try and bust out.

Finally on the right was a tall faceless pale creature. No ears nor muzzle nor tail, dressed in a suit, it stood near perfectly still in the center of its cage. One might mistake the creature for a mannequin if it weren't for the headache one gets by looking at it.

"These creatures," Loki says, "are some of the most powerful and dangerous creatures in all of Eagleland. I'm gathering them all and will take them with me as my unstoppable army. And soon you'll join them as my obedient servant!"

Lute is taken aback by the disturbing looks of these creatures Loki has captured, but even seeing these is not enough to deter him as with another glance at the very angry and scared Edgar, Lute knows he needs to stop this.

"Fine," Lute says. "But there has to be a way for me to reasonably win this match!"

"Of course!" Loki laughs before vanishing and reappearing right next to Lute, dropping a paw on his head. "See, this is all a game! Life is a show and we are the actors. It'd be quite easy, and quite boring for me to just snuff you out with all the dark power coursing through my old bones."

He pulls Lute's head down, covering his eyes. "So instead, how about a game of wits? Are you familiar with the ancient art of flyting?"

Lute pulls at the hat, trying to get it off his eyes. "I'm... familiar... with... the concept!" he says this as his hat comes off with a satisfying pop sound. The cages once again are swallowed by the darkness as Loki leans on his cane.

"Excellent! Then you should have no trouble fighting me." he smugly suggests. "In fact, I'll be a good sport, and let you go first. C'mon kid, the first shot's free, make it count!"

Lute isn't normally an angry person. Sure, he would be upset whenever Randy bullied him, and he did occasionally give in to his anger, but for the most part, he kept it under control. But here? The combination of the threats, the outfit, the Cheshire smug grin, and Edgar being locked up... it was enough to push him over the edge.

The silence of the tent is filled with another subtle beat like in the previous flyting contest, and Lute quickly manages to find the rhythm to it, swaying his body back and forth with it like a metronome. As the air fills with electricity, he envisions what he wants the magic to do and charges at Loki, fist raised.

"So you think you're cool, you think you're bad? Overall Loki, you're just sad. In this circus, you look like a clown. Now watch as I take you down!" He gives an uppercut, way too far away to make contact, but his fist was never meant to. Instead, as he swings, a line of mushrooms erupt from the ground, sprouting a wide variety of colored caps that glow and give off light.

These things are huge, ranging in size from a large pumpkin to that of a small table, the final one coming up directly under Loki as it launches him into the air. He seems overall unfazed by this as he sprouts wings from his back and begins darting around the dark ceiling. "Did I not mention, I can change my form? Now little bunny, prepare for the storm. I can tell from even one glance. In this battle, you stand no chance!"

As Loki counters with this, needles start to pour down from above. Purple in color and very sharp, Lute quickly ducks under the largest mushroom to get out of the evil rain. Lute's not an idiot, he knows he can't win with words alone, his attacks have to connect which they won't do while he's up there in the dark. He'll need to bait him down.

"What's the matter Loki, running scared? You're a lot of talking, not that I cared. Though I have to admit, this moment's soured. I never knew a legend could be such a coward!" That one got Loki's attention as more mushrooms sprouted around the edge of the tent arena lighting it up even more. They all seem to shoot off spores in time with Lute's words as if condemning Loki for being afraid of a kid.

Persephone and Freya get in on the action and cheer for Lute while Ishtar just chuckles at Loki. While not physically damaging, it is enough to hurt Loki's pride and make him land.

"You think I can't handle you, child?" Loki asks as his body begins to elongate and stretch and sprout out more legs, "This is my house, and here the joker runs wild! You're the one who's scared, your whole style is a joke, I'm gonna take you out with just one poke!" He shouts this as his lower body takes the form of a very large spider that skitters towards Lute. In Loki's paws is a very dangerous looking spear of magical energy he lobs right at him.

It nicks him in the shoulder and draws a bit of blood, but thankfully Lute manages to dodge the brunt of it in time as that same spear carved the mushroom he was hiding under clean in half and it topples over.

Lute clutches his shoulder and tries to focus. He needs just one, maybe two more verses for his plan to work. "Alright, alright, I hear you clear, I see what you're doing with that spear. Don't bother coming near, I can smell you from here. What? That's right I said it, you stink like bad cheese, when I'm through with you you'll be on your knees!"

This time a ring of mushrooms sprout up from around Loki's spindly legs and knock him off balance as they grow to the size of evergreen trees and poke against the roof of the tent. As they do, their spores scatter and fill the room with enough light that everything is visible again, from the cages to the entrance and the support beams in between.

Perfect!

Loki now seems more annoyed than ever, just at the mere thought that some snot-nosed kid can keep up with him, and less about Lute's bad insults. He manages to use his spider legs to slice his way through a couple of the mushrooms that topple over and crush the empty parts of the bleachers, and sprints at Lute again.

"Alright kid, I've had enough. You think you're smart, you think you're tough? Let's see how you handle it when I get rough. No more playin', no more disobeyin', pretty soon you'll be prayin', for me to stop this game, but I won't stop until your head I claim!"

As Loki shouts this he keeps circling Lute, shooting webbing out of his spider half, binding Lute in place and forming a cocoon so thick that the only things sticking out are one arm and his head. Loki moves in close. "Give it up kid, this is the end. Say to my will, now you'll bend."

Lute looks down, defeat written all over his face. This causes Loki to get perhaps a little too close so he can grin and gloat at the helpless bunny. His grin was cut down when Lute's frown turned into a smile.

"You know, I'm still amazed by all this magic, in the end, it's just tragic. I learned so fast it came so quick, now my words are gonna hit you like a brick. There's still so much out there for me to know, lots of room for me to grow. For now your face I gotta get bustin', and sure my rhymes are still adjustin', but here's the fact your flow's started rustin', combustin', and now you don't know where to go. Take it slow, feel the flow. You're gonna wind up on the floor, cuz old man, you're such a bore."

For someone with the monumental ego that Loki has, being called boring would be a slap in the face. Unfortunately for Loki, this time it was much more like a punch in the face by a corn cob that explodes out of the cocoon Lute's wrapped up in, the stalk springing out from Lute's pocket. It moved and bent in unison with Lute's arm as he curled up his fist and gave his hardest punch in the air, causing it to collide square on with Loki's face and knock him back.

He stumbles before collapsing the knockout punch living up to its namesake.

Defeated and unconscious, Loki's magic quickly fades from the surroundings, the darkness in the tent receding to the point where the mushroom's glow is no longer needed to see. The cages shields quickly dissipated like smoke, the first to break through was the strange bear that quickly snarled before running out, destruction of the whole circus could be heard as it rampaged away.

The gigantic moth was next, flying up, turning its face one last time to look at Lute as if to say thanks. It glanced around and stared at Edgar as he made his way out of the cage, and the moth hissed angrily before flying off. The faceless creature seemed to have vanished entirely, a blink of the eye and it was gone.

The women clap before hopping down from the bleachers. Freya quickly runs over to Loki to make sure he won't try anything when he gets up while Ishtar sets to work on freeing Lute from the cocoon and Persephone makes sure Edgar's in good health.

"Nice work kid," Ishtar comments as she slices the pod open. "I honestly didn't know if you had it in you."

"I thought you said I had to win?" Lute asks, shocked as he climbs out of the silk.

"I said that you needed to win." She corrected him. "If you lost things would have been..." she winces. "Bad. To say the least. Besides, what's a little double talk if it means giving you the confidence to win?"

So you lied? He wanted to ask her that question. The words burning in the back of his mind. Perhaps her whole speech earlier was just part of the lie to give him confidence, or perhaps there was something he didn't need to know or understand just yet. Regardless, Lute pushed the questions away as there was something more important to tend to.

He dashed over to Edgar and practically tackled him with a hug. "Edgar! Edgar, I'm so sorry! I shouldn't have left you alone in the tent."

Edgar keeps his wings wide, not returning the hug, it feels strange and alien and he doesn't truly know how to react to it. "It's okay?" He says this, unsure how to truly respond, "It's not like you're the one who stole me. It was Loki. I'm fine, I'm just...happy you're okay?" he smiles a little and breaks the hug. "Just uh... one moment."

Edgar walks over to Loki, who at this point has unconsciously shapeshifted back to his arctic fox form and is laid out on his back. Without missing a beat, Edgar stomps down hard on his crotch. "YOU WORTHLESS PIECE OF TRASH I HOPE YOU BURN IN A LAKE OF FIRE FOR ALL ETERNITY! IF I EVER SEE YOU AGAIN I'M GOING TO CUT OFF YOUR LEGS!" He finishes his rant by spitting on Loki's face. "Never put me in a cage."

Everyone just stared at Edgar as he did this until he turned to face them. "What?" Edgar asks. Freya burst out laughing at what just happened, her laughter was contagious and quickly picked up by Ishtar, Persephone, and even Lute. "What?" Edgar asks again, even more, confused as laughter fills the tent.

Waiting:

Top of her class. That's what everyone says. They're all so proud of Boe. Her parents, her aunts, and uncles, her teachers, everyone. Then why does she feel like such a failure?

The thoughts started intruding on her the day after Lute disappeared. She knew she shouldn't have let him go home, and yet she did. *And now Har is dead and Lute is gone and it's all my fault!*

She stops crying as she gets out of bed, she can't let her parents see her like that, they're already doing everything they can in their search. The search began immediately the night he ran away.

It was a suicide, the fingerprints on the gun, still tightly gripped in Har's paw was evidence enough of that, but the note was what troubled them. Lute had written it in his off-paw, so it was much less cleanly made than any of the work they could call on to check the paw writing.

Furthermore, while Boe wasn't supposed to see it, she overheard the cops mention it to Mrs. P that night. "Goodbye, I'm sorry, don't look for me." It was as if Lute wrote it knowing what was about to happen. The police decided it would be in everyone's best interest if they moved forward under the idea he had simply been kidnapped.

There is, after all, no clean-cut and logical way a child could cause his abusive father to commit suicide, and the idea that he had somehow planned it is even more farfetched. The case was immediately dumped off to the special victims unit, and they put as many resources as they could spare into the case.

As the days went on, the search only became more desperate, with some cops even following a supposed lead from a fast-food employee up in Horse Country, claiming the child had been there only two days before.

Meanwhile, a somber melancholy seemed to fall on Mrs. Fairgrove's classroom. While most didn't seem to really notice, Mrs. Fairgrove was wracked with worry over Lute, especially after hearing the full story from Mr. P. Then there was Randy, who decided to try and mock Lute, but this was quickly met with scoldings from other classmates who were already growing sick of Randy's behavior.

And then, there's Boe.

All alone. Lute's supposed friend, but she let him down. And now she's stuck.

Waiting.

That's all she can do.

She doesn't try in class anymore, and yet she still excels in it. She goes out searching on her own after school, looking anywhere she can think of in town that Lute might be, only to never find him. Her parents tell her it's a bad idea, and she needs to just be patient and the police will find him.

She just needs to wait.

But the waiting is killing her. Her over analytical mind, her active spirit, her deep-rooted desire to see her only friend *just one more time!* But no, she was alone, and the police had already made it clear that they're not going to find him.

And so she was stuck, waiting. Waiting as the search bled into a second week and the first of maybe ten days of fall and winter weather that Orange Bay ever receives each year hits. *It's early*. She notes it's *only September.*

The cold didn't bother her through her thick wool, though it did make her glad her parents had decided to wait for the weekend for her next shear-cut. If nothing else, it made her even more determined to find her lost friend than ever before.

She begins walking to her first usual stop after school, the gas station off of 8th street. She and Lute would sometimes go there for slushies when she got a bonus in her allowance. It was on her way there that she noticed someone she had never seen before.

To be fair, that's not that strange, considering that Orange Bay is one of the largest cities in Eagleland, but something about this guy caught her eye.

He is tall and lanky, the kind of body one might think of for a sickly high-school student. The black plumage of his downward pointed tail and shine of his beak let her know he's a raven. However, beyond that, absolutely no part of him was visible past his thick clothes. Wings tucked into his hoodie's pockets, and pants tucked into his boots, the hood covered much of his face to the point where no onlookers could even make out his eyes.

She felt uneasy as she approached him, almost like he was the neighborhood watch caricature made manifest. She kept her eye on him as she passed by.

"Don't look for him."

She could hear a pin drop. "What?" she breathed out and turned to face him, but he was already gone. She looks around frantically, *where did he go?!* She follows the sidewalk to the end of the street, running in the direction he went, and as she turns the corner, she can just make out a shadow rounding another corner at the end of this street.

This game went on for several more blocks as the buildings around them grew taller and taller, it was clear following him would only lead deeper into the city proper. Ultimately, she didn't care, she just knew, **knew**, he knows something about Lute and needed answers, regardless of the consequences. Finally, one last turn down a dead-end alley. Trash cans and a dumpster were the only things in it, a large fence on the far end was erected to keep cars from driving through, but the figure was nowhere to be seen.

She looks up, *did he fly away?* No, there's no one above, meaning he's here, most likely behind the dumpster. It's a trap, she quickly figures out. Stupidly, she approaches but makes sure to keep herself visible to the street behind her.

"Hey!" she shouts, "What did you say back there?"

"..." Silence. If he's there, he says nothing.

"Answer me!" she demands, her high pitched bleats are far from intimidating, but she'll take what she can get.

"He's already dead." A cold, almost robotic monotone of a voice says.

"What?!" She cries as she runs behind the dumpster, only to find the figure standing there as expected, he was just casually leaning up against it, not even like he planned to grab her, just as if this was normal for him.

He doesn't look at her, just stares up into the sky. "The future is already written kid, his destiny is set in stone, and that destiny is to die."

"What?" she asks, taking a step back from him, "What do you know?! Why do you think he's going to die?" she angrily retorts.

He shrugs, standing tall as he spreads his wings wide. "Because I've already seen it. If you go looking for him, all that will happen is that he'll die sooner." And with that, he takes off and flies away into the afternoon sky.

Boe P, now all alone on that street, alone in one of the biggest cities in the entire world, realizes there's only one thing for her to do.

She has to wait.

In the Hall of the Mountain King:

The next day came, all parties had agreed it was best for the kids to spend the night there and head out west again in the morning. In truth, the time spent there was much less than one might imagine. Less than a week has passed outside of the enchanted circus, yet to them it feels much longer. "Sorry, we can't help you, kids, anymore," Persephone says. And it was a shame too, though they kind of understood why. Freya had to take Loki back home and dismantle this circus, so she was at least excusable.

Ishtar for whatever reason had simply decided to refuse to help them, talking more and more about how "the future is always changing", and "they need to do this on their own". Though honestly, Edgar took this as her excuse to be lazy.

"I'd take you myself," Persephone offers, "But I'm not able to stay here anymore." she frowns.

Lute tilts his head. "What do you mean, can't stay here anymore?"

Suddenly, the ground shakes and rumbles, a small fissure smelling of sulfur and giving off a pale blue light appears behind Persephone. "I'm only able to stay up here half the year. The other half, well..." she eyes the pit. "It's nice down there! And hey, I don't have to deal with my terrible family, so that's a bonus."

She turns to head into the pit, and as she goes down she waves goodbye, "Ah, and happy winter! Make sure you bundle up!" As she disappears, she laughs and with one final shake, the hole closes and she's gone without a trace.

"Well." Edgar says, "Thanks for not taking us across sooner then!"

"Yeah, but if she did we wouldn't have gotten training." Lute points out.

"You guys will be fine," Freya comments as she walks over. "Just make sure you find a dry place to camp each night. Your fur and feathers will keep you warm enough so long as you don't get soaked."

She crouches down to meet with them at eye level. "That said, building a fire each night and whenever possible will be helpful, and you should start looking for camp early, maybe around two or three in the afternoon, since you'll want someplace you can defend easily."

"Thanks Ms. Freya." Lute smiles back at her. "But do you really think we'll be okay?"

She laughs and pets their heads, "Of course. If I didn't, then I would have called Thor or someone to babysit you two until you get to the other side. Make up for all the trouble we've caused."

"Oooh! Do you think we can still meet him someday?!"

"Hah! Maybe, tell you what, when the two of you become legends yourself, look me up, we'll party together! Old Snow style!"

"Freya, they're too young to drink." Ishtar scolds.

"Nonsense! Back in my day babes would drink deeply!"

"Yes, and your booze was a lot weaker. Now you two better get going. The longer you wait, the harder it'll be for you."

"Right..." Edgar says as he turns, "C'mon Lute, these two aren't gonna help us, and I want to find a safe place to sleep before night falls."

As they leave through the gate Lute turns one last time to wave goodbye, "So long! I hope we can meet up again soon!" And with those words, the duo head off westward again.

"...They're gone." Freya says dismissively. "Do you think we were right to send them off?"

"Maybe." Ishtar shrugs. "Honestly this is the best outcome for us regardless of what happens on the mountain."

"Sending children off to die for no reason?" Loki's slimy voice chimes in as he walks out of a nearby tent, "A lady after my own heart. Sorry, I'm taken. Though I am grateful that you've chosen to let those brats get eaten." he says this as he kneels over, "Damn punks, that really hurt. Now, I've done my part, where's my payment? No more snake venom..."

"Patience Loki. Your services may still be required." Freya sighs. "And we're not sending them off to die for no reason! We're not sending them off to die in the first place!" She eyes up Ishtar. "Right? They will live right? Astarte!" she calls out another name of her old friend. One of her newer ones, a kinder mask she started to wear some three thousand years ago.

"Oh yes yes," Loki chimes in, "Tell us 'Apphy' oh wise legend of love and kindness. Tell us all about how you know these children will be safe climbing a mountain in winter while fighting off a monster."

A tear rolls down the cheek of the lioness, her tail flicks slowly behind her but she refuses to face the lynx and fox. "I hope so." She manages to say. "Those two... they're so cute together... I just hope they'll be alright."

"Why do all this then?" Freya asks. "Why did we do any of this training if we're just going to let them go there and don't even know if they'll live?! We should have just taken them somewhere safe..."

"We could not." Ishtar holds her ground. "There's something about that bird. Edgar... the thing he's running from. Anywhere we take him it would find him. No. There are games being played behind the scenes now. Games across time and space. A new player sits at the board and has shown his wing. We all have our parts to play now."

She shakes her head and wipes her eyes before turning to Freya. "For now all we can do is wait, and prepare for our next move. If we get too involved then that one glimmer of hope may pass him by entirely. C'mon, let's clean this place up."

Edgar and Lute heard none of this. None of the arguments of what should and couldn't be done. Nothing of the remorse the legends have at the idea that even they can't get involved in whatever was going on.

They didn't hear as they lamented the fact that despite their roles as guardians and heroes, and all their history and power, they weren't able to interfere anymore as it would only cause the situation to get even worse than it already was. How this seems to happen quite often even, where there are many problems both magical and mundane that they could solve so easily, only to realize doing so would make things worse.

How this seemingly leaves them in a state of regulating their own world in pocket dimensions and other planes of existence and ever-shrinking back corners of the earth where magic can get away with being big and obvious. And how they reminisce for days long gone where their simple plans of big gestures of magic could solve most problems.

Instead the children were more wrapped up in their own conversation as they walked, trying to catch up on the past days, though there really wasn't much for Edgar to say. Having been trapped in a cage kinda limited his options. "After I used every spell I could think of to try and get out of it, and none of them worked I just decided to grind on some stones." he says as they return to the train tracks.

"Just more grinding?"

"Yep." He says as he pulls the aventurine out of his pocket. The unidentifiable lump it had once been had been smoothed and shined into a perfect green sphere the size of a large marble. "I uh... I made this for you." He smiles. "For when you came to rescue me."

Lute accepts it from Edgar and holds it up to the sun. "Woah... It's so pretty!" he smiles. "This is that one from the campfire right? You said it can boost earth magic."

"Mhm." Edgar says as he grabs the red carnelian and begins grinding it more. "I figured, where we're going and all, training's good, sure, but sometimes what you need is just a solid boost. And given how cold it'll be, chances are growing food will be hard."

"That's true. All we've got is corn and cabbage seeds, and neither of them can really grow in the snow... so how does this work?"

"You need to put it in something. Gems are used to either become objects like a ring," Edgar says as he shows the carnelian, now a thin cylinder with a small indent in the center. "Or they're put in other objects to give them power."

"Well, that's a shame." Lute sighs as he puts it in his pocket. "I don't really have anything right now. Maybe just having it on me will enhance my power?" He shrugs. "Though if my plan is correct we may not even need to worry about it."

"You have a plan?" Edgar says in shock. "Since when do you plan things?"

"Since you were captured and Freya told me running right in would be a bad idea. But regardless, I think I know what we can do! Look!" he says as he pulls the map out of their backpack. "This track we're on will cross a road up ahead. Once we get to the road, if we head north we'll arrive in Ashtown, just at the base of Big Smoke Mountain!"

"Alright... how does that help us?"

"Well, I may not have ever left Orange Bay, but I do know some landmarks from school. Ashtown is a tourist trap! It has like, a whole bunch of busses and cars and things that go up Big Smoke to the resorts and hotels up there. If we get on one of these, we can get a big chunk of the mountain out of the way in less than a day! And then we'll be working from near the top of the mountain going down, making the journey a lot easier!"

"That's..." Edgar stops in his tracks, trying to think of the right word. "Okay? More than that. Is there a word?"

"Good?" Lute offers.

"Sure. That. It's good! We'll do that!" he smiles. "Thank you for your good idea Lute!"

Lute can't help but smile at Edgar's attempts to understand basic Fogish and compliment him. Still, it's the thought that counts. They continue to walk along the tracks, and eventually, as they get ready to grow some lunch, they come to the road.

There's a good reason that they hadn't been traveling along the roads up until now. Trains aren't very common to run into. Sure, you can guarantee there's always one coming, but they're very far spaced out, easy to hide from, and hard to stop. If they got spotted by a passenger, that passenger would probably forget about them as quickly as they saw them. Cars however are a lot more frequent, the drivers can see you and be pulled over in as little as ten seconds. At least this time they didn't have to worry about a broken arm to make the drivers worry about kids in the middle of the woods.

The training had actually paid off pretty nicely for Lute too, he didn't even have to dance and within as little as five minutes they had a full meal from two cabbage seeds. They eat and drink from their water bottle before quickly heading back north along the road.

Cars pass by in hurried frequency as the sun dips lower into the early afternoon sky. A small chill fills the air as they continue their walk. The leaves on the trees have turned from the familiar greens of Lute's home to the darkened browns and reds and oranges of late fall. Leaves billow in the wind as they descend from the branches, a clear sign, no matter where in Eagleland you are, that October has come.

At about dinner time they arrive on the outskirts of Ashtown "Discover Incredible Sights." The sign on the side of the road reads as they pass by. While smaller than both Big Apple and Orange Bay, and perhaps even smaller than Horse County, the cats that make up the majority of Ashtown's population have done a wonderful job of making it feel large.

Indeed, this would also be Edgar's first time in such a large city. He had never been outside of his tiny home before escaping, and since then he had yet to encounter anyplace larger than the circus. As they walked along the road Edgar had questions about all the sights they had seen. He understood some things implicitly, such as cars basically being small and more mobile trains, about what cops were and why they should avoid them, and how some buildings could be so tall. But there were still things that boggled his mind, such as actions he saw people doing in stores as they passed by.

"What are they holding?" he would ask when seeing people using money. "Hey, it's that thing you did earlier." he would point out when a mother hugged her child. "Why don't we grab some food from one of these places?" he would ask as dinner time rolled around, only to be informed they would need money they don't have.

Lute was happy to answer all these questions as they searched for the right location, and it wasn't long until they found it. Big Smoke Resort Parking Lot. The booth and sign out front read. A bored looking tabby sitting there watching over the fenced off cars. A lone bus had just arrived in front of the lot and some various tourists were boarding. Thankfully the bus was a free service offered by the hotel, so they managed to just hop aboard without any questions asked, and took a couple seats in the back.

It takes off and begins its ascent up the mountain, which gives time for more questions to be answered. "So, if I have this right," Edgar says, "wealth is money, and that's the paper notes. I always thought it was like... shiny rocks and gems and stuff."

"I mean it kinda is?" Lute laughs, "Mrs. Fairgrove once said that Eagleland's money is backed up by gold in some big vault up north. I guess carrying around a lot of that stuff would be kinda heavy."

"Makes sense. So how do we get it?"

"Uh... work I guess? Before I met you, some people gave me money when I sang and danced in a park, so we could perform."

"I see..." he says looking out the window. "We'll just have to show off our magic then!" he laughs. "By the way, once we get to the top of the mountain, what's the next stop between here and Spectacle City?"

"Good question!" Lute responds as he pulls it out. "Let's see... It's... not here?" He looks again, he could have sworn he saw it on the map earlier, and can't remember how many times he's actually read the map, but he would have sworn up and down that Spectacle City was on it.

"It just stops." he frowns, "This map only seems to cover half the country!"

"Half?!" Edgar exclaims, "How is it only half?! How big is this place?" He thinks back on how long they've been traveling. Had it really not even been half the size of Eagleland? In a way he was glad to hear it, meaning that he would be able to get even further away now than he had ever even dreamed of before. "That's... bad right? We'll be moving blind once we get down off the mountain."

"Not entirely." Lute winces. "As long as we follow train tracks or roads, we'll reach another town eventually, which is a bonus. We just need to find some first."

"I guess..." Edgar winces. "I wish I could fly already, then I could just fly up and scout ahead."

"That would be so cool!" Lute laughs. "If you get strong, then you could just carry me on your back too!"

"Hah! Now that'd be something... hey, what's that?" Edgar says as he points out the window. The bus is pulling up to the lodge near the top of the mountain. There's a chair lift leading up to the summit, already powered off for the night as the sun begins to set. The hotel itself is a classic log cabin style lodge, large, yet cozy looking with warm browns and reds that make it feel welcoming. Over the entrance and around the windows hang decorations for the upcoming Halloween festival that occurs here every year to usher out fall and welcome the winter.

The bus comes to a stop before the main doors, and all the passengers disembark and head inside. The reception hall is large and inviting. A big glass window looks out over the frozen mountainside around them, evergreen trees covered in snow and carefully marked paths show where to go to get to the hotel's activities. There's a fire roaring in the pit next to the window, several couches and chairs encircling it with tables to their sides.

The front desk has an information kiosk next to it, and the other passengers are checking in, but the kids don't pay much attention to where. The receptionist, a white cat, is too occupied dealing with the adult guests that just arrived to notice Edgar and Lute enter and start to walk around. They walk straight past her, grabbing a pamphlet on the hotel's activities and services as they do.

"So what's our goal here?" Edgar asks.

"Mainly not getting kicked out or the police called as we crash here for the night." Lute responds as they walk through the endless series of hallways, at the same time he begins reading the pamphlet. "Let's see... Reception closes at eight, as does the bus service, but they leave the fire on all night, so we can sleep in there. As for food... oh shoot! They've got a gift shop!"

"Lute..."

"I'm kidding. They've got an all you can eat dining hall. Apparently the bill can get charged straight to your room."

"That'd be nice if we had a room." Edgar points out.

"Yeah, so I guess that's out of the question. Shame too, it's got a lot of really yummy sounding dishes..."

"Or..." Edgar offers, "We could always just... take some."

"What, like steal it?" Lute asks, after making sure no one was around.

"If that's the word for it." Edgar says as they approach the dining hall. "I mean, how can they tell where we're from?" Confident this plan of his would work, he leads the two into the dining hall and they look over the buffet.

The wonderful aroma of cooked seafood and fresh fruits and vegetables fills the air. There's a sweet scent of cakes and candies from the desert table, and black bean burgers still sizzling on the indoor grill. The boys' mouths water at the aroma, a far cry from their normal diet of instant grown crops or even the oversaturated and fat dripping foods they ate at the circus.

There's pulled jackfruit smothered in barbeque sauce and boiled shrimp next to a mountain of steamed crab legs, it smells and looks amazing from where they're standing, there's just one problem.

"Arm bands." A deep voice says. That's when they notice him. A tall racoon smiles down at them. He's broad shouldered and barrel chested, his long tail lazily whips back and forth behind him. As he looks them over from his podium in front of the entrance.

"Sorry what?" Lute asks.

"Hah. I said arm bands." he says, "'Fraid I need to see y'all's arm bands before you can go in. You probably got them from your parents when you checked in." He shows them the one on his arm, it's red and has the hotel's logo on the top of it. "They look like this, see?"

Lute looks over at Edgar nervously, but Edgar thinks fast and pulls one out of thin air. This one's deep purple instead. *Oh! It's his amethyst!* Lute realizes. *He did this before with Talos on the farm!* "Here, see it?"

"Let's see," the racoon says as he takes it from Edgar and tries to scan it. It doesn't work, obviously, but what's more interesting is that it actually crashes his computer kiosk. "Well, that's never happened before." he frowns as he gives it back to the kids. "This old hunk of junk... just tell me your room number, and I'll do it manually later." he offers.

"Um..."

"Two one seven!" Lute blurts out. A random number chosen completely off the top of his head, praying to whatever heard him that it was a room in use.

"Two one seven?" The racoon asks as he tilts his head. "Where have I... oh! You're the Gurdy's kids! Mr.

Hurdy said you'd be by later after you got tired of playing in the snow."

"T-that's right." Lute tries to keep up the bluff, "and this is Edgar, a friend from school who came with us."

"Very well, you two enjoy the buffet." He smiles.

And so the kids walk right past him and quickly grab their plates. They find a nice secluded spot of the dining area where hopefully no one will bother them and begin to chow down on the food.

It truly is a wonderful meal and they enjoy it immensely, each of them eating several plates full of their dishes of choice and glass after glass of sweet soda. As they keep eating they notice some others come in, mostly adults and a few kids who eye them suspiciously. *Please don't say anything.* Lute thinks.

Thankfully they don't as even those kids are overwhelmed by the buffet's many wonderful dishes and can't be bothered to react to the duo. Not wanting to stick around just in case however, when they've had their fill, Lute quietly and quickly leads Edgar out of the dining hall and into the gift shop.

They have some time to kill before reception would be closed and browsing the junk in here seemed like the best idea. Junk is also a very appropriate term for the stuff being sold here. They had your standard affair of towels, blankets, pillows, coffee mugs, and just about anything else you could think of with the hotel's logo slapped on it. Mixed in with the pens and stationary were some shirts and pants that caught Lute's eye.

The circus didn't exactly have laundry service, and even if it did, it was two boys in a dangerous place with their only company being three older women, so they've been wearing the same clothes for a couple weeks now. Edgar a bit longer than Lute, though that's a story for another day.

Regardless, the idea of clean clothes really made Lute wish he had some money, Edgar meanwhile was just more interested in the curious things he had never seen before, such as snowboards and umbrellas.

While most hotels only have bathrooms for the guests in their rooms, Lute managed to convince the gift shop worker to let them borrow the employee bathroom because their room was on the third floor and Lute didn't think he could hold it. One somewhat embarrassing lie later, and the boys found a new appreciation for indoor plumbing.

Edgar was oddly insistent on going in with Lute, but having Lute leave before he used it strangely enough. "Just don't watch me." Lute convinced Edgar. Either way they finished their bathroom stop and slowly started walking their way through the halls. No real goal or destination, just killing time and talking.

"You know, it's strange." Lute admits, "I think this is the first time I've seen snow in person."

"It's... not that good?" Edgar laughs. "Like, it's okay I guess but it makes finding rocks hard. Just about the only thing it's good for is charging up my milky quartz. Although..." He glances out a window at the end of the hall, the moon has already risen and it's dark out past the shine of the fairy lights of the motel. "This is probably not the best time."

"You can sense it too?" Lute frowns.

"Yeah, I've been ignoring it since we started eating. It's out there." He responds as they arrive back in the lobby, the receptionist locking the front door, a thick wooden barricade, leaving the giant windows as the most vulnerable parts between them and the outside.

"I thought Talos said it doesn't go near big crowds."

"It probably senses us." Edgar points out. "We're both a lot stronger than we were at the farm. It can probably tell we're in here and is just waiting."

"What do we do then?"

"They said it doesn't like light and fire right? Then we sit here." Edgar says, taking a seat on the couch right in front of the fire pit. "And we take turns sleeping. You can sleep first," he offers as he fishes out their blanket.

"Are you sure?" Lute asks as Edgar lays it out for him.

"Yeah, I'm not even tired yet. Besides, if that thing tries anything, you'll be the easier one to wake up."

"I suppose." he admits as he curls up in the blanket next to Edgar. "Alright then, just wake me up when you're tired."

"Right, right.." Edgar says. And with only the sounds and light of the flickering fire, Lute gently falls asleep.

Some time passes as Edgar is left alone to his thoughts, the slowly falling snow outside and cozy fire give him an odd sensation he doesn't quite believe he's ever felt before. Lute lays on the couch next to him, and there's a silent stillness in the air, but unlike the stillness he's used to.

Back home the quiet times were some of the worst, because it was a sign for him that trouble was about to hit. That he'd be denied food or forced to spend days locked up in that cold, tiny room, or worse still. But here? The room was large and larger still with the halls attached and open. The outside was frozen, yet here the fire was warm. He had just eaten and felt full and... safe. Despite the thing he felt outside, it didn't come any closer, it just stood stationary out there, waiting.

No word could come to his mind to describe it, he hadn't heard this word before, and his education, while good in terms of magic, was poor in almost every other category. He'd have to ask Lute about this sensation in the morning. A sensation so alien and strange it felt like it would defeat itself if he thought about it too long. Comfort. Comfort and Edgar were truly strange acquaintances.

At some point he must have dozed off himself without waking Lute, though it wasn't for long. He hadn't fallen asleep enough to remain asleep when the sounds of an acoustic guitar slowly filled the hall. Groggily, he rubs his eyes and notices the source immediately, the racoon from before.

"Howdy." He smiles as he strums the guitar on his lap. "Hope you don't mind me sitting here for a spell." It was at this point Edgar bothered to really look this guy over. He wore a red shirt and blue jeans, the uniform of the hotel, and a nametag reading "David".

"No." Edgar says after taking a moment to gather himself. "Um... don't tell our parents we decided to sleep here for the night?" He tries to lie.

"Haha, I imagine that would be difficult to do when they're not even here." David laughs. "Trust me kid, if you've been around as long as I have, you'd know a couple runaways when you see them."

"..." Edgar doesn't respond, terrified about what's gonna happen next. David simply sets the guitar down and grabs a stick and some marshmallows. Skewering one, he holds it over the fire pit.

"You seem tense. Can't say I blame you. You're in a bad situation kid. Ran away from home, stole food from a high-class hotel..." he trails off as he pulls the marshmallow from the fire and smears it on a graham cracker, adding a bit of chocolate to make a smore. "And now you're the target of that thing out there. Smore?" He offers it to Edgar.

"What thing out there?" Edgar tries to play it off.

"C'mon kid, I'm not an idiot. I could sense you when you were at the base of the mountain. It's alright, you're safe here. Take the smore."

Edgar does so and eyes it as the raccoon starts to make another for. "So you think you know us." He quietly responds, holding back his anger enough not to wake up Lute, "But if you know we're not supposed to be here, why didn't you kick us out?"

"I'm not about to let kids go hungry, and I'm certainly not gonna let you get eaten." he scoffs before setting the second one aside. Edgar takes a bite from his,

his eyes sparkling as he experiences the treat for his first time. Swallowing it down as he needs to focus.

"So you know about that creature. And you can sense us. So you have magic too? Just who are you?"

"Darn straight! Heh, this is MY mountain. Call me Davy." He salutes as he finishes his treat and goes back to strumming. "As long as I'm here, that guy won't come near. I've been keeping him at bay for years."

"Why not kill it then?" Edgar asks.

"If I could, I would. Truth be told, it and I are pretty evenly matched. So we've got a mutual understanding. After so many battles we've agreed not to go into each other's turf. I get this resort, and it can have the lower parts of the mountain."

"Hmph, so you're useless too." Edgar scoffs.

"Now hang on there son, I may be many things, but useless ain't one of them. I keep the people here safe, and that includes the two of you. That wendigo has you in its sights, so I'm gonna make sure it doesn't get you."

"You can't help us." Edgar says. "Those women told us we gotta battle that thing and no one can help us against it."

"I'm sorry, I thought this was Eagleland. Home of the free and land of the brave. Last I heard we had the freedom to do whatever the hell we wanted when we wanted, and some big cadre of old farts is not gonna stop me from helping a couple of kids pioneer their way forward to make a better life for themselves." David retorts.

Edgar remains incredulous, yet impressed that it seems he finally found someone that's actually willing to help them. *This sounds too 'good' to be true.* He thinks.

"So I want you to get some sleep, and in the morning I'm taking you to the peak via chairlift so you two can begin your descent and get out of here before that thing has a chance to even think about attacking you."

"Wait, how do I-" but before he could finish his question, David plays a note on his guitar and Edgar falls asleep mid-sentence.

Grief:

Everyone dreams. Every night we all dream. That's a scientific fact. If one falls into a deep enough sleep, they will dream, but whether or not they remember it come morning is a different story. Lute for example remembers his dreams because when not training with Culania, he normally has recurring nightmares.

Tonight was different.

Not a training night, so he knew to expect the nightmares, though, in truth, those had been slowing down ever since he left home. He still HAD them, but they were less intense. And this one was probably both the easiest and worst one he's had in a long while.

You see, there was simply nothing there. Just a big empty void. No monsters, no ground, no sky, not even his own body floating through all this nothing. It was just him, alone with his thoughts, the seconds ticking by.

Naturally, when faced with such a boring predicament, he does what anyone else would do, he gathers his thoughts and tries to cope with everything that's happened these past few days. It's all happened so fast, yet home feels like a lifetime ago.

He had been acting tough in front of Edgar, trying to keep himself together, trying to laugh off the monsters and dangers they've encountered. That was his thing. The class clown who laughs off the bullies, just on a much bigger scale. But the truth is he was absolutely terrified.

He's never fought someone before Loki, not really. The closest he ever got was the week of Tae Kwon Do he took before dropping out, and that was back in third grade. He's stolen, he's hurt people, he's done so many things he never thought himself capable of doing. Even back home, after his mom died and food became scarce, he never once thought of stealing money from...

And then there was that.

His mind kept coming back to that night.

Persephone said she didn't blame him, even if it was still bad. And it was still bad.

I killed my father. The thought always hits him like a semi-truck. *I murdered him.* If it was possible to be sick inside a dream of nothingness, Lute might have done so right then and there. For so long, he had tried to deny it. *He killed himself! He had the gun, he put it against his head, he shot himself while I just watched and...* sang.

Magic's not supposed to be real. You can't just start singing and dancing and make plants grow or fire start, yet that's exactly what Lute did. Magic IS real, both the good and the bad. Edgar's fear illusion is enough to drive legends into frenzied madness, if he didn't stop it, Freya may very well have lost herself to his darkness.

And according to Edgar, that's a basic dark spell.

He doesn't know advanced magic.

"It was self-defense." Persephone had said. "Magic can't be used to kill unless there's a good reason behind it."

So it was okay then right? It has to be, otherwise, it wouldn't have worked.

He tries to rationalize it, tries to explain to himself that he was in the right, but if he was right, *then why does it still feel so wrong?* He never had a close relationship with his father, and it always seemed like the feelings were shared, only worsened after his mom died and left him all alone with the monster.

He had tried for so long to hide his feelings, and get closer to him, but no matter what he tried, it seemed like he was never going to come around. Some small part of Lute, buried deep beneath his laid back nature and clownish attitude grew to resent, and perhaps even hate, his father.

He can't lie to himself. Especially not here in the void where there is nothing but his own thoughts. After killing his father, he did feel some immediate satisfaction. Akin to pulling a knife out of a wound, it felt good for all of a few moments before he got to the woods outside of Horse Country.

Back then, he was pretty sure he was going to die, maybe that's what he even wanted, a way to atone for what he did. It was only through sheer chance and fortune that he discovered he had magic and even more luck that Edgar had been nearby.

The void is calm and quiet. There's nothing in there to judge him, nothing to attack him, nothing asking him to pour out his soul, and nothing he feels he needs to be strong in front of. It's just his thoughts.

In the waking world, he's laying on Edgar's shoulder, his paws instinctively grab hold of the raven, refusing to let go. While his mind wanders, his body wants, **needs** something to ground it.

And so he just floats there in the void, thinking over and over how this is all his fault, how he deserves whatever is coming to him. How much of a bad person he is and how much he wants to find another escape.

And then a new thought struck him. What was that voice? The hot, quiet whispers that told him the words to his dirge. The ones that made all of this possible. Just what was it?

It certainly didn't sound like Lute's voice, heck it didn't sound like the voice of anyone he's ever met! It was so monotone and flat, the only cadence coming from them being the musicality from his dirge.

If the brain had a text to speech function hardwired into it, that would be a close approximation. Not just standard reading and speaking, but it sounded so much like a computer program reading off of a script.

It's certainly something to look into for the little rabbit, yet for now, one thing was certain. No amount of shifting the blame or searching for imaginary ghost voices was going to bring his dad back to life.

No amount of anger or sorrow was going to make things like they were before, he made his choice and now he has to live with it.

I killed my father. The thought hits him once again. *And I'm just going to have to accept it.*

Wendigo:

The morning comes, and David catches Lute up on the situation rather quickly. Edgar is understandably upset about the use of magic last night and doesn't trust him. "Why us? Why do you want to help us?" he asks. "You have nothing to gain from helping us."

"I don't need anything from you kids." David laughs. "Let me tell you boys something about the founding years of our great nation. See, our nation was born on an idea of life, liberty, and the pursuit of happiness. It is every Eagleander's duty and obligation to help those in need to overcome their problem."

David goes on about this over breakfast in the dining hall, telling the kids about how this land is full of good kind people, and they all want to work together to build a better future. However, neither of the boys truly believe him. The kids eat well, yet David doesn't even grab a single plate.

Lute stops eating his bowl of cereal, "I... I don't believe you." he reluctantly admits. "I want to believe, but... My dad was a reporter, and I saw what he reported on. There's a lot of bad stuff happening."

"Yeah, and my father is crazy. My whole family is insane! They sure seem like good people, don't they?" Edgar scoffs, not even slowing down as he eats his rice and beans.

"So you've met a few bad apples." David shrugs, "But they don't spoil the bunch. C'mon, surely you've met at least a few good people out there. Someone who was willing to help you when the chips were down. Friends or neighbors, teachers, anyone."

Lute thinks back to the start of this whole mess, Mrs. Fairgrove, Mr. & Mrs. P, Boe, heck even Talos who did try to help them. Persephone, Freya, and Ishtar and their magic lessons and training, even his traveling companion Edgar is a good person in his mind.

"I'm not gonna lie to you kids. This nation has its troubled past and dark moments." David frowns. "I should know, I've done my fair share of trouble in these parts, and some part of me is still trying to make up for it. You boys know where you're heading next right?"

"Spectacle City." Lute hesitantly replies.

"Ah, now that's a bit far off. Hang on, I think I have...." David fishes around in his pants pockets before pulling out an old piece of paper. "Aha. Here it is." He says offering it to them.

Unfolding it, the paper is revealed to be "A map?" Lute asks as he studies it.

"Made it myself when I was just a few years older than you boys. Took the time to mark all the hiking trails around the mountain and updated it over time to include the roads. Take this one." He points to one marked 66. "That road will lead you right to the reservation."

"Reservation?" Edgar asks.

"Yeah," David sinks down in his chair. "It's not my proudest work, and the people there are as stubborn as old tree stumps buried in the ground. But they're good people, if you ask the marshall there, he might just give you a lift to Spectacle City."

"Hang on." Edgar says, "Why can't you just take us there?"

"Oh yeah! That's a good idea! You have to have a car, don't you?"

"Nah." Davy says as he buries his face in his paws. "Truth be told, as much as I'd love to, I'm afraid I'm a bit... stuck. As it were."

"Stuck?"

"Yeah, the Wendigo, that thing is hungry. We discourage hikers traveling the mountain in winter, and keep everyone here inside at night. It knows to stay outside... as long as I'm here. If I were to leave, even for one night it would come in and slaughter everyone. Guns don't work on that thing, and nobody else here has magic, that's a fact. This mountain resort, it might as well be my prison cell."

Edgar winces. A cell is a cell no matter how big or fancy it is. Admittedly, compared to his past ones, he thinks he'd be happy to spend the rest of forever in this one with the gourmet food, running water, cozy fire, and other things he's sure this place has but he'll never know. Yet some part of him would be unsatisfied. Deep down, he knows this. If he was told by anyone, even himself, that he can never leave or cross some line in the snow, he'd do anything in his power to find a way to escape.

"What about what you were saying last night?" he asks. "What about freedom?"

"Freedom." David lets out a long slow sigh, as if reminiscing for days long gone or a love long lost. "This land was built on that idea, and I still hold it true. But for whatever reason, the people here seem to have forgotten that. They resign themselves to tradition, fear, and stubbornness, refusing to move forward in the name of progress and freedom."

"If I could, I'd leave this place in a heartbeat, get out there, and try and help more people. But I can't go nowhere till that thing in the snow is gone. Hell, I tried closing down the hotel one winter, that thing just went down to Ashtown and started attacking the people there. It's a smart son of a-" suddenly, an alarm went off on David's cell phone.

He checks it before immediately standing. "Right, lift's open, we need to get a move on." He pulls them from their meals. "No time to wait, we're burning daylight oil. Tell me, have either of you snowboarded before?"

Snow was something Lute had never seen before, and even until now he had yet to touch it. The entrance to the hotel has a covered driveway the bus pulled into when they were dropped off, and with how late it was when they arrived, they decided to go straight in. Taking his first step into the snow he found it was cold and wet, and really made him wish he wore shoes.

Having grown up in Orange Bay, his paws had adjusted to the scolding hot concrete and asphalt and sand, but this snow? The frozen damp cold that got between his toes like mud on a rainy spring day? It feels so bad. Like spilling a slurpee on his legs and then being told he has to walk for several hours with that on him.

Thankfully the chair lift was a short walk away, and he was the first to get on it and out of the snow. "I don't like that stuff." He says as the others get on..

"What, the snow?" Edgar asks. "It's not THAT bad."

"Maybe not for you, but I'm not really having an ICE time here!"

"Don't make me kick you off." David says as the chair lift takes off into the sky and begins climbing higher and higher up to the peak.

"Fine, fine," Lute smiles, "So you said something about snowboarding?"

"Yeah, when we get to the top, I'm gonna give you guys a sleigh and let you ride that down on the hiking trail. Keep to that and it'll reach the road you need to be on. Head west and you'll be fine."

"Can we really reach the base of the mountain before nightfall if we do this?" Edgar questions as he peers down at the evergreen forest below them, idly dreaming of being able to fly.

"With any luck." David says. "I can't promise anything but you might just make it out of that thing's range."

"And if not?" Lute hesitantly asks, "What do we do then?"

David is silent for a good few minutes as the lift nears the goal. "Then you either stand your ground and fight, try and run all night, or find a good place to hide before the sun goes down. You should be fine though." He half heartedly reassures them. "The sleigh will take you pretty far."

Something about the way he said that didn't quite sit right with the boys. Maybe it was the pause, or maybe it was how he practically ran off the chair lift to a supply closet to grab the sleigh. Or maybe it was the fact that neither of them were idiots and knew that eventually they'd run out of either snow or steep enough hills to keep using the sleigh, and would need to walk the rest of the way.

The sleigh is an old fashioned wooden one with a curved front made from planks of wood meticulously nailed together, which gave it the benefit of easier control. A toboggan is the official term if one was to split hairs, but it hardly mattered. What mattered more is that it seemed well used and aged, like it had possibly been there longer than the hotel itself, yet still in great condition. The long rope on it meant that by wrapping it behind Edgar, both the boys could help steer and guide it.

Despite David's uncertainty, taking the toboggan meant speeding up their escape, and they decided it was in their best interest to take any opportunity to do so. As they make their way to the trail and get ready to depart, a passing thought crosses Edgar's mind. "How come we can't sense you?"

"What?" David asks, almost taken aback and caught completely off guard by the question. "Why bother asking such a question." He quickly responds. "There's no need to concern yourselves with such things."

"But if we could hide our magic like you, then the Wendigo couldn't track us." Edgar points out.

"Hey! That's a brilliant idea! Can't you teach us real quick?" Lute asks.

"There's nothing to teach." David sputters. "I keep my magic hidden by not using it at all."

"But you used it last night." Edgar points out. "When you made me fall asleep on the couch... and wait. You said you keep that thing away at night, everynight. When do you sleep?"

"During the day." David tries to reason. "Look kids, you're putting way too much thought into this. Look, there's the trail, just get on the sleigh and go."

The kids know when not to argue. Well, Lute knows when not to argue, Edgar would gladly spend hours in the snow ranting and raving at David for trying to tell him what to do, but there were more important matters at wing. With not a feather more ruffled, the duo clamber onto the sleigh, Lute taking the back as Edgar takes the front.

"Alright kids, good luck out there." David smiles. "And if you ever get stronger, consider coming back and helping your friend on the mountain!" he laughs before shoving them off down the trail.

Now a bit of context for this trail. The first part is like any other skiing or sledding path, it goes down a slightly curved path between clearly marked flags and will return near the hotel below. Looking further ahead as they begin picking up speed they see the hiking path they need to take. It's narrow, and not the straightest path around. Tall evergreen trees are on either side, which while they wouldn't be fatal to crash into, certainly wouldn't feel good.

It's a bit of a trick shot even managing to get on the trail, but it's far enough away for them to learn how to steer the sleigh a bit. It was harder than it seemed in the movies Lute used to watch around Yule time, and they have to work together leaning in the direction they want to go as Lute pulled on the ropes for extra steering.

They nearly careen right into a pine tree as they make their way onto the hiking path, Edgar's keen eyes giving him the ability to see the path ahead a bit easier. It's hard to hear one another over the sounds of rushing winds and plowing snow, so they keep the conversation short to words saying what they need to do.

"Left!" Edgar will shout, and Lute will lean to the left with him. "Right!" He says, and they list to the right. They regret not having a good way to slow down, with their only option being Lute hugging Edgar tight and sticking his legs off either side.

While slowing down isn't something they want to do, it can be a bit of a necessity so they don't fall off the path or ram into a tree. It's hard work, but the paths are clear since they've been closed for the past week, and they feel they've made it pretty far down the mountain.

As they go and get more used to controlling the toboggan and relax, Edgar's mind begins to wander as he thinks back to David and the hotel. *If he sleeps during the day, then why was he awake before we got there? The drive up the mountain took a while, and he said he could sense us when we got to town. Does he sleep? And why didn't he eat? I suppose he could have gone back to the hotel and eaten then, but still, it's strange.*

Some time later, about an hour or so after they started sleighing, they're starting to really feel the chill, clouds start to roll in, and both of them are ready to get off the ride. Thankfully they enter into a long and mostly flat stretch of trail and coast to a stop. Deciding to take the opportunity, they get up to stretch their legs.

"How far do you think we've come?" Lute asks.

"Well..." Edgar looks around, between the trees he can see the peak of the mountain, "Given the size of the mountain top, it looks like we've gone pretty far, at least further down than the hotel was."

"That's good right?" Lute smiles. "What do you think, should we try to keep going, or find somewhere to hunker down?"

"I don't know what time it is." Edgar frowns. "The clouds are too thick to see the sun, but it has to be pretty early still, right? I'm not hungry, are you?"

"No, I suppose you're right. I'll watch the sky as we go, see if I can't spot the sun."

"Good call. Now come on, there's a lot of mountain to go."

Climbing back on they shove off again, it's a bit of a slow start, but they pick up speed quickly again. The wind rushing by their heads and stings Lute's eyes, the clouds don't seem to be letting up, and soon enough it even begins to snow.

Dread and worry begin to fill the children as they spiral further down down down the mountain. A creeping worry that neither of them can really talk about right now, and hope that soon will be behind them. They can both feel it. The Wendigo. It sleeps for the rest of the year, but in winter it is awake all day and night.

It can't follow them easily, even in the snow and cloud coverage, the light is strong enough to hurt it. They can feel it following. Rapidly running between trees and through underground cave systems. It's chasing them and managing to keep up with the sleigh, following an uncomfortably close distance behind. Just knowing it was on their tails made them feel even more cold.

We shouldn't have stopped. Lute thinks. *It was a bad idea, it's gonna cost us time.* He shakes the thoughts out of his head. There's no sense in worrying about it now, if they want to make this work, then they **need** to stay positive, they need to keep going and hope for the best. That thing feels as strong as Loki did, and the only reason he beat Loki was, to his knowledge, because he got a power boost from the duel.

Edgar meanwhile is more focused on the path ahead. Get to the bottom of the mountain, find the road, head west, and get away. He considers taking the toboggan off the track, through the trees and down the mountain faster, yet no place seems wide enough to safely pass. Even if it were, then they'd be screwed and lost at the base of the mountain. If only they had a way to speed it up.

A new thought crosses his mind. Ice magic. He knows it exists, the Wendigo is proof enough of the concept. If he could tap into ice magic perhaps he could use it to freeze the snow under the sleigh and speed them up.

He thinks about it, then thinks better after he nearly hits a tree because he got lost in his focus when the path suddenly turned. *Bad idea. If we go too fast we'll crash for sure.*

As more time passes, and the snow starts to get heavier, the sky begins darkening even more. Unsure of the time, all the boys know for sure is that once it gets too dark, the Wendigo will abandon the shadows and run right after them. The fact that it's able to track them makes them even more afraid of it.

We can't hide. Lute thinks as he peeks over his shoulder at the ever shrinking mountain peak.

We can't run. Edgar realizes as a quick glimpse upwards shows that the storm is only going to get worse as the afternoon sets in. Their only saving grace is the fact that as they go down, the snowfall would naturally be less as it slowly warms up, but the storm is intense enough that it hardly matters.

As they keep descending the storm gets so bad that they nearly crash twice more, unable to see the area ahead enough to avoid sharp turns. After a third time the toboggan starts slowing down again as they reach another flat part of the trail. Considering they had to have been going for at least three hours now, they imagine to be pretty low down the mountain. Deciding not to risk it anymore, the boys pick up the toboggan and hold it above their heads as they continue walking the rest of the way.

"At least this will keep the snow off." Lute points out.

"Worst case scenario we can use it as firewood," Edgar adds.

The boys continue their march down the mountainside, the snow making their steps slow and awkward as they go. They try their best to keep to the path, unable to really even see the sides or edges, and mainly deciding to walk straight in the direction they were going until they hit a tree, then turn in the nearest walkable path.

The wendigo is hunger. The wendigo is greed and hunger and pain and icy cold wrath. It eats people. It tears them apart limb from limb as they die. It steals their magic power as it eats them. Consuming them to strengthen itself. It's feral. It's no longer the person it was who knows how many years ago.

It doesn't even remember why it keeps eating other than the fact that it hungers. If you had been there back when it started its yearly hunt. Back when the eagles and horses were the dominant species, and the idea of crows and rabbits and dogs and cats were not even thought of on these lands. Before hundreds left the old world and came across the ocean on their massive wooden ships to take this new land, and the tribes of old were scattered and left in certain small locations to call their own.

One might have met a native back then. What species? None alive can fully say for sure, though there are some who claim it to have been a horse. And this horse was a powerful mystic who used his magic much as Lute does now. He would dance to bring in the bountiful crops and stoke the fire, to keep out the chill of winter and heat of summer.

Then a war between the mountain tribes came. It had been a conflict for decades between the tribes, who or what started it, nobody remembers, nor is it important. All that matters is that the tribes both had magic and both used it to attack the other. The mystic was not strong enough to save his tribe. In a fit of anger and rage, he sold his soul to some demon of grief and sorrow and was forever cursed with his new existence.

His body emaciated as his skin peeled away from the sharp cutting cold of years of icy wind. His skull grew horns of a stag to help him mutilate the mages and natives that killed his tribe, and anyone else that stood in his way. His mind flayed from grief and loss and the trauma of his vengeance against those that did nothing. His very soul shattered as he sleeps and dreams the years away only to return every winter to consume anyone on his mountain.

For nearly two hundred years now he's starved even more than usual. That raccoon. It wouldn't die. No matter what the wendigo did to it, it would just keep fighting. It kept the wendigo away from the people who live in the city by keeping it baited in the mountain. But the bait this year is nothing compared to the feast that was now walking down the mountain unguarded by that raccoon.

Finally, after so long of taking only the occasional one or two random powerless hikers on the mountainside. Finally after years of waiting in patience and hunger.

It can feed.

The storm doesn't let up. It can't let up. It's not natural. The snow falls down in thick sheets, so dense and thick that even the kid's makeshift umbrella isn't enough to keep it from clinging onto their clothes and fur and feathers. It slows them down even more, each step harder than the last as they continue. They're not able to slide down anymore, so the storm's intensity stays with them and gets stronger.

It was so clear this morning. Lute thinks as he strains to stare at the back of Edgar's head. *David wouldn't have let us go if he knew a blizzard would have formed right? He wanted to help, surely he would have let us stay there for another night.* And that's when the realization hit him like an icicle through the skull. *It's causing the blizzard. It has ice magic. This storm is it's way of trapping us!*

But what could he do to fix this? The storm was too strong, the road ahead too far, and they both began to feel their own hunger grow from breakfast, the physical labor of needing to push through the ever piling snow burned through their calories like mad. He begins to panic, trying to think, figure a way to escape, to get out of this situation.

"Hey Lute!" Edgar calls out from upfront, snapping him out of his spiral. "There's a cave, we're going in!" Peering around Edgar's head Lute saw this 'cave'. In truth, it wasn't much of a cave or tunnel, more a deep outcropping in the rocky hills and mountainside. That said it was relatively big, about the length of a school bus and about as wide and tall, with plenty of room for them to get into.

The snow stopped a few feet into the cave, and Lute collapsed to his knees upon transitioning to the dry dirt floor of the cave. *I hate this snow!* Edgar however quickly takes the toboggan and shoves it against the cave entrance. It's just big enough to cover it.

"With any luck, the snow will pile up against it, and keep us buried for the night." He says as he pulls out the carnelian again and sets it on the floor. "Bada..." as he whispers that the rock catches fire, it's small but bright enough to see the walls and warm enough to get the chill out of the room.

"That won't work," Lute says. "It'll find us." Tears begin forming in his eyes, *this was a stupid plan*, he thinks. *Why did I have to leave?* His thoughts continue to race as he questions everything. *Why couldn't I just keep quiet and stay with Boe? Why couldn't I just tell someone what Dad was doing? Why did I have to kill him?!* Tears roll down his cheeks as he spirals downwards into what very well might be a panic attack.

Edgar meanwhile just stands there. At first anyway. He hasn't seen someone act like this before. That's not to say he's unfamiliar with what Lute's doing, it's simply the first time he's seen anyone other than himself doing it, and the sight catches him off guard. He doesn't know how to react or what to do but knows the feeling is terrible and there has to be a way to make Lute feel better.

Awkwardly, he approaches and sits down next to Lute, wrapping his wings around Lute's shoulders. "Don't cry," he says, parroting words he's heard countless times before in similar situations, though his are much softer. "You're right, it can find us here, which is why we need to set a trap."

His logic falls flat on stone bunny ears as Lute just holds tight to Edgar's side. "I... I'm so afraid," he says after a while of just hugging and sobbing. "Just this morning, everything seemed to be going fine. We would get down the mountain, we wouldn't have to fight, and wouldn't have to kill to live, and I just..."

"It's okay." Edgar says, "You managed to beat Loki on your own, and now you have me at your side. We can beat some old deer."

"Can we?" Lute asks, staring Edgar right in the face, their eyes making contact as if their very souls were staring at one another.

"Yes, we can." Edgar forces a smile. One thing he learned a long time ago was how to best lie and make sure everyone else will believe him, even if he didn't believe himself. "But we have to work now. I don't want to die." he frowns as he stands and faces the entrance. "And if we're going to live, we need to fight. I'm setting some traps. With any luck, they'll be all we need."

Lute let go of Edgar as he stepped up to the cave entrance and began channeling his magic into his wings. He's setting up the spell from before. The drunk spell. Lute knew that just by watching him. *Is he really planning on fighting? Does he really think we can win?* He looks down at his paws, the outside cold and flakes of snow still in his fur are enough to send shivers up his spine.

There's no sense in sitting there and crying.

A voice in the back of his mind says to him. It's quiet and Lute can just barely hear it. It's familiar, though he's not sure from where. *You can not die here. Not after how far you've come. Now get up, and help him.* The voice commands. He brushes the tears out of his eyes. Where had he heard this voice before?

That question is perhaps best saved for another day, provided he lives to see it, so Lute does what the voice tells him to, and stands. He fishes around in their backpack and finds their seeds, and begins sprinkling them all about the cave. *I don't want to die.* His mind echoes Edgar's words. *But I really don't want YOU to die. Edgar... I'll make sure you live.*

The kids keep laying traps, as many as they can in the tiny cave, Lute growing the crops to act as food and barriers when the wendigo strikes, as Edgar strategically places a few pieces of quartz around the room. After taking a small break to eat, they make their way to the very back of the cave and wait.

As the sun goes down, and darkness rises, the storm blots out the final remaining rays of twilight, it leaves the shelter of the shade of trees and the nooks and crannies it has in its ancient home. It runs, as fast as it can, like a cannonball fired fresh from the barrel, straight at the boy's cave. They sense it as it approaches, keeping an accurate measure of where it is and when it'll arrive.

Through the layer of earth and snow and traps, the boys can hear it as it lets out its monstrous roar. "**Garoooooooooooooo!**" it cries as it punches the toboggan. Nobody had warned them about the roar. Upon hearing it Edgar takes a step back, as Lute's blood runs cold. The sound was enough to trigger a fight or flight response, and both of them wanted to fly.

The wendigo quickly and easily pushed the snow away as it clawed at the makeshift door. A few good punches with its incredible strength and the toboggan shatters, cold air, and snow blowing inside and creating frost on the plants nearest the entrance. It howls again as it takes its first monstrous step inside, "**Garoooooooooooo!**"

The kids are hiding. The plants and darkness are enough to make them hard to spot, even for one who has lived countless years in eternal night. They make no sound as it fully enters the cave. Magic sense is an art form. It is difficult to pin down the exact location of the source for even the best of mages, even more so when you don't know what it was. In training, the boys learned to sense Ishtar because they knew she was the source. Lute could and still can sense Edgar because he knows Edgar's dark energy and can feel the difference between it and other dark energies like Loki's.

The wendigo was once a wise shaman. He was once brilliant and cunning. Some small fraction of that remains, yet over the centuries, his mind has gone feral, wild and unfocused. It knows they're somewhere, but it can't pinpoint them. It keeps its long bony claws low to the ground as it steps forward again.

And right into Edgar's drunk trap.

If dark magic gave off light, perhaps there would be a flash. A flash of shadows that would be easily noticeable on a bright day, now they only blend in with the rest of the darkness of the cave. The weak moonlight is blotted out by these tendrils of shadow as they wrap up the body of the Wendigo and into its skull.

It stumbles a bit. Off-balance, but otherwise seems undisturbed. Perhaps it was already used to seeing the world differently, perhaps this trick had been used before on it. Or perhaps its senses were good enough that it could close its eyes and still roughly know where they are. Regardless of the reason, it only stumbled for a moment before proceeding forward again. The tendrils of darkness vanishing.

Its ears are sharp. It makes it halfway into the cave and can hear them in front of it. Their tiny breaths or small steps as they shift and move between the stalks of corn and heads of cabbage. It lets out a low growl as it gets deeper into the cave. Now it stands where the pebble for the fire once was, the time has come.

"Hey!" Lute steps forward and shouts. "You want me? Come get me!" The Wendigo knows exactly where he is now. It charges him and grabs him by his overalls. Lute struggles against its grasp, but it's too strong. It lifts Lute up to its skull, its deep socketed eyes and rotten mouth mere inches from his face as he tries to break free. It screams in his face as it opens its maw wide, "**GAROOOO!**"

"Be afraid," Edgar whispers. "BE VERY AFRAID!" he shouts. Once more his shadow launches out before him. The visage of a large bird of prey on the shadow's head as it penetrates the Wendigo's torso. Suddenly, a bright light fills the room.

"**GAROOOOOO!**" it bellows in pain from the light as it shrinks down and tries to cover its body, dropping Lute as it does.

He gets to his feet quickly, "Run!" Lute shouts as their trap goes off, the wendigo crying out as it confronts its greatest fear. The blinding light of the midday sun that only it can see. The boys quickly run past it and get outside of the cave. The combined work of several hours of growing crops can finally pay off.

"BOOM!" Edgar shouts as he throws the Carnalean into the cave. It lands and shatters into a million tiny pieces, a fireball launching itself from the remains and igniting all the plants. The light and heat from the fire intensify the pain of the wendigo as it continues to scream. Everything was planted so close together that the fire spread to every plant in there until the entire cave became a furnace.

They need to know that it won't come after them again, exhausted from all the magic they had used, the kids just stand on the path and watch the fire burn until that thing's screams fade into nothing.

Ghost:

As the fires burn out, and the horrible screaming ends, the unnatural storm subsides and the clouds recede into the distant sky. The moon and stars peek out from behind the treetops and allow the two to see the path down the mountain as well as back up to the cave they had just been in.

Racked with fear and worry that their plan may not have worked, they spend a moment frozen in the snow just eyeing each other and the cave, wondering if either would be brave enough to approach and see what sort of corpse was left behind.

"I... I guess it's cooked." Lute hesitantly says. "C-can't be anything to see, can there?"

"I'll go look." Edgar gulps down the building vile in his throat as he offers. "I... I've probably seen more dead things than you."

"No," Lute grabs his wing. "Don't go. Not alone. It wouldn't be fair."

Edgar squeezes Lute's paw before letting go as he takes a step forward. "You've gotta stop making up words, Lute." He flashes an uneasy smile back at his friend. "Besides, it's safe, right?"

As Lute reaches out to grab at Edgar again, something catches his eye. A low glow, coming from the cave. He gasps out in shock as he watches a shape begin to form in the light. Edgar turns his head to watch it as it slowly reforms back into the shape of the Wendigo.

"No!" Edgar cries. "That's not..."

The Wendigo should be dead. The Wendigo **is** dead. Nothing more now than a spirit, a curse left behind by that demon from so long ago. As it emerged from the cave, the boys could see the trees and stars through it, as if only partially there. It turns its head towards them. It has no skin on its mouth, no eyes in its sockets, and yet they both see it grin at them.

"GAROOOOOOO!"

Once more it bolts downwards at the boys, but they are paralyzed with fear and exhaustion, and can't move! *This is the end.* Lute thinks. *Edgar, I failed. Persephone, please don't be too mad at us.*

He flinches as Edgar raises a fist to punch the Wendighost. If he was going down, he was gonna fight.

Suddenly, dropping out of the sky, someone lands on top of it, knocking it to the ground. "Ya'll did some mighty fine work." A familiar voice says. "Think it's time I showed this thing who's the real king of the mountain."

It was David, the raccoon from the inn, he was pinning it down as it bit and snapped and howled at the boys. "Yeah, YEAH! HOW'S IT TASTE BEING INCORPOREAL!" he spits on it. "You're not going anywhere 'sept straight to hell you little monster!"

"D-David?!" Lute asks in amazement. "What are you doing?! How did you find us? Have you been following us this entire time?" A million questions raced through Lute's mind all at once, but Edgar only had one.

"Why can I see through you?"

It was true, much like the creature he had pinned, the kids could see right through him to the night sky beyond. "Can't you tell, kids? Same reason you couldn't sense me, and now can't sense this beast. I'm dead!" He laughs. "Don't worry, I'm sure one day you'll be able to sense ghosts."

"W-when did you die?!" Lute asks in horror.

"Oh, you know... 1836... dang spicers killed me in battle, hang on kids, I need to deal with this first." He punches the back of the wendigo's skull. "Now listen here you son of a bitch! You're gonna leave these kids alone and bind with me. YOU HEAR ME?!" he shouts as he shoves a paw into its back.

It howled once more, clawing not to attack the kids, but seemingly out of fear, and desperation to get away as it slowly became more transparent until finally, it was gone, just an untouched patch of snow with David crouched down in it.

"What?" Lute asks, "David? Where did it go?"

"It's gone kid. But it still might come back. Heh, thanks for all your hard work, I couldn't have done it without the two of you." He smiles warmly at the kids, a falling flake of snow passing through his tail as it lists back and forth. "You kids should be perfectly safe traveling down the mountain now. For me, it's time I left."

"You're gonna leave, just like that?" Edgar fumes, "you just show up and leave? What's the point!?"

"I'd love to help you boys, but I've got a one way delivery to make. This thing, the wendigo, it's more than any normal monster, it's a curse." Edgar clammed up as his heart dropped from hearing that. He knew curses well. "When you kill a wendigo, its spirit is free to find a new host, usually whoever was strong enough to kill it."

He clutches his glowing chest as he drops down to his knees. "I took it for you, and now it's gonna make me the next one. But I won't let it! Hear me you punk? This is the spirit of Eagleland! We don't surrender to monsters." He says all this while he looks racked with pain, Lute tries approaching, but David calls out. "Come no closer! It's fighting hard. I'm going to cross over now."

A red light engulfs David growing up his body as it spreads. "Keep your chins up kids. I'm gonna make sure this thing gets the punishment it deserves in the pit. Maybe that'll redeem me of my crimes. All the spicers and gulls I killed back when I was stupid. Now get out of here! And remember, The world is what you make it. Keep going, and one day you might be a legend too!"

And with one final laugh, he vanishes, leaving the boys alone on the mountainside once more. It's quiet, and cold, and dark. They're tired, and all their food was burned in the fire. They dig up some snow at the base of a tall tree, wrap their blanket around themselves, and try to fall asleep.

The morning comes, early light and frost waking the kids, Lute already upset with himself that he used all the seeds last night, and they hadn't had the time to save any new ones. The walk down is easy enough for them as they take stock of supplies in the cold morning air.

They're out of food, their fire starter is broken, as well as an amethyst Edgar had planted in the cave mouth to enhance his spells. Their clothes are disheveled and coated in dirt and snow and ash. Their stomachs rumbled and growled louder and louder as the day went on, eventually, like crossing a threshold, they got out of the snow and into a greener hillside. Lush grass and thick bushes surround the trail broken only by the neverending sea of evergreen trees.

Down down down, they continue to march on empty bellies as the sun rises high into the sky and slowly starts to trundle down again. Eventually, they reach the end of the trail, or at least where the road intersects it.

"You know... we went faster with the sleigh right? How far down were we?" Lute asks.

"We must have gotten down near the bottom. The path kind of evened out back there for a while. Heck, I think we went over a hill an hour ago." Edgar responds.

"Okay, so I didn't imagine that from hunger." Lute laughs, "Here I thought I was going crazy."

"Can't go where you already are." Edgar grins as they start walking along the highway towards the desert of the west. "So we're going to a big field of sand next?"

"Yeah, if I remember my geography lessons right. Not much out there other than sand. Shame too, I always hated getting sand in my dessert."

"Lute... please stop those I am going to scream." Edgar can't help but smile.

"Never!" he cheers and runs off ahead. Edgar manages to catch up, and as the grass starts to turn browner and browner, the kids are delighted to find a truck stop diner on their side of the road. While Lute would make the argument that he shouldn't go in there because there might be cops, and they don't have money for food, the growling of their stomachs and empty water bottle basically decided for them.

The diner is the classic affair that makes anyone think of 1970s Eagleland, complete with red leather seats and checkerboard floor. Some big horse and dog truckers are sitting along the counter while most of the booths are empty. A bell dings as the kids enter, alerting everyone they were there. It wasn't the cleanest affair, and it looked like there was a thin layer of dust on the windows and ledges, but the kids didn't care. There's a small tv hanging over the order window playing the news. Some local channel played news about the upcoming election, or other things the kids had no interest in.

They find a corner booth and take their seats, Lute quickly showing Edgar how to use a menu, (though it wasn't that hard to figure out), the sole waitress approaches them. She was a somewhat perky calico cat dressed in the diner's red and white uniform. "Welcome to the Davy Crockett Truckstop!" She smiles at them before quickly realizing the lack of parents. "Say, where are y'all from?"

"Town." Lute poorly lies. "Can I have carrot juice, please?" He tries to brush her off. Edgar finds the drink section and adds a Kuba Cola to that order. The waitress, quickly putting two and two together or at least being suspicious enough to know she should get help, simply accepts and goes to get their drinks.

After delivering them and placing their orders for food, the waitress leaves them alone as she silently alerts the police to come to pick them up and take them into protective custody.

"So." Edgar breaks the silence, "We... won that?"

"Yeah, hah, I guess we did?" Lute starts to giggle, and soon enough they break out into laughter, the sheer amazement that they somehow made it this far absolutely mystifying them. "You were so cool back there! Those spells of yours are amazing! How'd you know that would work?"

"I didn't! I just had no other ideas! Hahaha! I mean I knew the fire would, but I just had to think that it'd get scared enough to not kill us! And then there was David, did you know he was a ghost? I didn't! And I've seen other ghosts!"

"No! I had no idea! It's just..." He glances out the window, his eyes immediately drawn to the logo of the shop on the sign by the road. *Davy Crockett Truckstop*. The name wraps around the picture of its mascot, a smiling raccoon in old cowboy gear. "Edgar, look!" Lute points to it, Edgar's beak immediately drops.

"He was a legend too?! Just who was he?!"

"I heard about this guy in school! He was some pioneer who, like, went on adventures and fought the eagles, and..." his eyes widened, "He died in the battle of Cottonwood fort!"

"So... he's famous for dying?" Edgar tilts his head, both of them growing quiet as the waitress delivers their meals, not wanting to draw too much attention. Platters of

Spice Island rice and beans, great food for long treks through the desert.

"Nah, he's famous cuz of all the things he did while alive, he was a hero and soldier... the south coast would belong to the Spice Archipelago if it weren't for him! Orange Bay included!"

"Orange Bay? That's where you're from right? What's the Spice Archipelago?" Edgar asks as he starts eating.

"What? C'mon dude, I know you don't seem to know some words, but how do you not know about other countries?"

"There are OTHER countries?" Edgar stops mid-bite. "As in... MORE than Eagleland?"

"Yeah! There's like... hundreds of other nations, the world is huge!"

Edgar drops his fork, it clatters on the floor. "D-do..." the words fill his beak, but can not cross the edge, he gathers his thoughts and tries again. "Do you think we might be able to go there someday?"

"Maybe." Lute laughs, "It's a funny idea, are you okay Edgar?"

"Y-yeah, I'm... okay. Just... I never knew." He goes back to his meal, using his spoon instead.

"You... Did you ever go to school? I mean, I know it sucks butt, but have you ever been?" He notices the cop car pull up and starts shoveling down mouthfuls of rice.

"I've been educated. But I'm gonna guess, 'school' doesn't kick you if you get the questions wrong?" He sees the car arrive too, the cop, some young eagle, doesn't get out yet.

"What even. No seriously, what even is your family? Edgar, I know you don't want to talk about them, but like... that's not good. That's really bad."

"That's because THEY'RE really bad!" he slams his wings on the table. "I don't talk about them because I'm so SCARED that they'll find us. Do you remember the hall of mirrors? They broke after I looked at them because I saw my family in them. Each one a different person, I just... I nearly broke there. Just seeing them."

"Edgar..." he places a paw on Edgar's wing. "I'm sorry. About all of it, I... you don't have to tell me. I think I understand. And I promise you don't have to go back. I won't let them."

He smiles a bit, the promise, while genuine, felt hollow to him. Not because he didn't believe Lute, just that he knew, or at least feared, Lute would probably be useless against his family. The fact they killed the wendigo and beat Loki, he just attributed to a mix of teamwork, stupid plans, and dumb luck. And if he knew about Loki before, he would probably be even more skeptical.

He quickly shoves the last of his meal into his beak as the cop hops out of the car. Lute meanwhile heads over to the counter and asks for the bathroom key. The waitress hesitates, though she realizes the cops are already here, so what's the worst that could happen, and gives it over.

The boys exit the diner and are immediately cornered by the cop. "Hang on there boys, where are your parents?"

"Inside?" Edgar lies.

"Riiight, well, I got a tip alerting me that there were two unsupervised children here. But if you say your parents are here..." he shrugs, "Look, kids, the jig is up. Just get in the car."

"Can't we go to the bathroom first?" Lute asks, showing off the key. "We've been holding it in all morning."

"Fine. Better there than in the car." he leans back on the hood of the car. "Just don't try anything, alright?"

"What could we possibly do?" Lute asks before the two head in and lock the door. The bathroom is dirty, the level of grime and filth that one would expect for a middle of nowhere truck stop. No windows and a healthy level of dirt seemed to coat everything. The sink drips slowly behind them as they stare at the door. "Do you have a plan?"

"I say we zap him with some fear magic and run."

"Edgar! We can't do that!" Lute scolds, "Yeah, we can't let him take us, but he's not doing anything wrong. He's just doing his job."

"He's an adult! I don't see why we shouldn't."

"Yeah, but what about Ishtar and Persephone and David? They were adults too."

"And there was Loki and Talos' mother, they were adults that tried to kill us!" His feathers ruffle as he growls. "Not to mention everyone back home. Look, Lute, I say he's bad news."

Lute just sighs, "Be that as it may, we can't just go around attacking people for no good reason. Would... wouldn't that just make us like the wendigo?"

Edgar goes quiet, realizing Lute's right. "So what do we do then?"

"Run?" Lute shrugs. "If we can get away, we could just hide."

"Isn't there a desert down the road we need to cross? Pretty sure it'd be hard to hide in an open sand field." Edgar points out. "If we're going to Spectacle city, then going back to Ashtown is only going to make the past two days worthless."

"Hmm, I've got an idea. Wait here, and listen outside, trust me." Lute says before quickly heading outside. Edgar does trust Lute and does as he says, putting his ear against the door. "Hey, Mr. Cop guy!" Lute says. "Where are you gonna take us anyway?"

"The station, so we can find your parents." He responds matter of factly. "Is the other one done yet? You're not trying anything, are you?"

"Not yet!" Lute says in his sing-song happy voice "And we know we can't get away from you here. Neither of us is stupid." He laughs, quickly shifting over to pouting and stomping his foot. "And which station? It kinda matters if I'm gonna call my mom!"

The cop scowls a bit, "You have a cellphone?"

"Duh! Who doesn't?" Lute laughs, "Money too, we were gonna pay for our meal and everything!"

The cop may or may not have bought his bluff, though it hardly matters to him. "My station is the nearest, it's in Phoenix Outpost down the road. Near the reservation."

Perfect. Lute thinks. "Oh wow! I've never been there before!" He knocks on the door. "Edgar, come on! It's time to go!" Opening the door, the boys quietly pile into the back of the cop's car and begin traveling down the road. Traveling on foot through hot sand or on even hotter asphalt would, in Lute's own words, *blow chunks.*

Sure, Edgar has boots, but just like back in the snow, Lute's bare feet would be exposed to both, and while he was somewhat used to hot asphalt back home, this might be a bit much. Even more so if they actually had to spend hours on the road, or worse, go overnight. Meanwhile, a car ride with the police made for a much quicker trip across the desert.

"Right, go ahead and call your parents then kid." the cop says to Lute.

"Ohhh. Right, I lost my cell phone." Lute tries to lie. Edgar then pulls a cell phone out of his pocket.

"You can borrow mine, here." He offers. Grabbing hold of it, Lute quickly realizes it's actually one of his pieces of quartz disguised as a cellphone. Catching on Lute quickly pantomimes using it as a real cell phone.

"Mom? Hey Mom! It's me! Guess where I am? In a cop car!" He starts acting, "N-no Mom, it's just a misunderstanding- Yes Mom. Phoenix Outpost. Yes. Yes. Edgar's with me. Okay. Love you." He gives it back to Edgar, "Mom said she'll pick us up after work."

"I'm sure," the eagle responds, "now, do you care to tell me why you're traveling alone and unsupervised, or why you decided to steal from that restaurant?"

"We were hungry." Edgar shrugs, "And we were gonna pay! As for why we were alone, it's because Mom's at work."

"And why weren't you in school?"

Crap. Lute thinks he doesn't even know what day of the week it is. "We're uh... homeschooled?"

"You kids don't know how lucky you have it." The cop begins to lecture, "You have a family that loves you," these first words immediately made Lute fall silent, though almost made Edgar laugh. "The ability to come and go as you wish, no bills or responsibilities, and yet you resort to petty theft? If you're hungry, go home."

The eagle's speech goes on for a while like this down the road, a lot of circular logic and empty platitudes expected from someone lecturing someone else about something they don't know the full story of. Combined with some things that are either plain untrue or otherwise hurtful to say because he refuses to acknowledge the obvious reason why they're here.

The boys pay enough attention to the speech to know how they need to respond when they arrive at the other end to try and make for a quick escape, and only occasionally give responses to him.

As they pull up to the outpost, they see how unimpressive it is. The main road only has about three or four buildings on it, the police station, another gas station, and the rest they assume to be part of the tiny motel for truckers and other travelers. A side road branches off of the main, and in the distance they see what looks to be a proper town. Not as big as Ashtown, but still fairly decent sized. *That must be where David told us to go.*

He parks the car in front of the station but leaves the boys locked in until he can come around and pull them out to make sure they can't run away. "And don't even try it kids, you're not going anywhere until your parents show up." He grumbles as he drags them by paw and wing inside.

The outside air is hot and dry, and there's this feeling of dust and dirt just caking into your fur as you walk around. Inside, the air is very still, and it's very quiet, but at least there's air conditioning to make it more bearable. Another eagle is working at the desk, and by working, of course that means playing solitaire on her ancient desktop.

It becomes clear that given the tiny size of the station, that either not a lot of crime happens in these parts, or the criminals are quickly shoveled off to some larger prison elsewhere. The lone cell that looks like it has been there for the past two hundred years sits across from two offices and reeks of the same smell Lute is all too familiar with from his father. The eagle shoves the boys in before closing it. "Wait here for her to show up," he orders before returning to his office.

"Well. That could have gone better." Edgar growls as he grapples the bars. "Another cage, how wonderful."

"Okay yes, there was a small snag in the plan, but hey, we're a lot closer to our goal right?" Lute tries to comfort him.

"Yeah, no, I'm still calling this a failure," he responds as he tries to bend or shake them loose. "Since now we're stuck here waiting for someone who doesn't exist."

"Okay yeah fair." Lute frowns, "Okay, what if-" before he could finish his thought, the door to the other office opens and he goes quiet, not wanting to let the cops in on his plan. Emerging from the room comes a third eagle, this one seeming a lot less angry than the last one.

"Well, I'll be. Sam actually did it." He approaches the eagle behind the desk, "Kai, did you see? Sam actually brought in someone this time." He laughs. "Look kinda scrawny for criminals though."

"He did indeed," Kai responds, not taking her eyes off her game, "I suppose this means you won, and I owe you dinner."

"Well if you insist. It's getting to be about that time, and there's that diner in town that sells really good Fogland food..." He suggests.

"Fine." Kai retorts, "but I'm taking the car, it's too hot out to fly."

"Drive safe." He smiles at her as she leaves. "Now what do we have here," he says, turning his attention to the kids. "Let me guess, a couple of dwarf backpackers traveling the world only to run out of money?"

"No?" Edgar annoyedly replies.

"No? Then perhaps you're gnome mobsters from Marbleland that just happened to get lost and tried to rob a gas station?"

"No," Lute says, just tilting his head at the accusation.

"Ah, I see. Then you must be a pair of kids that ran away from your respective homes and met up on the road, only to get caught by Sam for being unsupervised kids in the middle of nowhere on a school day."

Neither of the boys responds, and that is all the answer that this new eagle needs to confirm his suspicion. "Well then, glad we got that part sorted. Tell you what, if you can tell me why I shouldn't call child services on the two of you, I'll let you go."

Edgar lets go of the bars, dragging Lute to the back of the cell so they can whisper and figure out what their best shot here was. "We could threaten him," he offers.

"Edgar, we can't just threaten or attack him, it's not right!"

"Right? What does direction have to do with this?!"

"I mean right as in the opposite of wrong! It's bad to just attack people." Edgar goes quiet at Lute's words, he honestly knew deep down that Lute was correct, even if he never had the words for it before. "Why don't we try the truth? It's gotten us this far."

"Yeah, because we've been stupidly lucky!" He shouts before going back to whispering, the Eagle just smiling at him. "I got out of my cage because of luck, we met by chance and encountered a minotaur and the carnival at random. We were gonna meet David no matter what because of your plan, but it's all been so much luck. And we're gonna run out eventually."

"Alright," Lute agrees, they have been very, very lucky and if they push it too much it'll only make the situation worse. "What should we tell him then?"

"Don't keep me waiting, boys, I can only offer this until Kai returns." He kneels down to their eye level and leans forward, cupping his beak in his wings. "Why shouldn't I send you home?"

"BECAUSE THERE'S NO HOME TO RETURN TO!" Lute cries out, he's not sure why, but it's as if a form of pressure had been building in him and it finally blew. Like all the things he hasn't said, and all the things he's done these past few weeks finally boiled over.

"Lute..." Edgar tries to comfort him, placing a wing on his shoulder.

"Don't you get it?" Lute sniffles as he wipes tears from his eyes. He grabs his left ear and starts fidgeting with it. "My parents are dead, there's no one back home for me. I left because there was no one there for me." he half lied. "I had one friend back home. She trusted me, she wanted to help me, but I betrayed her! And now I can't go back."

He looks over at Edgar, "And that's nothing compared to him! I don't know the whole story. I don't need to know. Not until you're ready to tell me. But your family is bad news. I don't know why they hate you so much, but if you go back, they'd kill you, wouldn't they?"

Edgar is silent, he looks away, his tail feathers brushing against the floor. He doesn't know how to respond to him. There's nothing he needs to say, at least as far as Lute's concerned.

"I ran away because I had no one." Lute turns his attention back to the eagle. "And now... I have Edgar! If you send us home or put us up for adoption... I'm gonna lose him!" he cries as he quickly grabs onto Edgar, pulling him into an embrace. "I can't lose him. I can't let him die. Please, don't separate us!"

Edgar slowly but surely hugs Lute back. He grabs the white rabbit in his wings, holding him tight. He brushes Lute's head, his black feathers like the soft touch of a pillow on Lute's back. It's strange. Some new feeling takes hold of him. Something Edgar had never felt before. Anger, rage, fear, sorrow, 'comfort', 'joy'. The emotions and feelings he had known for so long and the ones he had just recently discovered, it was as if he was feeling all of them at once.

Comfort and joy from hugging Lute. Fear and sorrow at the idea of being separated and going home. And blinding rage as he looked up at the judgmental eagle that held their fate in his wings. He pulls Lute back a bit, positioning himself closer to the eagle.

It's curious. *I felt something like this before.* A stray thought hits him. *Back in the cave, when the wendigo grabbed him. But not as strong. I felt in control back then. Like I knew the plan would work. I didn't worry about losing him. But now...*

"...Don't touch him." Edgar hisses at the cop. "I won't let you."

The cop stands up and leans on the wall across the hall. "So that's all you've got to say is it?" He stares up at the ceiling. "Sounds like a rough story, if it's true of course. Though I've gotta be honest, there's not a lot in this town for kids like you. This is our land, and a lot of our people still don't like your people. You won't get a job, won't be able to go to school. You'd be seen as parasites on society." He glares at them. "You'd starve or die of thirst if you stayed here. Unless you've got some kind of magic."

He laughs and shakes his head, "Ah, but the people around here can tell you how worthless magic is. If it had any use, we probably wouldn't only have a wingful of towns. Did you kids ever hear about that stuff? They say our ancestors had some kind of super-powerful wind magic and could control the weather. Heh, if that were true Eagleland might still belong to the eagles."

"Ah, but I'm rambling. Besides, what do I know, you might just be passing through. Though there are problems with that too. Even if you could cross on foot, you'd need a lot of food and water, foraging's out unless you like cactus, since nothing else will really grow out there," he continues to ramble.

"You could always try to get a bus out of here, though you'd need money, and something tells me you're not gonna try stealing again." He says as he unlocks the cage. Opening it, he finishes his monologue, "There's a small park in town. Keep it clean, and don't cause any trouble, or I will turn you in. Do I make myself clear?"

Neither of the boys says anything, they silently nod and quickly make their way out of the station before either

Sam comes out, or Kai comes back. They decide to sneak off to the side of the building to wait for Kai to return so they wouldn't be spotted on the road. They take this time to calm down and think.

"Looks like we got lucky again." Lute smiles a little bit as he stares across the barren planes of sand, lonesome plateaus rising up in the distance. "But he is right, I don't think I could even grow food in the sand. We could try stocking up before leaving..."

"Yeah, maybe," Edgar says, his mind focused more on the feeling he had in there and the words the cop had said. *He seems like he's done something like this before...*

"Wait! I've got it! Edgar, your amethyst! We could use it to create a fake bus pass for the first bus out of here and heading to Spectacle City! If we do that, we could be there by morning! Why didn't I think of this back in Ashtown?" Lute kicks himself.

Edgar thinks for a moment, trying to piece it all together. Lute is right, that small illusion spell would be enough to get them there. If it can create a water bottle, an electric key, and even a cellphone, then it could easily make a bus pass. "I'd have to see one first," he admits, letting Lute in on the secret of the spell. "Can't make something I haven't seen."

"That can't be too hard, now can it? It's just a piece of paper after all. We get on and we'll see someone else's ticket or pass and then you can just copy theirs!"

"True." Edgar comments, though he's still distracted, finally something clicks for him. *Why did David tell them to come here?* "Hang on a second." He says,

"Why don't we stay here for a bit?" The words almost made him shiver, even as they left his beak. Surely he was at least far enough away here that he'd be able to spend some time not moving.

Lute tilts his head, a puzzled expression crossing his face, "Huh? Why?"

"That cop in there. He mentioned something about old magic, right?" He questions.

"Yeah, I think I saw a cartoon in like third grade about that once. Like, okay people came over from Fogland and The RK to Eagleland and war broke out between them and the natives. The RK and Fogland guys had guns and stuff while all the eagles still used mostly stone tools. The eagles said they would 'curse' the others with their magic." Lute explains. "It was just them not knowing how science works." He shrugs.

"Lute, we KNOW magic is real though. And the stuff we're doing is the basic stuff. You've seen what Ishtar and her friends can do. What if these guys did have some sort of super-powerful magic they just never got the chance to use?"

"That's..." Lute trails off, he hadn't really thought about it. He knew Freya and Loki in passing from the comic books, and just about everyone in Eagleland knew the story of Davy Crocket. Edgar can control shadows and cut objects with them, and he himself can make crops and plants dance and grow. Legends are real, myths are real, strictly speaking, he knows curses are real because Edgar put one on him!

"Fair," he finally says. "That's very fair. So what are you thinking?"

"What you said back there, in the cell and truckstop. You're wrong," he frowns. "My family wouldn't kill me if they caught us." He grabs Lute's shoulders and looks aways, holding tight he manages to quietly tell Lute the truth. "But they will kill you, and when they do, and see me cry over your corpse..." tears well up in the young raven's eyes, Lute just standing there paralyzed in fear.

"I can't even begin to describe what they'd do to your body to torture me more and keep me from running away again. I can't let that happen." He turns his head to face Lute, looking deep into Lute's eyes. "I **won't** let that happen. We beat the wendigo by luck and planning, but if my family catches us off guard, we're dead. We're not strong enough to fight them."

He lets go of Lute and takes a few steps towards the town, pointing at it, he proclaims, "They might have what we need there! That eagle said they can control the weather itself! Shadow illusions and dancing plants are one thing, but dropping a tornado on their heads is something much better!"

As the tears dry up, he smiles at Lute, extending an open wing to his friend. "You're the one always saying 'trust me', or how friends help each other. So I'm asking you as a friend, come with me, we'll spend a few days here, and see if we can't learn something new."

Lute thinks, for only a moment, but the hesitation is quickly wiped away. He smiles and grabs hold of his wing.

"Wherever you go, I'll go too!" he smiles back. "That's what friends are for!"

Curtain Call:

"So? What happened next? C'mon, don't keep me in suspense!" Culania playfully pouts, another night, another dream, and after everything that's happened the past few days, Lute's more than happy to have someone else to talk to.

Lute found himself back in the creature's bedroom, it was a comforting sight to be back here as opposed to the stage or dance hall that he would normally enter into for their usual training these past weeks. The darkly colored walls, the soft carpet, and the faint smell of lavender that hung listlessly in the air made him feel at ease.

"Not much to say," he shrugs, "We didn't actually go into town until the next day, we were really tired, so we just went into the motel next to the station, we got a room, and just kinda... collapsed. Heh, you should have seen Edgar's eyes sparkle when he lied down on the bed, he looked so happy-"

"Wait, hang on, how did you afford a hotel room? I thought you didn't have any money," Culania puzzles.

"Well... we might not have MONEY, but we do have Edgar's amethyst. He managed to disguise it as a fifty-dollar bill, so it'll cover the room for the night."

"Won't the innkeeper be suspicious when he sees a rock in his register in the morning?"

"Eh, perhaps. But we're kinda planning on going into town and seeing if we can't earn some money tomorrow. That cop said he won't arrest us if we don't cause trouble, so if I do some singing and dancing... without magic, I might be able to earn a small profit, and we can spend another night in the hotel. Besides, it's not like he can say the rock came from us. He'll probably just think he was robbed."

"I guess that works then." Culania smiles as he gets up to rummage around his bookcase for something. "Just promise me you guys will be safe."

"Hah! After fighting that wendigo, I'm sure we'll be fine. Food shouldn't be too much of an issue. Just need to get a salad tomorrow from a restaurant, and then we'll be able to grow food in the park when no one's around." He stretches before flopping down on his stomach, revealing just how tired he is. Even in this dream, he feels like he's going to fall asleep. "What are you looking for anyway?"

"My dream chart," the purple creature says before pulling a book from the shelf. "It shows me who's asleep based on location, it's how I met you." He says, flipping through the pages as he waddles over.

"Neat." Lute laughs, "why do you need that?"

"Well..." Culania stops at a specific page and places it in front of Lute's face. "Ever since you met this 'Edgar', I've been trying to enter his dreams too. I figured it'd be nice to make more friends, you know?" He flashes a small smile, though it doesn't last for long, quickly turning into a frown. "See that picture of you there? That's where you are in the waking world. If Edgar's asleep, he should be appearing right next to you. But he's just not there."

"Maybe he's staying up later? He seemed to really like the bed... and we have a tv in the room! I was just really tired." Lute shrugs it off.

"Yeah, but... I've been looking over this for a few weeks. While you were singing or trying new dance moves, I kept glancing at this. He's **never** in it. Never! I'm not sure he even sleeps."

"That's ridiculous." Lute scoffs, "Of course he sleeps, I've seen him sleep. Maybe your book is broken?"

"Maybe..." Culania shuts the book. "I'm just worried, you know?"

"Yeah..." Lute frowns, "I am too. I trust him with my life, so it's not him. I've told you everything that I know about him. You know he's a good guy right?"

He hesitates and puts the book aside, laying down next to Lute, Culania places a paw on his shoulder. "I don't know," he admits, "but I know you're a good guy! And if you trust him, that's good enough for me." He smiles to comfort his friend.

"Then maybe you know something that could cause this? Like maybe his family did something?" Lute offers.

"Maybe..." Culania thinks, "It would be like, really powerful dark magic if that was the case though."

"That's bad right?"

"It could be. For now, let's not worry about it for now. You must be so tired." Culania stands and grabs the blanket off his bed, laying it over Lute.

"Yeah, I think I'm gonna skip training tonight, and hey, I'm sure he'll tell me what's up when he's ready. There's nothing left to do now but wait and see."

And so the two dreamers sit together on the castle floor, spending the night relaxing and recovering. In the waking world, Edgar is asleep on the bed next to Lute, tossing and turning, whimpering, and even crying. So very much afraid of what might yet be, and of all the things left unsaid. Time is marching ever forward, and soon, all too soon, it'll be the end. But overall, even if it does end when he wakes he will be happy. His twelfth birthday comes at the end of this month, and it'll be the first time he has ever received a gift.

A friend, a new life, and freedom. And though the fear may make for dreamless nights, fear that it may all end or go away, or he may yet lose it all, as the sun rises and he awakens, he knows that if only for this short time, he is happy.

They smile and wash up, a first in a long time for Lute to enjoy such a pleasantry, and potentially a first-ever for Edgar. While they do have that nameless song Culania taught Lute, it's nothing quite like the feeling of a warm shower and clean soap. There was also the bonus that despite not being able to see Lute in the other room, upon exiting the shower, Edgar realizes he knows exactly where Lute is. Their training has paid off it would seem.

Their pasts behind them, they set out down the dusty road to the old reservation. What new adventures await them there, only time can tell, but for now, their future is looking bright!

THE
END

Made in the USA
Middletown, DE
02 December 2022